KJELL OLA DAHL

Translated by Don Bartlett

◆

LITTLE
DRUMMER

Complete and Unabridged

ISIS
LARGE
PRINT

ISIS
Leicester

First published in Great Britain in 2022 by
Orenda Books
London

First Isis Edition
published 2022
by arrangement with
Orenda Books
London

First published in Norwegian as *Lille tambur* by Gyldendal in 2003

This is a work of fiction. Names, characters, places and incidents are either products of the author's imagination or are used fictitiously. Any resemblance to actual events, locales or persons, living or dead, is entirely coincidental.

A catalogue record for this book is available from the British Library.

ISBN 978–1–39912–535–2

The Crab

She stopped the car. At first, they sat in silence, staring across the sea. It was so shiny and still. The glacially polished rockfaces of two huge boulders were mirrored in the water with such sharpness it was almost impossible to see where reality finished and the reflection started.

'I'll never get used to this,' he said.

'To what?'

'To nights being so light.'

She opened the door and got out. There wasn't a soul in sight. Nor a sound to be heard — until he opened his door, stepped out and closed it. She walked ahead, turned off the path and followed a narrow track between the rocks. 'Short cut,' she said.

Down by the grass, she flipped off her shoes and continued barefoot. The feeling of dewy grass beneath her feet made her stop for a few seconds, stand with her eyes shut, enjoying the sensation, before she set off at a run across the greensward with her arms outstretched.

He watched her with a smile on his face. 'Watch out for dog shit,' he shouted.

She stopped and turned, breathing heavily. 'Come on.'

He bent down, loosened his shoelaces, took off his shoes and followed her. When she crossed the narrow strip of sand and waded into the water, he paused to roll up his trouser legs. 'I wish I could go swimming, like you,' he mumbled.

1

She held up the hem of her skirt and waded out further until she found a white area of sand among the seaweed. The sea reached above her knees. She stared through the water at the sand. 'Why can't you?'

'Actually, I can't swim.'

She straightened up and tried to remember what this admission reminded her of. Magnus, she thought. But the image of Magnus had faded. So she began to study Stuart; she knew him better now: the almost feminine curve of his spine; the trousers that seemed too big around his slim waist. The slightly inquisitive, humorous glint in his eye, the smiling lips in his slender but symmetrical face. What he had just told her made him seem more tangible, yet more mysterious.

'You remind me of my cousin,' she said, proffering a hand. 'Come on.'

'I daren't.'

They eyed each other. After a while he tossed his head lightly and said, 'The place we just drove past is the most beautiful in the country.'

'The folk museum?'

'The houses are the same as at home.' He took a hesitant step toward her, raising his arms to keep his balance. 'Is the log house called an *årestue*?'

She nodded, but corrected his pronunciation.

He said: 'In the log house the women were cooking over an open fire, like at home. In the folk museum I saw white pigs in the flesh for the first time. At home we have black pigs. When I was small and saw pictures of white pigs, I thought the connection was obvious.'

'What connection?'

'White people have white pigs; black people have black pigs.'

He burst into laughter. It began as a splutter and

continued as a long, almost soundless gasp.

She waded in further, leaned forward and, collecting her long hair in one hand, began to search for shells. A flounder shot away; all she saw was a shadow darting across the sand. Tiny bubbles rose from where a crab had buried itself, and she spotted the almost transparent creature sneaking away from her toes. She poked the sand above its air hole. The sand crab appeared, anxiously brandishing its small claws.

She looked up. Something had sparked a little tension between them. In his eyes she read seriousness, anxiety and what she interpreted as passion.

'There's something you have to know,' he whispered in a barely audible voice.

She guessed that he wanted to say something that would change the expression in his eyes and answered: 'This minute?'

'I've done something wrong,' he whispered.

'We've got plenty of time,' she said. 'The night is long, and everything's quiet.'

'But I want to tell you. It's important.'

'Not now,' she breathed, reaching out for his arm. 'I have to show you something.' To see the movements of the animals in the sand more easily, she focused on a round stone just under the surface of the sea. She had stood like this many times as a child, and this realisation made her mind go blank for a few seconds.

He waded closer. 'Show me what?' The bright morning sun shone from a low angle behind his head, and in the strong light the contours of his body were lost — it was as if the sun had spoken, not him. He took another step and reappeared. The water reached up to his knees. The capillary forces in his trousers slowly drew the water up his legs and turned them

3

from orange to black. Then she saw the little crab again. She grabbed it, hid it in her hand, straightened up and passed him her dripping fist. His fingers gripped her hand and opened it.

'Holy shit.'

Stuart gave a start as the crab fled into his hand. He lost his footing and lurched into a backward stagger to the shore — completely off balance. And even though he had let go of her hand, she allowed herself to fall with him. The water soaked everything they were wearing in a second. When Stuart began to thrash around, she held his arms. 'It's not dangerous,' she gasped, laughing at the same time. His arms wouldn't quieten down until she had placed her mouth on his. Then they lay in the sand, in thirty centimetres of water, lips on lips, as the sea became colder and colder, making the outermost layer of their skin beneath their sodden clothing hypersensitive as their bodies touched. And, a little later, when the sun had begun to ascend, they laid their clothes to dry on the smooth rock, two boulders that, between them, formed a cleft so narrow that only wayward rays of sun could find their way down to where she held his black body in hers.

When she finally released his lips, she whispered: 'Now.'

'What do you mean, 'now'?'

'Now you can tell me everything.'

PART ONE

THE WOMAN IN THE UNDERGROUND CAR PARK

window again. It was slow work because all her muscles were tense. She locked on. The digital signs on
the ceiling flashed to indicate that the level was
full and potred. [?]
There are [?] the people. There wasn't a living soul

Transfixed

There were some situations Lise Fagernes hated:
entering unfamiliar, enclosed spaces was one of
them. It rekindled a feeling she had first experienced
when she was eight years old. The children in her
street had dug a cave in the huge pile of snow left by
the ploughs. It was a long, narrow tunnel, so cramped
that the snow pressed against your body as you wriggled through and out the other side. When it was her
turn, some boys wanted to have a bit of fun. They
had lain on their backs by the opening and kicked it
full of compacted snow. That was all she could
remember. Just the sense of heart-pounding panic.
So, she always went to great lengths to control this
panic, to keep it at bay. But fighting panic had
become something she loathed. It made her feel
weak and pathetic. It made her dread driving down
into underground car parks. However, now, as she
reached the building, she took a deep breath and
braced herself. She came to a halt in front of the
barrier, rolled down the window and took the ticket
from the machine. She clung to the steering wheel as
the barrier opened, and, feeling the sweat break out
on her forehead, drove in with the window open,
even though she could smell the stale air coming into
the car. She breathed through her mouth and automatically switched off the radio when it lost the
signal. Only when she had driven down to the lower
floor and checked in the mirror that no one was
behind her did she make the effort to wind up the

window again. It was slow work because all her muscles were tense. She looked up. The digital signs on the ceiling flashed in orange to tell her this level was full and pointed downward.

Where are all the people? There wasn't a living soul around, only tightly parked rows of empty cars. After manoeuvring her way around the third bend, she slowed down. *Please don't make me drive all the way down. Let there be a space here, right here.* But there wasn't. The arrows continued to flash downward. She was forced to continue, forced to pass car bonnet after car bonnet — another bend, the last, down to the lowest, emptiest level. She depressed the clutch pedal and let the car roll around the bend and down until it stopped on its own. Here, at the back of the dimly lit bottom level there were spaces. For a fraction of a second her mind was blocked: she wanted to turn around, drive back up, into the open air and away. She repressed her desperation and stared out: water was dripping from a vent in the ceiling; immense drops were hitting the windscreen, dissolving and running down to the wiper, obscuring her view with a blur. A flickering neon tube was sending blue and yellow light across the car roofs. The dashboard clock showed 09:52. She had eight minutes to make it to the interview. She reached back to take her mobile from her bag. *Ring them and say you're delayed.* No. That would anger the man. A disgruntled interviewee makes for a bad feature. *And all because you're afraid to get out of your car in an empty car park. But why is there no one else here?* She rammed the car into gear and manoeuvred her way into the nearest space.

Looking right, into the next car, she was startled to see a woman. The sight gave her such a shock it took

8

her breath away, and she placed a hand on her chest. *Relax, it's only someone sitting in a car. Take it easy.* She switched off the engine, turned round and grabbed her bag from the back seat. Fumbled inside until she found her lipstick. She took it out and craned her neck to see her reflection in the mirror, but stiffened when she saw the darkness behind her. *What am I expecting to see?*

Lise Fagernes breathed in, painted her lips red, checked the result and pressed her lips together as she opened the door and pushed it — a little too far. It hit the other vehicle. She squeezed out and closed the door. The echo resounded around the enormous lower floor. *Relax. Once you're around the bend you'll see other people. You'll meet all the others going to the shops or important meetings or . . .* At that moment she thought about the woman in the adjacent car and bent down to look through her car windows into the next vehicle. The woman was still sitting there, her head resting at an unnatural angle.

Her nose and half-open mouth were pressed against the glass, but there was not a drop of condensation. The woman in the car wasn't breathing.

Lise Fagernes — a full-time employee at *Verdens Gang* who now had six and a half minutes to make her appointment with the middle-aged social commentator whose career was in such steep decline that he had written a book — felt with every pore of her being what her consciousness would not accept: this person was not alive.

For a second Lise was rooted to the spot. The feeling of panic that she always kept under control finally had the upper hand. It started with this paralysis, which gradually wore off under the pressure of her

9

surroundings: the echo of the underground car park, the vibration of a stray grain of sand knocking against the wall of the ventilation shaft, the hum of the neon tube flashing incessantly above the blue metal door covered in graffiti tags. Lise was alone with a dead body, forced to inhale the nauseous smell of concrete and stale exhaust fumes. As her gaze shifted wildly from car to car, she felt a frosty finger bore between her shoulder blades and into her body, an icy chill that spread down her arms and spine, where the feeling changed and became warm, making a cold sweat break out on her skin. She gasped and instinctively took two to three clumsy steps to the side then, as if in a dream, set off at a run between the rows of cars, terrified, not daring to turn to examine the cause of the terror that was propelling her legs. She passed bumper after bumper, the click-clack of her shoes echoing in her ears, and she cursed her high heels and the ridiculous outfit she was wearing for the interview that would never take place, while her breathing lacerated her lungs, as if with a sharp knife. There wasn't a soul around, until she turned the bend and saw a young mother unloading a pram from the boot of a Volvo. The sight of this woman, the sight of such harmony, poise and self-assurance, allowed Lise Fagernes to regain her composure. She pulled up at once and stood gasping for breath. Now she knew what she had to do. She took the mobile from her bag and tapped in a number.

She called Verdens Gang. Lise Fagernes was a journalist. What she needed now was a photographer.

Looking For Leads

As the woman had neither ID nor any other personal possessions on her, it was down to the senior duty officer at Oslo Crime Squad to start making the necessary enquiries that might establish the identity of the victim. The car she had been found in was apparently owned by a certain Kjetil Sandvik. The duty officer rang Sandvik from his desk. It turned out he was a retired pilot living in Heddal. He was extremely ill at ease at being called by Oslo Police, but was able to inform them that his car was being used by his youngest daughter, Marianne, who was studying literature at Oslo University. He hadn't driven the car himself for more than a year.

While Sandvik was talking, the duty officer tapped his forefinger on a biro, the rounded end of which he had placed in his left nostril. This was a habit he had developed when he was on the phone and no longer listening. What he really wanted to do was hang up. However, this conversation had put him in a difficult position. From the police report, it emerged that the car park staff had called the police, who in turn had called A&E. The doctor who arrived with the paramedics in the ambulance concluded that the woman's death had been caused by a self-administered dose of heroin and had issued a death certificate to this effect. Between the fingers of the victim hung a syringe, pointing down to the floor, where the duty officer had found the rest of the junkie's standard kit: a spoon, a cigarette lighter and some silver paper containing traces of heroin.

It was, therefore, highly probable that the deceased was the car-owner's daughter. But it wasn't certain. And it was the job of a priest or someone suitably qualified to pass on the sad tidings, not the lot of an impatient policeman like himself. Having no wish to get himself into deep water, he stammered out an apology for ringing Sandvik, knowing full well that this would not put the car-owner's mind at rest. He failed to ask Sandvik about his daughter's appearance or her use of drugs. Instead, he made out that his call was due to a parking issue, which in a sense was true, as the car was at that moment being towed out of the underground car park and taken to Oslo Council's impoundment lot for illegally parked vehicles in the district of Sogn.

After the conversation, his sense of unease developed into annoyance, and he soon knew what he would do. For some time now, he'd had a bone to pick with a certain police inspector, and because he had just received another complaint regarding the man's wilful smoking habits, he decided to let the man — Inspector Gunnarstranda — sharpen his wits for a few hours on a bog-standard OD case.

* * *

As the duty officer marched into the office shortly afterwards, Gunnarstranda was fighting to stifle an unpleasant coughing fit. These bouts were getting worse and worse. If he let them have free rein, he would end up choking, which would finish him off entirely. And he didn't want to give anyone the pleasure of that sight, least of all the man towering over

his desk right now: the kind of guy who only artic-
ulated his thoughts as he spoke them, and for that
reason repeated every sentence aloud, as if to confirm
to himself what he had been thinking and saying.

Gunnarstranda observed him in silence.

After a while, the ploy started working. At first, the
man stopped talking. Then he began to scratch his
groin. When Gunnarstranda went to shake hands, the
man put down the papers as meekly as a teenager
handing over a poor school report.

Gunnarstranda waited until he was alone in the
office before he began to read. Afterwards he mused
for a few moments, then picked up the phone.

The deceased still hadn't been identified. If the
woman belonged to the drugs fraternity around
the Plaza Hotel or Oslo Central Station, her name
would already have come up, because she would be
an 'old friend' of the police and the paramedics. The
equipment in the car suggested she was a junkie.
And Gunnarstranda didn't want to dispute the doctor's conclusion about the cause of death. But if his
superior officer had decided to delegate this job to
him Gunnarstranda would have come up with several
possible interpretations. One was that the death may
be suspicious.

He phoned the Forensic Institute and commissioned an autopsy of the body. The use of sorely
needed funds for the autopsy of a typical OD case
would irritate both his boss, the budget holder, and
the man who had just left him. But it was probably
the latter who would be left holding the baby. The
satisfaction of paying a senior officer back for a delib-
erate slight and also precipitating a row between two
people who occasionally riled him put him in such a

good mood that he determined at once to do some field work and clarify the identity of the victim.

★ ★ ★

The car-owner's daughter lived in Bjerregårds gate, in one of the brick tenement buildings by the Maridalsveien intersection. There was a smell of frying in the stairwell and a blue cardboard disc on the door. Two names, Marianne Sandvik and Kristine Ramm, were written in red.

The door was opened by an overweight blonde in her early twenties. She wore a sweet, heavy perfume. Her hair was on the thin side, and she had broad features with a prominent chin, which lent her a friendly but also anonymous appearance.

'Are you Marianne Sandvik?' the inspector asked after introducing himself.

'Yes, I am.'

'Are you in possession of a Honda Civic?'

'Yes.' The expression of mild curiosity that had hitherto characterised her broad face gave way to a trace of anxiety.

'Is it missing?'

'Not as far as I know. From here, in the stairwell.'

When the policeman didn't react to her tone but continued to look at her with a blank expression, she added: 'Have I parked illegally?'

When the policeman still didn't say anything, she continued nervously: 'It's usually parked a bit further up Bjerregårds gate . . .'

'It's not there now.'

The woman's face began to colour. 'Ah,' she said with a brief, strained laugh. 'Kristine must've taken

14

it. You see, we share the car. But as you're the police, perhaps I can guess what's happened. Has it been stolen?'

'Kristine who?'

'Kristine who lives here.' She pointed to the blue disc and the name of Kristine Ramm.

'Have you got any ID?'

Marianne Sandvik hesitated for a few seconds before turning and going inside. Gunnarstranda followed her in as though it were the most natural thing in the world. The flat was bright and inviting. It smelt of boiled eggs and fresh rolls. There were the remains of a half-eaten meal on the table. The sunlight from the windows filtered through the leaves of a ficus plant in a pot and gently cast its rays over some posters on the wall. One, of a dance at Smuget, showed the backlit silhouette of a female body. Next to it, Audrey Hepburn posed between Bogart and Holden, both wearing dinner jackets. The last poster showed Elvis Presley in a white, fringed jumpsuit. When Marianne Sandvik went through a bedroom door, Gunnarstranda opened another door leading out of the lounge. He entered a tidy bedroom. A few textbooks and notepads on the desk revealed that this room belonged to Kristine Ramm.

When Marianne Sandvik appeared in the doorway Gunnarstranda was lying flat on the floor beside the bed, stretching one arm under it as far as he could.

'What are you doing?' she asked in dismay, as the inspector's glasses slid up onto his forehead, undoing his carefully arranged comb-over. He squeezed his eyes tight until, with a groan, he reached what he was after. Standing up, he shook open a plastic bag and dropped a Nokia phone inside. Then he brushed

15

some dust balls off his jacket sleeve, while Marianne regarded him sceptically from the door and the traffic in Maridalsveien droned past.

'It must've slipped down the crack between the mattress and the wall,' he concluded, studying Marianne's ID and confirming that she was who she claimed to be. 'Thank you,' he said, and passed her driving licence back. 'Have you got a photo of Kristine?'

'If you come with me.'

She rummaged through some drawers in a long bench placed against a wall in the lounge. At length, she produced a photograph of a smiling woman sitting on a sofa. The flash had lit up both retinas, turning them red. People shouldn't smile at photographers, Gunnarstranda thought. Smiling faces expressed nothing more than the smile, not the appearance. 'Can you describe her?' He could read from Marianne's expression that she was beginning to put two and two together. As her suspicions of the gravity of the situation slowly dispelled her initial nervousness, she became more distant. The flush had changed to two pink spots on her cheeks. She stepped forward and glanced down at the photograph to describe the features in more detail: 'Kristine has dark hair, shoulder length. She's quite slim and, well, about the same height as me. One seventy two.'

'Brown or blue eyes?'

'Blue.'

Gunnarstranda slipped the photograph into his inside pocket and asked: 'Has Kristine ever taken drugs? Heroin, recreational drugs, amphetamines?'

'No, are you crazy? No, she hasn't.'

'Sure?'

16

'Absolutely.'

Gunnarstranda eyed her suspiciously.

'A hundred per cent,' Marianne Sandvik said.

'What about alcohol?'

'She drinks beer and wine, like everyone else.'

'A lot?'

'No, the usual, at parties. Why can't you tell me honestly and directly what this is about?'

'Has she been hanging out with any dubious types recently?'

'Not as far as I know, no.'

'When was the last time you saw her?'

'Yesterday morning.'

'When?'

'At about six, half seven, in the morning. We met in the hall here. I was just back from a late-nighter. She was also arriving back from some party or other. Her hair was wet. She'd been in the sea.'

'At six o'clock on a Sunday morning?'

'Yes — I asked her. 'Have you been swimming?' I said, and she replied, 'Yes, in Huk.' 'Alone?' I asked. 'No,' she said. 'Who was he?' I said. 'Wouldn't you like to know?' she said. And she laughed. She seemed to be in love.'

'How do you mean 'in love'?'

'She was a bit hyped up, in a good mood. My impression was that she was talking about a guy she'd met and the emotions were flowing.'

'Did she say the man's name?'

'No, that was the end of the conversation. She went into the shower. I sat down and had a smoke. Afterwards I went to bed. I could hear that she did the same.'

'Do you know what she was doing the previous

evening? On Saturday?'

''Fraid not. I was away all last week, so we haven't talked much recently.'

'And how late did you sleep — on the Sunday?'

'Erm, now you're asking. I went to work at four. I must've eaten a bit first. I'm a waitress at the *Lekteren* in Aker Brygge.'

'Was Kristine here when you woke up?'

'No, she'd gone out.'

'How long were you at work?'

'Until twelve, midnight.'

'And then?'

'Then Knut picked me up. We went back to his place. And I stayed over until today.'

'Knut?'

'Boyfriend. He works for Storebrand. Knut Radér.'

'Do you know what Kristine did after she came home yesterday morning?'

'I'd guess she had a sleep. But I'm getting quite curious now as to what this is about.'

'Do you know if Kristine has had any problems recently?'

'Such as what?'

'A death in the family, romantic problems, bad grades at university or general depression . . .'

'No, not that I know of.'

'Would you say you're close?'

'Yes, as close as . . .'

'What does she live off?'

'She's a student, like me, and works a bit on the side.'

'What's she studying?'

'Folklore studies and social anthropology. She's going to major in social anthropology.'

'Where does she work?'

'In a bar, a sort of pub, not far from Bankplassen. I think it's called Joyce or Voice, or something like that.'

The policeman angled his head as he made notes. 'Have you known her for many years?'

'No, we got to know each other here.'

'Here?'

'This is my flat, but it's expensive, and as there are two bedrooms I put some ads up at Blindern University, in the café, to find someone to share the costs with me. A few girls phoned. I chose Kristine because we got on well. Same wavelength.'

'A long time ago?'

'Soon be a year.'

'Do you know her well?'

'So so. It's always good to have a little distance from the people you live with. We agree on that. That's one of the reasons I chose her.'

'You're not on very close terms then?'

Marianne Sandvik took a deep breath: 'This would be easier if you were more open about why —'

'How close?' the policeman interrupted.

'A little. Not very, I suppose.'

'Not close enough for her to reveal the name of the man she'd been with the other night?'

'She would probably have told me eventually if I'd pushed, but I don't do that. And that should tell you something about how close we are.'

'Where's she from?'

'Molde. Somewhere just outside. Near Hustadvika. Bud, I think the place is called.'

'Has she been in Oslo long?'

'Can't tell you, but I think she moved here because of her studies.'

'What sort of people does she hang around with?'

'All sorts. Students, people she knows from Vestland.'

'Has she got any brothers or sisters?'

'She's an only child. I think her parents are divorced. Her father works on oil rigs. In the North Sea. I don't know anything about her mother.'

'This Honda's actually owned by your father, isn't it? Does anyone else apart from you and Kristine use it?'

'No.'

Gunnarstranda considered what to do. 'I'd like you to come with me for an hour or so,' he said at last.

She frowned hesitantly. 'Where to?'

'The Forensic Institute.'

★ ★ ★

After a shaken Marianne Sandvik had confirmed that the deceased was Kristine Ramm, Gunnarstranda drove her home. And once he was finally back in the office, his next job was to ensure that the priest in the parish where the woman's relatives resided was instructed to inform them of her death. He found the telephone number of the appropriate police station and by chance talked to an officer who vaguely knew the family. The man was able to tell him that Kristine Ramm's mother was divorced and had reverted to her maiden name. She was on her own and receiving benefits.

Gunnarstranda told the officer Kristine Ramm probably died of self-administered heroin poisoning, but there would be an autopsy anyway.

After ringing off, he had actually nothing left to do.

20

At first, he sat staring at the wall, then he glanced down at the mobile phone he had found in the woman's bedsit. And without considering what he was doing, he began to fiddle with it.

Orbit

Hanging tremulously over Nesoddland peninsula, the sun made the sea resemble a tray covered with crinkly gilt paper. Frank Frølich squinted through his dark glasses at a bottle of water. In it, he saw the sun reflected like the head of a yellow clout nail.

He sat with his face turned to the people streaming up and down the waterfront promenade in Aker Brygge and reluctantly had to confess that he was somewhat indifferent to whatever undiscovered beauties there might be in the crowds. Instead, he caught himself craning his head at the sight of long, black hair falling in a particular way or felt his stomach flutter when he saw a dark-haired, long-legged woman in the queue by the ice-cream kiosk. His unease would become so acute that he was half tempted to stand up and walk past, glancing over his shoulder to make sure, to find out if it really was Anna standing there, to quieten his unease — until it dissipated of its own accord because the person changed posture in a sudden fit of boredom and revealed that she was someone else. *What the hell am I doing?* he thought; this was like the time he had rung her at home and, sweating profusely, spluttered out some ridiculous excuse, before engaging in a bizarre conversation.

When he spotted Gunnarstranda walking up the jetty he was thinking about Anna's eyebrows. They were like two perfectly silhouetted wings of a bird. This image melted away as Gunnarstranda's pale, creased, balding head filled his field of vision. To celebrate the glorious day, his eyes were obscured by a pair of sunglasses that any artist or teenager hunting for cult objets d'art would have paid a fortune for. The glasses were large and shaped like raindrops, reflecting in them colours ranging from black to mauve to light-blue, in a gilt plastic frame.

'How much do you want for them?' Frølich asked.

'For what?' Gunnarstranda said, casting around for a free chair. He found one at an adjacent table and took it without hesitation. The two women sitting at the table exchanged astonished expressions at the man's impudence. 'It's taken. We're waiting for someone,' one of them blurted.

'For your sunglasses,' Frølich said, knowing that Gunnarstranda was deaf to that kind of objection. 'They must be at least fifty years old.'

'Twenty-five.' Gunnarstranda sat down and placed a newspaper on the table. 'I bought them at an Esso garage. Easter of 1977. In Fagernes. Let me show you something.'

Frank Frølich watched two pairs of broad hips and two erect necks stand up and move. The two women found another table further away and glared furiously at himself and Gunnarstranda, who was now opening today's *Dagbladet*. He licked his forefinger and flicked painstakingly through the newspaper, page by page, until he found the right place and pointed to an article. Frølich leaned over and skimmed through it. He had read the same report in the previous day's evening edition of *Aftenposten*. A foreigner had been reported missing, for three days.

The waitress, a well-rounded young woman with her hair gathered in a ponytail, came to their table. 'Ah, it's you,' Gunnarstranda said in a friendly voice.

'How's it going?'

'So so,' she said.

Gunnarstranda removed his glasses and asked for a large beer. He glanced at Frølich, who shook his head and pointed to his mineral water.

When the waitress ambled off, Gunnarstranda pointed down to the newspaper and said: 'How about us two looking for this missing man?'

'An asylum seeker on the run?'

Gunnarstranda stood up and scanned the waterfront. Soon he was waving to a familiar figure in the crowd: Emil Yttergjerde, who was strolling muscularly down the quayside toward them.

'He's not on the run. He's a respected scientist.'

Emil Yttergjerde was wearing tight jeans and a bicep-flaunting white T-shirt. His head was shaven and he had organised his sparse stubble into a pointed extension of his chin. Before going to find a chair, he announced in a loud voice that he always sat with his back to the ostentatious buildings in Aker Brygge.

Frølich studied the glittering surface of the water while waiting for Yttergjerde to finish.

'Swindlers and packs of thieves, the whole lot of them. We invest all our energy into building a case against them and then they delay it by . . .'

Frølich wished he would lower his voice.

'We should be living in the Middle Ages,' Yttergjerde waffled on, wriggling on his chair. 'They knew what to do. If some bigshot got up to any knavery, they'd whack him on the noggin and cut off his bollocks. Afterwards he had to play the jester in front of the finer folk. If he was funny, they threw him peanuts and patted him on the head.'

Gunnarstranda stared at him with a deep frown.

'Where have you heard that?'

'I've seen it on TV. Besides, it's true. They used these bastards instead of monkeys. And if that didn't work, they just cut off their heads. Simple as that.' Yttergjerde pulled at his fingers, one by one, until they cracked.

'Tell Frølich about Takeyo,' Gunnarstranda said impatiently.

'The guy's twenty-seven and is working on some kind of doctorate. He's from Kenya and has come to Norway via some aid project in Uganda. He studied at the University of Kampala, which is the capital. That's all we have in the reports. The details are a bit unclear, but he was reported missing by two different women. One's called Ingunn Løvseth. She works with Takeyo at the university. But by the time she'd pulled her finger out, a woman called Evelyn Sømme had already rung the station. Apparently she's known this guy ever since he was small, and they were supposed to be going out to eat on Monday. But he never showed up.'

While Yttergjerde was talking, Gunnarstranda had rolled a cigarette. He lit up, took a speculative puff and turned to Frølich, who asked:

'Why are you interested?'

'Several reasons. One is that the man will soon have been missing for four days.'

Gunnarstranda leaned back as the waitress placed a tray of foaming beer glasses on the table. He waited until the waitress had gone before continuing: 'She . . .' He nodded in the direction of the waitress. 'She and I talked on Monday. She shared a flat with the girl who OD'ed in the car park on Ibsenringen.' He produced a phone from his pocket and laid it on the table. 'This

25

phone belongs to the dead woman, Kristine Ramm. She used it to call Takeyo's home number five times on the day she died. The same day he disappeared.'

'Tragic,' Yttergjerde said. 'When did she die?'

'On Sunday, the fourth of August.'

'That was the boiling-hot day I went swimming in Svartkulp,' Yttergjerde said.

Frølich frowned. 'Svartkulp?'

'Sorry,' Yttergjerde said, self-consciously. 'I meant Lake Sognsvann.'

'At 21:05 she rang Takeyo for the last time.'

'Jesus,' Yttergjerde interrupted. 'I meant Lake —'

Gunnarstranda cut him short with a raised hand. 'The day after, so Monday the fifth, Stuart Takeyo didn't turn up for work. And, so far, he's been missing for four days. Before disappearing, he was contacted by this woman, who later died of an overdose.'

'A narco case,' Frølich said.

'Exactly. And I was delegated to clear it up: to find out who snuffed it after a jab in the arm. And then down from the sky flutters a missing-person case, an African who this young lady calls again and again before departing this world. And in her circle of friends everyone gapes because no one has any knowledge of her doing drugs. She was as clean as a whistle — and the person who most probably sold her the heroin has conveniently vanished.'

'No parents believe their children are on drugs until the shit hits the fan and there they are.'

'I've never ever been near Svartkulp,' Yttergjerde insisted.

Gunnarstranda sent him a stern glare.

'It's just that —'

'You've made your point, Yttergjerde. Thank you

26

for your input.' Gunnarstranda turned to Frølich. 'I'm going to check out Takeyo's flat right now.'

'Now?'

'Well, as soon as possible.'

'Who's driving?'

'You are,' Gunnarstranda said, sipping his beer. 'Because you haven't been drinking.'

* * *

'What do you reckon about Yttergjerde?' Frølich asked as they drove out of the roundabout by Bislett and up Theresegate. 'Is he a closet gay?'

'Why does it interest you?'

'The slip of the tongue. He said he'd been swimming in Svartgulp. That's a gay cruising ground.'

Gunnarstranda shrugged. 'It's so modern now to be gay. It'll soon be as normal as going on a demo. First it was in to be anti whale-catching. Then they marched against police violence. Before you know what's going on, we'll have to look to women for our protection. Here,' he said, pointing to a free parking space beside a black Saab. They got out. There was no one around.

Shortly afterwards, a dark Passat passed them. The driver waved, continued to the block of flats and parked as if he lived there. The taxi sign on the roof was extinguished. The man who struggled out of the driver's seat had once had curls. A long time ago. The remaining hair clung to his scalp like cotton wool. It was as though someone was holding an invisible vacuum cleaner over his head. He was broad in the beam, and his ears stuck out like tuba mouthpieces on either side. Introducing himself as Jon Legreid, he

27

brandished a huge bunch of keys in front of him, then waddled ahead to the front entrance at the corner of the block.

Gunnarstranda had a choking fit on the way up the stairs and hung back.

Legreid spent a long time over unhooking a smaller keyring from the main bunch and opening the flat door. 'You can keep the keys,' he mumbled. 'Pop them into the post box on your way out. It's got 'Legreid' written on the front.'

'Is the furniture the tenant's?' Gunnarstranda asked, taking the keys, still panting.

'It's all mine,' Legreid said. 'I let the flat furnished; that's what it says quite clearly in the contract.'

Gunnarstranda absent-mindedly arranged his own hair before entering. The flat smelt stale and fusty. The hallway was long and narrow. The plaster walls were still unpainted, which didn't improve the impression. Apart from the hallway and the bathroom, the flat consisted of one large room with a sink, a stove, a sofa bed and a desk.

Gunnarstranda opened a window. A tram screeched to a halt at the stop outside. 'No fridge?' He glanced over to the owner, who was still standing in the door-way. 'There must be food rotting in here. You, as the owner, should consider the danger of rats.'

Legreid shouted: 'Anything else? I don't have time to stand around.'

'When did you last see the tenant?'

'Not since we signed the contract.'

'And when was that?

'Before Christmas last year.'

'How do you get the rent?'

'Bank transfer. No hassle with the guy. Pays on time

28

every month.'

'And otherwise? Comments, complaints?'

'Not a squeak.'

Legreid left.

'If there's any smack in this place, we'll find it.' Gunnarstranda put on plastic gloves.

The computer was an older model. Dust had collected around the tower and the screen. Gunnarstranda opened the desk drawers. They were empty apart from a stack of biros and a ruler. He slammed the last drawer shut. There was nothing attached under the desktop. On top, there was a scientific journal, beneath which was an edition of *Playboy*.

Inside the magazine was a NOR bank card with the Visa logo on one side and a photograph of Stuart Takeyo on the other. The picture had been taken in a booth and was not very sharp; it gave them little information about his appearance except that he was young, had regular features, a narrow chin and very short hair. The man's eyes were half closed, which lent him a lethargic appearance. The card was valid until November.

'Vegetables, fruit and ham.' Frølich lifted a plastic bag with the contents almost liquid now and held his nose.

Gunnarstranda waved the bank card.

Frølich went over and studied the *Playboy* article. The glossy pages showed a big picture of black men cleaning fishing nets on a white sandy beach and smiling. It was an article about nature and fishing.

Gunnarstranda went over to the bookshelves, and examined the books and what was between and behind them. On one shelf there were some sheets of paper. Compactly penned notes in neat, elegant handwriting. Gunnarstranda stuffed all of them into a carrier bag. Afterwards he went to the wardrobe. There were three shirts hanging inside, all brightly coloured. The suit jacket had worn sleeves. On the floor were two pairs of shoes. Gunnarstranda lifted them to see what size they were. 'What do you think?'

'Forty-three or forty-four,' Frølich said, busy with the kitchen cupboards.

Gunnarstranda read the label: 'Bata,' he muttered.

'Look at the soles,' Frølich said. 'Cheap plastic. No support in the sole. This man's not exactly well off. Look here.' He took out an empty nylon travel bag with the destination label still tied around one handle. 'Travelling without a bank card and a bag?'

Gunnarstranda continued into the little bathroom, where he examined the classic hiding places: the toilet cistern, under the bathtub, behind the sink and the trap underneath. It was beginning to stink of putrid water. On the sink was a toothbrush and a well-used bar of soap. On a shelf under a medicine cabinet containing a packet of plasters were a razor and a tube of shaving cream.

'This guy's planning to return at some point,' Frølich said from the doorway. 'He didn't take his clothes, bank card or toiletries.'

Gunnarstranda returned to the main room and inspected the sofa bed. Frølich helped him to lift the mattress. Underneath was a green passport issued in the name of Stuart Takeyo, and the ID photograph was the same as on the bank card.

Frølich scrutinised the seams of the mattress in case something had been sewn inside.

Gunnarstranda pointed to the telephone on the bedside table. 'Is that a red light I can see?'

'The answer machine.' Frølich went over and took out the little tape. He pressed a button. Immediately there was a scratchy message coming from the loud-speaker.

'. . . *This is Stuart speaking. Please leave a message . . .*'

A loud peep was heard before the tape wound scratchily on: '*Hi. It's me again. Where are you? I don't want to do this alone. Not now. Please hurry . . .*'

The scratching continued and then went silent. Then there were several calls, but each time the connection was broken without a word being said. It happened six times. The seventh and last time was a familiar cough.

'That was me,' Gunnarstranda said. 'Play the tape again.'

Frølich rewound, the scratching noise repeated itself and the same woman's voice spoke via the loud-speaker.

'She must've rung before. And that time they must've spoken.'

'They've arranged to meet,' Frølich said. 'But after he's left she's become impatient and rings again. And there must've been something new. 'Not now'. Something has happened.'

'It could be something to do with her. We don't even know if it's Kristine Ramm talking. But bring the tape. Marianne Sandvik will tell us if it's Kristine's voice.

★ ★ ★

After sealing the door to the flat and trudging down the stairs, they stopped in front of a line of post boxes. On the left, at the bottom, there was a dented post

31

box with Takeyo's name on it. Gunnarstranda fumbled with the bunch of keys until he found one to fit. The box was half full. Among the advertising there were a few bills, but there was only one letter. Stuart Takeyo's name and address were typewritten on the envelope. The two officers exchanged looks. Gunnarstranda, who was still wearing plastic gloves, took a penknife from his pocket. Without the slightest embarrassment, he cut open the envelope. There was a single sheet inside — a computer print-out. There were only five words, written in Courier and block capitals. The message was concise and left no room for misunderstanding:

        YOU'RE A DEAD MAN, NIGGER!

Breathing Difficulties

She told him to strip to the waist. Gunnarstranda turned to the mirror and obeyed with a grim expression. He didn't like undressing in front of a mirror. It was bad enough undressing in front of a woman without having to witness it himself. Pensive, he stood for a few seconds viewing his lean upper body before turning to her.

The first time they met, he thought it would be their last. For him it didn't matter that she was of Pakistani origin; his misgivings were more about the femininity she always radiated — the make-up around her deep-brown eyes, the dark-red, filed nails, the painted lips and the long ringlets, the pattern of her bra that could be discerned through the material of her white coat, all wreathed in heavy perfume, which could easily have knocked out lesser men and given them hallucinations.

But she had met his condescending arrogance with composure, looked him in the eye and performed her first examination without showing a single sign of professional or personal discomfort. He had liked this, and now, standing close to her, like a schoolboy next to the teacher's desk, it struck him that she was probably one of the women he liked best, of those he had any contact with.

She took the stethoscope from around her neck and listened as she told him to breathe out: 'Harder. Deeper . . .'

The coughing fit came unannounced, as always. He

held his hand in front of his mouth and succumbed.

When it was finally over, and he had straightened up, she was sitting back in her chair, arms crossed, her brow stern rather than concerned. 'It could be chronic bronchitis, as we discussed last time,' she said. 'But it isn't. You've got pulmonary emphysema. Chronic shortness of breath.'

As Gunnarstranda said nothing, she continued: 'The tests don't lie. The walls between the air sacs in your lungs are damaged.'

'How can I get rid of it?'

'You can't.' She chewed the inside of her cheek thoughtfully. 'But you can stop the damage spreading.'

'Spreading?'

'Well, stop the disease developing. With medication and a number of other measures.'

'Measures?'

'Giving up smoking.'

He grimaced at the suggestion.

'Do we have to breathe to live?' she asked.

'You think we do?'

'It's the first thing you have to do. But you mustn't just give up smoking, you have to do exercise too, avoid pollution, head south in the winter.'

'I do do exercise.'

'Such as?'

'I swim now and then.'

'You have to do it regularly. You have to change your lifestyle.'

'I don't like going to southern Europe and I don't feel like giving up smoking.'

'Let me make myself clear. If you don't try to give up smoking, I don't want you as a patient.'

She met his gaze head on.

'I mean it,' she affirmed.

Gunnarstranda stood up and put on his blue shirt.

'Are you out of breath after the slightest exertion? Do you have breathing difficulties and the sensation that you can't get enough air? Is that happening more and more often? Phlegm? Coughing fits?'

Gunnarstranda buttoned up his shirt, got to his feet and tucked it into his trousers.

'This is about your life — in the best-case scenario, the quality of your life.'

'And what was the medication you were going to suggest?'

'Medication to help you breathe. Corticosteroid inhalers.' She swung round on her chair and reached for her prescription pad. Her hand was small. She crossed her legs: sandals on her feet, slim ankles and chubby toes. She was the most feminine creature he knew. Usually just seeing her put him in a good mood, and he looked forward to every appointment. And now here he was, considering whether to drop her as his doctor.

'You know,' she said, as she concentrated on writing, 'it's not hard to give up smoking. That's just a myth. It's all about not taking the next cigarette.' She tore off the prescription and handed it to him. 'The first's for inhalation every morning and evening. The second's for more acute shortness of breath. And when you come here next time, I want a full report on your strategy for giving up smoking.'

'Just giving the next cigarette a miss?'

She grinned and revealed a glimpse of white teeth. The sight would have taken his breath away if he had been twenty years younger. 'You can stop smoking at night, can't you?'

'No.' He shook his head. 'I wake up and have a few drags every night.'

'But if you had to sit here with me for the rest of the evening without tobacco, what would you do?'

'Is that a genuine offer?'

She smiled. 'There you go. If that's how easily your mind is led, then there's hope for you yet with regard to smoking. Just imagine you're putting off your next cigarette. But you're putting it off for more than ten minutes. You're deferring it for the rest of your life.'

'Hang on,' she called as he was about to leave.

He turned and met her gaze. She did it every time, and from the laughter in her dark eyes he could see she liked the ritual as much as he did.

'What is it now?' he growled sulkily.

Her smile became even broader. 'Your next appointment,' she said, pointing to the printer; his appointment slip squeezed out like a white tongue.

He folded the sheet and put it in his pocket.

'Gunnarstranda,' she said.

He turned again.

'Have you ever thought of treading the boards?'

Biology

The sun was beating down as Frank Frølich strolled up the hill between the Munch Museum and the university's botanical garden. A light breeze took hold as he turned in through the main gates and gave him a shove in the back, like a giant but gentle hand, alongside the brick Botanical Museum building. As he shielded his eyes from the swirling dust, he heard an old Neil Diamond song — 'Cracklin' Rosie' — waft through an open window. Diamond's rich rendering of *ba bapa bapa ba* faded slowly as he rounded the corner and caught sight of a young woman in work gear calmly pulling a lawn mower behind her. The wheels clattered on the tarmac. When he ran up the steps to the Botanical Museum and knocked on the big entrance door, she shouted at him to go straight in because no one would hear him knocking.

Ingunn Løvseth had an office on the first floor. She had bristly blonde hair that hung in strands on either side of a triangular face graced with round, rimless glasses. Between her eyes was a stern furrow that reminded Frølich of Little My from the Moomin stories.

'Stuart's project is about biological control of weeds,' she said. 'Shall we go for a walk in the garden?' She grabbed a white lab coat hanging on a hook behind the door and walked ahead with short, energetic strides.

'Is it for the doctorate?'

'Yes, it's about ecological imbalance, an Eichhornia

hybrid . . . Sorry, I don't suppose you know what that means. It's a plant, also known as a water hyacinth. This aquatic weed spreads exponentially, and for a while it invaded harbours and caused problems for fishermen.' Little My carried on talking as she walked.

'Where?'

'Lake Victoria. Stuart's from Kenya, but the problem's just as big in Uganda and Tanzania. Originally the plant comes from South America — the Amazon — so it doesn't belong in the African biotope.' She stepped lightly down the stairs. On the radio, further down a corridor, John Lennon had taken over from where Neil Diamond left off: 'Mind Games'.

'Stuart was busy comparing biological schemes to measure the effect of a particular initiative,' she said.

Frølich held the door open for her. The bright sunlight was blinding.

'In other words, to measure how effective it is to reduce the spread by introducing a natural enemy of the plant. As the water hyacinth originally comes from South America and has no natural enemies in Africa, over the last ten years it's been able to grow at an incredible speed over the whole continent. Shall we find a bench to sit on, or should we look for a table in the café?' She pointed up at the magnificent, old, yellow building.

'Café sounds good to me.'

'Little My' Ingunn continued to walk and talk at the same brisk pace; her voice had even found a conspicuously semi-aggressive undertone: 'In some places the water's cleaned mechanically. Uganda in particular has achieved good results by using barges to remove the plants. But a biological method to combat the plant would be to introduce a weevil — Neochetina something. Let me see. I can't remember exactly what it's called . . .'

'Never mind. I'm only interested —'

'Please don't talk for a minute. I can't hear myself think. *Neochetina . . . Neochetina . . . Neochetina bronteria* it's called. I usually get it. Eventually. Anyway, it's a beetle, a kind of tick, which attacks plants and sucks nutrition from the leaves so that they can't flower, and so can't breed.'

Frølich followed Little My across the shingle until they found a table in the sun. 'So nature can be used to control nature,' he concluded.

'Exactly.'

'But why would an African travel to Norway to research this when the lake, the plant and the beetle are on the other side of the globe?'

'Stuart's a statistician. He writes a thesis and needs related material — figures and documentation from other places — to say something general about this kind of measure. I don't know much more about it, but I can find you the project description if you need it.'

'And this kind of project exists in Norway?'

'Goodness, yes. For example, ladybirds have been used in agriculture to control aphids. And the Russian king crab spreading down the Norwegian coast is not native to our shores, and it has no natural enemies. And then we have the problem with American lobsters threatening our lobsters in Oslo fjord. No one can predict the consequences. That's probably the difference: as far as the water hyacinth's concerned, the problems are very obvious.'

The atmosphere in the café was drowsy and summery. A few customers were drinking from porcelain

39

cups and eating cake in the sunshine. 'Do you know if Stuart has a lot of friends?' Frølich asked, donning his sunglasses.

'Stuart's a nice person, but it wouldn't surprise me if he doesn't have any friends. The Botanical Institute at Blindern is his real employer. Perhaps he's fallen between two stools or he's a bit on the outside. I don't know. It's probably the case that the university milieu is not the easiest. Here we go home or pick up kids from school when the working day's over.'

'Sports team? Chess club? Does he have a hobby in his free time?'

'Not as far as I know. But he probably goes to the bars and pubs where Africans hang out. He talked about it once, somewhere in Oslo where he usually meets people he can communicate with.'

'Do you know if he's been worried about anything recently?'

'How do you mean?'

'Someone threatening him and he's had to move away?'

'No. I can't imagine anything like that.'

'He's never said he felt unsafe?'

'Never.'

'Has he received any threats because of his colour?'

She shook her head. 'Not that I know of. He would've said. That's so despicable.'

'No harassment or clashes here, at work?'

'Are you out of your mind? No.' Little My smiled at the question.

'Did he seem tense or anxious in the days before he went missing?'

The angry furrow in Little My's forehead deepened as she hesitated.

40

Frank Frølich waited.

'He might've been a little more stressed, but I don't really think so. I suppose when something like this happens, you ransack your memory, searching for signs or signals, but I can't say that he behaved any differently last week from how he normally is.'

'You said he might've been a little more stressed in the last few days. Could he have been under the influence? High?'

'Why would he be high?'

'Well, he might've been taking drugs.'

'No chance.'

Frølich said nothing.

Little My looked at him, unsure.

'Have a good think,' Frølich said.

'About what?'

'Whether he showed any signs of drug use. Whether he'd been jumpy, irritable or unstable at work. You said he might've been stressed . . .'

'Are you serious?' Little My seemed genuinely offended. 'Do you mean that?' When Frølich still said nothing, she began to search for words. 'If you'd met Stuart, you'd know that he was completely . . . completely . . .' She couldn't finish.

'Did he have visitors at work, people who wouldn't fit into academic circles?'

'I don't think anyone has ever visited him at work.'

Frank changed the subject: 'Is he in a relationship?'

'I don't know.'

'Has he mentioned the names of any Norwegian women?'

'Not to me, as far as I can remember, no.'

'Has he ever mentioned the name Kristine? Kristine Ramm?'

41

Little My, who still seemed confused, sat shaking her head.

A bird began to chirrup in the tree above them. Little My scuffed a shoe in the shingle. The sunlight shone through the foliage and dappled people's faces a yellowish white. On the path that disappeared behind the main building Frølich recognised the woman in green with the lawn mower. Now she was alongside a young man with a ponytail. He was taking off a pair of gloves.

'And you, did you have a lot of contact with Stuart?'

'Stuart and I have worked together quite a bit, but that contact's limited to professional matters.'

'When did you report him missing?'

'When he didn't turn up on Monday, I rang his home number, but all I got was an answer machine.'

'Did you leave a message?'

'No. But afterwards I called the police. I felt stupid, but . . .'

'You reacted quickly.'

'He's a little helpless,' she said hesitantly. 'Sometimes it's like Stuart has no other interests than work. He gives it everything. I've always thought it must be something to do with his background. He comes from poor circumstances and is very focused on his studies and his career. So, he's a bit inhibited by his culture. Meeting women scientists, for example, was very difficult for him at the beginning. He asked me who I'd paid to get the job I had. And I don't know if he believed me when I said there's no corruption in Norway. And his own research grant — well, the whole concept is a budget expense. Stuart's appointment is fixed-term and I'm not sure it will be extended, let me put it like that. And he's obsessed by that. He's always asking whom he has to bribe to keep the project going.'

'Bribe?'

'Yes, I suppose he wants to make sure everything works as it should, and at the start he took it for granted that someone in the university would have to be bribed.' Little My laughed. She had short teeth spread far apart, like tree stumps on the ridge of a hill.

'Is he corrupt?'

'You misunderstand,' she grinned, removing her glasses and wiping the corner of her eye with the back of her hand. 'It's his culture, and for him it's an absolutely innocent approach. Think of it like this: you'd probably be on your guard if you were working with colleagues in the African police. Nothing is free, we say here in Norway. For Stuart that statement has real meaning. He has such a literal, naïve attitude to things. That's why he seems helpless and on the periphery.'

Frølich had no more questions and politely took his leave of Ingunn Løvseth, who made a beeline for a group of colleagues at another table. Frank rounded the corner, walked behind the building and continued between low, trimmed box hedges, past a fountain and down an oak-lined avenue leading to Jens Bjelkes gate.

The Clinic

Inspector Gunnarstranda wrinkled his nose as he turned into Bamseveien and parked by the wire fence. The place confirmed all the class prejudice that had built up inside him when he first read the address: big houses, housewives taking dogs for a walk, remote-controlled garage doors, spoiled children and second car for the wife.

As he was about to get out of the car, his phone rang.

He stood with one hand on the open door while studying the screen and thinking: *Why does this woman bother calling me?* He let it ring, trying to remember what rules he had broken that would be worthy of a reprimand. And when he did, he accepted the call and asked her to be brief.

'With pleasure,' the voice said. 'I have one question: Are you in the habit of contesting experts' conclusions in areas where you have no competence?'

Gunnarstranda closed the car door and strolled toward the wrought-iron gate in the distance. 'What do you mean?'

'If you are not,' the voice said with equal froideur, 'would you be so kind as to explain why you commissioned the autopsy of a body where the cause of death was obvious and certified by a particularly well-qualified health official?'

'Are you telling me the autopsy report is ready?' Gunnarstranda asked.

The answer was a while in coming, and he suddenly

realised he had left his prescription at home. 'Shit,' he muttered.

'Don't you take that tone with me.'

Tone? Gunnarstranda was annoyed. 'Is the autopsy report ready or not?'

'I'm asking the questions here, Gunnarstranda.'

'And I have a job to do. We'll talk when the report's ready. Goodbye.'

Gunnarstranda opened the gate. When he pressed the bell, his phone rang again. Same number. He switched it off and stuffed it in his inside pocket. 'Evelyn Sømme?' he asked the woman who opened the door. She was Gunnarstranda's age and had clearly come from working in the garden, wearing light-green shorts, a tight-fitting yellow top with an embroidered poppy on the front and soil-covered rubber gloves. Her hair was covered with a checked scarf. 'I've come about Stuart Takeyo,' he continued and introduced himself.

Evelyn Sømme, who kept her gloves on, raised one hand in the air and rubbed her cheek with her upper arm.

'You reported him missing, our records say,' the policeman explained. 'So I assume you know him well?'

'That's correct.'

As the woman didn't make a move to let him in, he got straight to the point: 'Did Stuart Takeyo ever say to you that he was frightened of something or someone, or of some event?'

Evelyn Sømme unrolled her gloves. 'Come in.'

A box of plums by the cellar door gave off a sweet smell. *They're early*, Gunnarstranda thought, wondering what type they could be.

She guided him into a small office, where she sat down behind an imposing desk and indicated that he should take a seat in an armchair with a foot-rest, by the window.

'Stuart's more likely to be frightened of being served lutefisk or sheep's head for dinner at a Norwegian's house than he is of being in any physical danger. And I've never heard him say he was frightened of a particular person.'

Gunnarstranda plumped down on the chair. 'He's never felt threatened?'

'Not to my knowledge.'

'Are you a nurse?'

'Was once. Now I'm more of a therapist, here, at the clinic.' She looked for somewhere to put her gloves. They landed on the floor.

'Clinic?' Gunnarstranda looked around: one room with this armchair and a desk, and a computer and ink-jet printer on the shelf below the window.

'Homeopathy and reflexology.' She nodded toward a poster on the wall. It showed the sole of a foot divided into sections by dotted lines, like the county borders on a map of Norway.

'A kind of layer-on of hands?'

She gave a tired expression and then sent him a patronising look before answering: 'I treat people and write natural medicine prescriptions to alleviate complaints and tensions. You should try it. You look as if you need it. I'm sure your foot is so tender you can barely walk barefoot over the bathroom floor.'

They eyed each other.

For an instant he wondered whether she'd tactically shifted the focus onto him.

'Don't tell me you don't dare,' she said at length.

46

'Dare to do what?'

'Take off your shoes in here. Your breathing's laboured, you've probably got inflamed bronchioles and your shoulders are much too high. No doubt you smoke too much. I can stop you smoking with a few weeks' intensive treatment.'

'I'm investigating a case; you're a witness. It's inappropriate for a witness to massage my feet, especially not in her home.'

The answer earned a condescending, somewhat arrogant smile. *This woman is bloody pigeon-holing me*, he thought with irritation, then coughed and said in a controlled voice: 'Perhaps some other time. We were talking about Takeyo . . .'

They exchanged looks again. She didn't say anything, but from her expression he could see that she had finished analysing him and he had been labelled: a neurotic, work-obsessed, socially dysfunctional man with poor self-knowledge. And she was right of course. But because her conclusions couldn't ever include a fraction of what he suffered — stress, neck pain, sleeping problems, and self-contempt that increased by the day — he felt that the slightly infantile view of humanity that she represented made him more sympathetic than annoyed. And this strange sense of sympathy in a way undressed her in his eyes, and in turn this nakedness embarrassed him, made him turn away and drown his emotion in a question: 'If Stuart Takeyo's life was under threat, what do you think he would do?'

'He certainly wouldn't decide to disappear,' she said at once — as though she had sensed his embarrassment and wanted to smother the unpleasantness of it. Then she sat thinking — and Gunnarstranda

47

could clearly sense that she would rather try to understand what had just happened between them than
talk about Takeyo's personality. 'My guess,' she said
slowly, 'is that he would either talk to me or Jan. Jan
Groven's a man he's attached to. Stuart would talk
about the situation, perhaps with both of us, and I
know he hasn't.'

'Could he have taken his own life?'

'Definitely not.'

'You seem very sure.'

For some seconds she stared down at the desk.

The walls of the room were painted a light yellow.
They were decorated with pictures of poppies as well
as the reflexology chart of the foot. A watercolour
showed fields of poppies in a landscape that was redo-
lent of Provence. On the facing wall, there was a large
study of the proud style stalk of a poppy, towering up
between scarlet petals with a coal-black background.
Behind her back hung a colour photograph of hairy
Arctic poppies. The silence in the room began to feel
oppressive. They both seemed to realise it at once.
Evelyn Sømme tilted her head as they exchanged
glances.

'Why are the police suddenly interested in Stuart?'
she asked.

'We haven't at any stage been uninterested.'

'But you haven't done anything.'

'We've carried out a systematic probability assessment — eliminating possible solutions to his
disappearance,' said Gunnarstranda, who didn't want
the conversation to degenerate into general dis-
satisfaction with the police. 'We haven't recorded any
accidents that Takeyo might have been involved in. So
he may've left the country of his own free will. And, if

48

so, that's his business, not the police's, so long as he hasn't fled because he fears for his own safety. But his passport was in his flat when we searched it yesterday. And we've contacted several airlines, but none of the flights has his name on its lists. Accordingly, it's unlikely he's left the country. His name and description have been given to all local police stations.'

'So what? If he isn't on the streets, it won't help if the police are keeping an eye open for him. You have to search for him through the newspapers.'

'Stuart Takeyo is a grown man and can travel freely without having to report to either you or me.'

'But —'

'Formal search ads are of no interest to me,' Gunnarstranda interrupted her impatiently. 'But several of the national newspapers have followed the case, so in a sense that is a search. And now I'm here to get closer to an answer.' He paused for a few seconds and then asked: 'What are your thoughts about all this?'

'Anything could've happened. One day you think it must be a crime; on others you think the whole thing is a misunderstanding . . .'

The policeman produced a copy of the written threat he had found in Takeyo's post box and passed it to her: 'Seen this before?'

Evelyn Sømme took the sheet of paper and her eyes widened. 'My God . . .'

'If he'd received this, what do you think he'd do?'

'As I said, he'd contact someone. But . . .' She handed him the sheet back. 'Where did you get it?'

'From his post box.' Gunnarstranda folded the sheet of paper. 'Has he ever talked about racism in this country — to you?'

'No.' She shook her head, shocked by the discovery.

'I would know if he had,' she added.

'And you don't know if he's received other threats like this?'

She shook her head.

'Of course, Takeyo may've gone underground somewhere in Norway for completely unknown reasons. But that's just speculation. One option with a tiny degree of possibility is that he's hiding from the police. But Takeyo may also have taken his own life. For the moment all we have is this,' Gunnarstranda said, waving the piece of paper, 'which may suggest that Takeyo's involved in something criminal.'

'Hiding from the police? Do you mean Stuart might've actually committed a crime?'

'I don't mean anything. I'm just working on probabilities.'

'And you really should do something to de-stress,' she said, staring at him distantly: 'Cut out coffee, drink herbal tea. Camomile or valerian.'

Again, she was trying to control the conversation by changing the subject, away from suggestions that Takeyo might be a criminal.

'How long have you known him?' he asked.

'From when he was a little boy. I was once stationed in Homa Bay, as a health worker. It's a town by Lake Victoria. Many years ago now. But in those days a lot happened there. A radio station was built, for example.'

'Oh, yes?'

'That was why Jan went there. Jan Groven — he's an engineer. A widow called Ruth lived nearby — Stuart's mother. She had lots of children and was very poor. I became very attached to her; so much so that I decided to pay for the education of one of her

50

children. And that was Stuart.'

'And your contact since then?'

'I left in eighty-two, when he was seven years old. Since then, we've stayed in touch via letters. We met again two years ago, after he'd got his master's; I was visiting Homa Bay for the first time in many years. His results from Makerere were fantastic.'

'Makerere?'

'The university in Kampala.' And she added with a smile: 'So his mother was happy. This photo was taken then.' She passed him the framed photograph on the desk. There were three people in the picture: a man and a woman flanking a younger black man, who must have been Stuart Takeyo. Evelyn Sømme, sun-tanned and smiling, was on the right. The man on the left had a trim, grey beard. He was standing with his hands on his hips, staring at the photographer.

'The man on the left?'

'Jan Groven. They're very close. Stuart has never known his biological father.'

Gunnarstranda passed the photograph back. 'Do you know why he chose to come to Norway?'

'He was given a grant by the university. It's something to do with biology and data processing.' She rested her chin on her hand, thinking. 'Believe me, it would never occur to him to take his own life. Africans with his background don't get the typical depressions we decadent citizens in the rich part of the world suffer from.'

'What depressions?'

She looked up. 'Eighty per cent, at least, of my patients have symptoms that can be reduced to a single common denominator: an emptiness, a sense of not being able to cope, a lack of something they can't

51

define. They suffer from what professionals in the social sector call 'melancholy' or 'burnout'. You don't need to pretend that this is new to you. It's at this level we find one of the biggest differences between the northern and southern hemispheres in human terms. For us, there's nothing at stake anymore; we barely notice that life is a challenge. The only time we meet the brutality of existence is when we see hurricanes, floods, fires and drought on TV. The most daring thing we do is catch a plane to New York, Paris or London to go shopping. And we breed people who can't bear this emptiness, people who parachute off mountains, paddle canoes down waterfalls, throw themselves off bridges tied to an elastic rope — just to get the kick that tells them they are alive. It's not like that in the southern hemisphere. Death, or ruin, is a real entity for poor people in poor countries. There's no safety net, no social care, no social security. If you have an accident or lose your job, you're literally on the slippery slope, and without a parachute or elastic tied around your ankles, please note. For him, Norway is a golden opportunity — a gate to the ideal world he has only heard about. Try and discuss the concept of depression with him and he won't understand what you're talking about.'

'And he didn't react negatively to a freezing-cold Norwegian winter?'

'It would never occur to Stuart to kill himself. You'll have to show me a suicide letter before you can make me believe that's what's happened. And even with that I'd have to think it through. Why would he? A broken heart? Don't forget that Stuart, with his academic background and all the status he's acquired, would be a privileged person in his home country.

The concept of a broken heart in this context is an empty cliché. Besides, it's anything but a polar night here now — it's light all day and almost as hot as in his home country. I think he's been having a great time.'

'Do you know anything about his love life?'

'He's your gay bachelor — gay in the old sense.'

'Has he ever mentioned a woman by the name of Kristine?'

Evelyn Sømme's eyes sharpened again. 'Are you telling me Stuart has a Norwegian girlfriend?'

Gunnarstranda fell silent.

'Is that why you're here?' Evelyn Sømme asked coldly. 'Has this Kristine been raped by a man of foreign origin?'

'Has Stuart Takeyo ever mentioned the name Kristine or Kristine Ramm to you?' the policeman repeated.

For a brief moment their eyes met across the room. Evelyn Sømme looked away and said: 'He did sporadically mention names of people connected with the university, but I've never heard that one.'

'When did you last see him?'

'Must be a few weeks ago. But we've been in contact via email. We were supposed to be going out for a meal on Monday.'

'Have you tried to contact him since?'

'I've rung several times, but I only get his answer machine.'

'Have you left a message?'

'No.'

'When did you call the police?'

'Late Monday night, when he didn't show up. You know, Stuart's reliable — one hundred per cent reliable. The fact that he didn't show up and didn't answer his phone was alarming.'

'You said you usually email each other. Can I see your emails?'

'Why?'

'To try and find a clue as to what's happened.'

'But there's nothing —'

'We're only trying to solve the case in everyone's best interests,' the inspector interrupted. 'It's important to see if he mentions any names, places of special significance . . .'

'If he had, I would've told you.'

'If you refuse to hand over material that would further our investigation, I would have to consider a court order.'

'I'm not refusing. I just can't see —'

'Leave that to our judgement,' Gunnarstranda said as gently as he was able.

Evelyn Sømme stared at him. 'I can send you Stuart's emails,' she decided at length, with an apologetic smile. 'I don't want anyone sniffing around my hard disc. I have patients . . .'

Gunnarstranda stood up with difficulty.

She accompanied him to the door. There, in the doorway, she inhaled deeply, as if she had remembered something.

'Yes?' the policeman said.

She shook her head and said: 'You should take your health problems seriously.'

He smiled back weakly. 'I'll give them some thought. There's one more thing . . .'

Evelyn Sømme raised both eyebrows.

'Does he take drugs?'

'What?' she said, astonished.

'Is it at all possible that Stuart Takeyo takes other intoxicants than alcohol?'

Evelyn Sømme stared at him for a good while without speaking: 'For me, that's inconceivable. What makes you ask?'

'Have you ever seen him inebriated?'

'He's very fond of beer, but I don't think I've ever seen him drunk, actually. Why do you ask?'

'Are you sure he doesn't have any connections with criminal groups?'

'What sort of groups?' she asked fiercely.

'Please be so kind as to answer my question.'

'At the very least you should be more specific about what you're suggesting.'

'Let me formulate the question in a different way. Can you imagine that anyone in Takeyo's circle of acquaintances has taken drugs?'

'No!' Sømme spat the answer out. A saliva bubble stuck to her trembling lower lip.

'Did Takeyo seem testy, uncommunicative or different recently?'

'No.'

Gunnarstranda observed her. The friendly woman who came to the door from her gardening was gone. In her place was a furious and apparently affronted woman. 'I assume —' he began, but was unable to finish what he was going to say. The door had closed.

'. . . that you will contact us if you hear from him.' Gunnarstranda said to the door before turning and walking back to his car.

Evensong

'What a strange man,' Tove said.

'I thought so, too,' Gunnarstranda said, flipping off his shoes and walking in his stockinged feet into her sitting room. As always, the TV was on. It was a dose of the usual Valium served to viewers as the weekend approached: a bunch of celebs were being interviewed about themselves by a celebrity journalist, everyone doing as little as they could to feel ashamed of the role they'd chosen for themselves.

'So, are you off work?' she asked, fetching a fat bottle from the glass cabinet beside the sofa.

She had been sitting outside. The veranda door was open, and there was a half-smoked cigarette on the edge of the onyx ashtray on the glass table.

'I'm probably about to be ordered off the case I'm investigating,' Gunnarstranda answered. He sat down on the sofa and stretched out his legs.

'Why's that?'

'My use of police resources and my pig-headedness.'

'And the money went on . . . ?'

'An autopsy.'

She showed him the bottle and read out the label: 'The Balvenie. It was on offer at Heathrow. It's single malt and may be a bit fiery.' She showed him the label, with a grin. 'It's only ten years old.'

'Let's try it,' he grinned back.

She went onto the veranda and brought in the ashtray and the cigarette.

He fetched two glasses from the cabinet and sat down.

'And you're putting up with that?' She removed the top and poured.

'Putting up with what?'

'That you might be taken off the job.'

'I don't have much choice. But it's annoying because the case was just beginning to get interesting.'

'*Skål*,' she said.

Gunnarstranda swirled the whisky in his mouth for a while before swallowing.

She stared at him with raised eyebrows.

'You first,' he said.

'Not bad,' she said.

'It's brilliant,' he said.

'But have you been?' Tove asked.

'Have I been what?'

'Have you been taken off the job?'

'Not yet. There'll probably be a row when the autopsy report comes out.'

'When's that?'

'Anytime now.'

With a devilish glint in her eye, she asked: 'Anything I can do?'

The TV celebs roared with laughter.

Gunnarstranda reflected, raised his glass and looked at her through the golden-brown liquid. 'You could turn off the TV . . .' he said, leaning back on the sofa.

Sedative

Frank Frølich grabbed her around the waist. She put her arms around his neck while he held her with one arm. He pressed her back against the wall and used his other hand to lift her legs. She wrapped her thighs around his waist and hooked her feet together. He took her nicely rounded buttocks in both hands and penetrated her. When she covered his mouth with hers, he woke up, staring straight into the sun shining in his face. He had a taste of beer in his mouth and a huge erection. He twisted his head to see the clock on the bedside table. The hands showed a quarter to five. He tried to remember who the woman in the dream had been, but failed. He was wide awake and realised he wouldn't be able to go back to sleep, so he got up, had a shower and went to work.

One and a half hours later, in the office, he saw his boss's tobacco pouch on the corner desk under the window. Gunnarstranda had already been in.

At almost eleven o'clock the heat of the sun coming through the glass panes was unbearable. Dust was dancing in the beams of light angling into the room like yellow stripes. Frank could feel his trousers sticking to his thighs and was wiping the sweat from his brow when Gunnarstranda burst in, excited, his comb-over in disarray, and threw a pile of papers on the desk.

'I've been thinking,' Frølich said. 'There's no evidence to suggest the girl was a junkie, nothing to suggest the missing researcher was a junkie. What are you grinning about?'

'The autopsy report.'

Frølich was lost.

'Congratulations.' Gunnarstranda was smiling beatifically. 'Murder. Premeditated. Malice aforethought.' He interlaced his fingers behind his back and paced to and fro along the wall, head down.

'She was murdered?' A razor-sharp pain entered Frølich's temples, and he knew all too well what Gunnarstranda's restlessness signified. To gain time, he asked, 'How do they know she was murdered?' At the same time, in a seemingly casual manner, he cleared his own desk, stood up and placed the pile of papers and journals in his hands on the corner desk, hiding the tobacco pouch.

Gunnarstranda rummaged through his pockets and agitatedly stroked his lips. 'So, I ordered the autopsy just for the hell of it, did I? For the sheer hell of it? Well, Schwenke now says, while the girl did in fact die of an overdose, she was sedated first. She was unconscious when she was given the shot. She didn't inject herself. Someone else did it. But what makes this murder is that they used *ether*.'

'Ether?' Frølich pretended to stretch his arms and sat back down at his desk.

'Yes. Chloroform. That means it wasn't a nice pal giving his girlfriend her first shot either, because if that had been the case the other toxin that came up in the tests would almost definitely have been Rohypnol. And Schwenke wouldn't have reacted to that. He says most ODs happen in combination with Rohypnol. This was ether. No drug addict injects with ether.' Gunnarstranda cast around nervously. 'Could it have been a robbery . . . ?' He paused as he

59

searched through his pockets. 'But that doesn't help us, because there's no evidence of one. And we don't even know whether there's anything missing from her car. There was nothing except for the syringe and the other drug-taking equipment. And a rape is also unlikely. Although there were traces of sperm in her vagina, she was dressed. And, according to Schwenke, there were no cuts or bruises to suggest she'd had sex against her will. Robbery and rape are therefore just speculation. What is definite is that heroin was used to kill her *while she was unconscious*.'

Gunnarstranda pulled out the drawers of his desk, searching for his pouch. He slammed the drawers shut, lifted the books and papers, but without finding his tobacco. His hands were trembling and his eyes swept the room like radar.

Frølich breathed in, feeling the stuffy air around him, his headache increasing. He cast a stolen glance at the corner table to assure himself that his superior officer's tobacco pouch was still well hidden. Then, with a serious expression, he looked up at Gunnarstranda, who continued with renewed energy:

'If she'd been sedated with Rohypnol before she got the heroin injection, the pathologists wouldn't have reacted — addicts often use Rohypnol to intensify the heroin high. So we have to ask ourselves why the murderer used ether instead.' His lips were quivering, which indicated that the arrow on his nicotine-addiction gauge was alarmingly close to the red. He lifted the pile of papers on his desk without finding the tobacco, moved to the shelves and checked between the files and magazines.

'Time?' Frølich suggested tensely, forcing himself not to look at the corner desk. 'The murderer may

60

not have had enough time to get Rohypnol — or there was nothing to drink around . . . Coke or beer. Or perhaps it simply wasn't possible to knock her out with sleeping tablets.'

Gunnarstranda continued his search for the tobacco pouch, head down, arms by his sides, like a crow hopping about on a rubbish heap. 'Exactly. So it could've been Takeyo. He works at the university, where they have access to unusual chemicals, and now he's vanished. The whole business with the ether seems a little primitive and may accord with my prejudices against science nerds. But the problem remains: if the aim was to sedate her, why give her a shot of heroin in the arm as well?'

'Could it have been the other way around?' Frank considered standing in front of the desk to make sure his boss wouldn't find the tobacco and pollute the air in this cramped room even further. 'Heroin first and then ether?'

'Out of the question. It was the heroin that paralysed her breathing. If she'd had heroin first, she would've been spread-eagled on the floor, and there would've been no point with the ether — there would've been no point sedating her any further. No. The murderer got ether to sedate the poor woman and heroin to kill her while she was unconscious and unable to defend herself. The idea was to camouflage the murder as a standard OD case — another statistic. And then I had an autopsy done for the pure hell of it.' Gunnarstranda whinnied with self-satisfaction. 'A reprimand was on the cards — a dressing-down in the back room, but then it transpires it was a premeditated murder after all. What about that, eh?'

Frank stood up and ambled casually over to the

desk where the tobacco was hidden behind and partially under the post-mortem report.

Gunnarstranda watched him. 'If I hadn't been irritated, if I hadn't *demanded* an autopsy, she would've gone to her grave as a suicide case.'

'Pure luck. If you hadn't had the autopsy done, I assume her parents would've demanded the same.'

'True. But the autopsy reveals that the goal for the murderer must've been twofold. One, to kill her; two to kill her there and then, that Sunday evening. She was in the passenger seat of a car she'd most probably driven herself. So, she could've been with the murderer in the car.' Gunnarstranda was breathing heavily and leaned against the window frame.

This was the moment Frank had been waiting for. He strode out and stood in such a way that he was screening the view of the corner desk, and said: 'We'll have to impound her car. It'll have to be gone through with a fine-tooth comb for evidence.'

'Precisely.' Gunnarstranda rummaged through his pockets for the nth time. 'Bloody hell, you haven't seen my tobacco, have you?'

'We have to concentrate on this.'

'I can see it in your face. You've hidden my tobacco.'

Frank ignored the accusation and said: 'We've had the autopsy done. We've been dealt a murder. If this bastard is as calculating as you say he is, he must've imagined this was a possibility.'

'Nope. We've just been lucky. The ether was discovered by chance. There was an alert pathologist who smelt an irregularity when Schwenke opened the body. Then he carried out a test that was more comprehensive than the usual ones. That means they were looking for other toxins in her blood. If luck had been on the murderer's side, they would never have found the ether. And the murder would never have been discovered.' Gunnarstranda flashed a white smile and said cheerfully: 'And there's my tobacco. Do you mind if I have a smoke?'

'Do I mind?' Frølich sighed heavily.

'First sedated, then killed, before someone quite simply put the syringe between her fingers to simulate a suicide.' Gunnarstranda licked the roll-up paper, lit the cigarette and spoke in a cloud of blue smoke: 'This murderer is single-minded, efficient and presumably devoid of feeling.'

'By the way . . .' Frølich began.

'Yes?'

'It *is* Kristine Ramm speaking on Takeyo's answer machine.'

'Who says so?'

'Marianne Sandvik.'

'This is like solving a crossword, isn't it, Frølich.' Gunnarstranda grinned through another cloud of smoke. 'Woman killed, the man who was supposed to meet her legs it. Do you see how the cards have fallen?'

'But Marianne Sandvik had never heard Kristine talk about Takeyo, never heard his name mentioned. She didn't think Kristine was particularly interested in black men,' Frank said, and added hesitantly: 'And there's another matter that could be problematic.'

'What's that?'

'A journalist rang in to ask after you a couple of hours ago.'

'I don't talk to journalists.'

'But this is the one who found the body — Lise Fagernes. She works for *Verdens Gang*.'

63

Gunnarstranda shrugged. 'So? I hope you told her how things are? Nothing new?'

'I did, yes, but she'd somehow heard about the row blowing up over the autopsy and asked what it was about. I told her the truth. I hadn't heard about any row and the autopsy was performed because we needed to be sure about the cause of death.'

'Write a press release and say the woman was murdered. It'll leak out sooner or later anyway. And send a copy to VG while you're at it,' Gunnarstranda said, lost in thought.

'And if she calls again?'

Gunnarstranda turned to the window. 'I don't talk to journalists. It's all too easy to let the cat out of the bag or say something wrong. And once you've done that, it's bloody impossible to unsay it.'

Femina

At first, Frølich didn't notice the woman standing by the reception barrier. But he stopped when the security guard motioned him over. The woman was around thirty with hair that was so blonde it looked bleached.

'Frølich?' A pair of slim designer glasses made her look like a jet-setter. As she stretched her arm he caught a glimpse of a wristwatch — steel and a top-of-the-range design.

'I keep asking to see your boss.' She stared up at him, straight into his eyes, and stood so close it was unpleasant.

'Oh, yes,' he said, automatically retreating a step.

'Oh, sorry, I was forgetting myself. Lise Fagernes.' She followed him as they shook hands. She was now as close as she had been before. There was something hungry about her designer gaze, and something familiar too — even the facial expression.

'And you're the lady who found Kristine Ramm,' he said. 'We've already spoken.'

She nodded, without letting go of his gaze. 'Dreadful experience. Leaves its mark.' She beamed, but he, unable to take the pressure, looked away. And when he tried again, she was back and just as relentless: 'From what I gather, the death's being regarded as suspicious and you're looking for a man who has disappeared — this Takeyo, a Kenyan who's in the country on a contract with the university and the Ministry of Foreign Affairs.'

65

'She was murdered,' Frølich said, 'And that's all I can say.'

'The woman in the car? So it wasn't an OD but murder? Tell me more.'

'I've just sent a press release. Read it.'

'But I'm here, aren't I.'

Frølich was getting tired of bending his neck and pressing his chin down to hold the gaze of this woman who came up to the middle of his chest and stood so close. He raised both hands in defence and backed away again.

She followed him. 'I have just one question.'

'I'm sorry but I don't have the authority to answer.' He hurried toward the exit.

She ran after him and tried to stand in his way. As this didn't work, she continued in the same direction that he was going, but walked backward, smiling. 'You haven't heard my question yet.'

'There's no point. It's not in my remit to answer journalists' questions.'

'But the answer to this question's a simple yes or no.' She had stopped in front of the door. He would either have to grab her and push her aside or wait until she'd had her say. 'Do the police think there's a link between the murder of Kristine Ramm and Stuart Takeyo's disappearance?'

'I'm sorry,' he said, forcing his way past her and out. The heat stuck to his skin and the sun dazzled him as he headed down the footpath to Grønlandsleiret.

'Come on,' she said, panting after him. 'It's impossible to contact your boss.'

He stopped when she seized his arm. The narrow glasses made her seem arrogant and a little cold. She wasn't exactly attractive, he thought. But he liked the way her top lip curved, and the mole on the left of her mouth automatically drew his gaze. Her blonde hair cascaded down her shoulders.

'Now listen,' he said earnestly.

'OK,' she said. She readied herself, back straight, bent at the hip. A button had come loose and revealed a sun-tanned stomach for a second. Looking up, he saw she had magically conjured up a small biro and a notepad. 'I'm ready.' Her caricatured pose made him laugh.

'There are three possible answers,' she said while he focused on the mole by her mouth. 'Yes, no and don't know. Which is it going to be?'

Her eyebrows formed an interrupted sine curve. Again he was struck by something familiar he couldn't place. 'Yes,' he said, and could have bitten off his tongue immediately. 'I mean . . .'

She allowed the silence to persist for a few seconds before answering herself: 'So the answer's yes. Now, that wasn't so difficult, was it.'

They stood looking at each other. Her blue eyes now took on a caustic glint. She knew she had him where she wanted him: she had wound him around her finger, another example of a male who had allowed himself to be charmed by a mole and a glimpse of a navel.

She spun round abruptly and slunk down the footpath with an exaggerated swing of the hips, as if it were a catwalk. It only lasted for a few moments, then she swivelled round, waved goodbye and continued on her way, walking normally.

Frølich was annoyed with himself for the fiasco. First of all, he had been seduced by the sight of bare flesh, and now his phone was ringing: his mother asking him to drive her to her sewing club. He gave in, of course.

★ ★ ★

Driving her when she was alone was usually fine, even if she was forever reeling off the latest news about her grandchild, whom she had visited at Frank's sister's place ('she's so intelligent, she's just like me'). He had no problem with his mother's subsequent complaints about his unmarried status, either. Nor the usual satirical comments about Gunnarstranda; Little Napoleon, as she called him. But when his mother's friend, Edna, joined her on the back seat, it was too much to bear. This time Edna was out to make him part of the conversation by hook or by crook. She leaned forward, patted him on the shoulder and began to initiate him into the idiosyncrasies of her family:

'You know, Frank, Aunty Kitty, my Aunty Kitty, was only one metre fifty tall, that was why we called her kitty, you see, she was no less impressive than Aunty Maiken, in the looks department, that is, but Maiken had the height, long legs, you know, Aunty Maiken was a Miss Oslo — we always said that when we ate out, in the rotunda in Theatercafeen, we only ate in Theatercafeen, we did, and always in the rotunda, and stared at all the people in Stortingsgaten, just to spot Aunty Maiken trooping up in all her splendour.'

Frank pretended he wasn't listening. He knew that to survive the rest of the journey he would have to think about something else. *I have to concentrate*, he told himself, trying to drown the voice from the back seat by putting on the radio.

'Please, Frank, turn the music down.'

'Well done, Edna. I'm impressed you can still recognise music, and you don't tell your children to let the cat out because it's yowling.'

Their laughter rocked the rear seat. 'Karin! Where *do* you get it from?'

I insisted to the journalist that there was a link between the murder and the missing-person case. But all we know is that Kristine Ramm was in the passenger seat of a car she must have driven herself. If it was her who arranged the meeting with Stuart Takeyo, there could be a link. She could have met him in the underground car park, got out of the car and been doped; but then there's probably a video of this — the car, the perp, whether man or woman. The car park has CCTV . . . And why the hell haven't we checked if the murder was caught on film?

'Don't be so moody, Frank. Come on, give us a smile. Edna, Aunty Maiken was the one who married Eilert, the ladies' underwear manufacturer, wasn't she?'

'Well, in those days we didn't think it was strange that a man was head of a factory producing lingerie, it was completely natural. And they were the ones who made the little miracle, you know, those lovely chiffon knickers with lace, they were so popular, and they made Aunty Maiken even more attractive, to men, that is, who were thinking about the delights she had underneath.'

I have to go there and as fast as . . .

Frank glanced at Oslo Stock Exchange as he passed under the pedestrian bridge. There, behind a transformer station, were two youths with leather belts around their biceps, ready to share a syringe.

'Do you remember Eilert's sister, the one with the

crooked nose? She had a joint at the top. Whenever she got angry, her nose went up and down, quickly, as though she was wagging a finger, in the middle of her face.'

'What? She was born with a cuckoo clock in the middle of her mug?'

'Oh, Karin, the things you say.'

There's a possibility the CCTV caught them both going in and out ... And he was an African. There can't be so many black men leaving the car park on a Sunday evening or night ...

'Didn't she die of cancer?'

'No, that was Ivar, her other brother, but that was the doctor's fault. Ivar was in pain for several months, but do you think the doctor did anything? He just prescribed painkillers. He had no idea the man had cancer. The idiot even wrote in the paper that people shouldn't ring in the middle of the night and bother doctors with unnecessary call-outs. Call-outs, I ask you. He jumped on his bike with a panier full of pills and blood-pressure instruments ...'

'And there was Ivar dying of cancer in front of his nose. I mean to say.'

The whole mystery can be solved by the bloody video. With our luck the duty officer has already filed it and someone thought it was a confiscated porn film and has taken it home, and then his fifteen-year-old son has wanted to watch it too, with his mates ...

'But wasn't he bonkers?'

'Ivar?'

'Yes, I heard he was bonkers.'

'No, that wasn't Ivar. That was their father.'

'Well, they were a funny lot, all of them. You know, if anyone went to their farm they all ran into the forest.

70

You saw a grey trouser leg disappearing over a fence, and there they sat, up a tree, until the visitors had gone again. Perhaps they were bonkers, I don't know. At any rate, that doctor should be shot. By the way, he comes to our hotel with that married jezebel. And, goodness me, you should hear them. She screams so loud you'd think . . .'

Of course, that's it. There's a video that's bound to contain lots of clues and if the perp left the multi-storey in a car, he must have paid to get out.

'Who screams?'

'The one with the thin legs and no bra, walking around and flaunting herself.'

'Well, we were all young once.'

Bloody hell, Frølich thought.

'Frank! Remember to turn off here, it's Gamlebyen.'

Please, do me a favour, Frank thought.

'Yes, and now look at Aunty Kitty. She lived half her life as a dancer, smoked like a chimney and in the end sounded like one of those black women who sing with orchestras. Once, I remember, we were eating, and she took a slice of bread, she was a bit senile, you know, and after lifting the bread, but before it reached her mouth, she'd forgotten what she was going to do and started screaming.'

Frank admitted defeat, it was impossible to think. Confused, his eyes vacant, he slowed down in front of the roundabout. A car hooted behind him. Frank changed gear. 'Mother,' he pleaded.

'What was that again, Edna?'

'Mother . . .'

Frank didn't have a chance to finish his sentence, his mother's indefatigable friend continued: "Oh-oh-

71

oh-oh . . .' she screamed. 'What was I about to do?' We had to push the whole slice in her mouth because she'd forgotten she was going to eat.'

'Yes, I remember that. But was it Aunty Kitty?'

'Yes, it was. She used to forget to get dressed and all sorts of things. The worst was the telephone. When it rang, she didn't know what the sound was and didn't know what to do, so she ran around the house shouting, 'Help me, help me, help me."

Frank gripped the wheel tighter. *If Kristine Ramm wasn't with Takeyo that night*, he forced himself to think, *then she was killed by someone else. If someone else set out to murder her . . . they will still have had to enter the car park . . .*

'Hey, Frank. Don't forget to stop.'

From the car, he watched them walk away, two broad-hipped, elderly ladies waddling along and slapping each other on the back and roaring with laughter, excited and ready for a long afternoon of coffee, gossip and cards. He waited until they had gone through the brown door before picking up his phone and calling the car-park security company.

Film Script

After waiting for around ten minutes at reception, Frank Frølich was welcomed by a man in his mid-twenties. It must have taken him a long time to gel his hair in such a way that he looked as though he had just got out of bed. He had that parvenu expression that makes you alternate between wanting to pat him appreciatively on the head and give him a good slap. He was wearing a white shirt with the brand logo on the chest and a yellow silk tie with the same blue pattern as his neatly pressed trousers. And Frølich was immediately passed a brochure for the security company with the young man's business card.

Frølich thanked him for taking the trouble as it was a Saturday and the weekend . . .

'That's fine,' the man said. 'We're well known for giving that bit extra.' He pointed to the company logo.

Frølich didn't understand.

'Our business slogan. Give that bit extra.'

'Aha.'

They were sitting in a bare meeting room with a small TV monitor.

The young man asked Frølich if he wanted a biro.

'Thank you, I have one.' Frølich patted his shirt breast.

'Have one anyway,' he said generously. It boasted the company logo as well.

'I've found the car,' the stripling said, winding forward. It was a black-and-white recording with typically poor picture quality. When the young man pressed

73

play you first saw a freeze-frame of walls and car bonnets. On the right of the picture was the entrance ramp with the two barriers and the ticket machines. A car drove in and stopped in front of the barrier. The young man froze the picture. It was a Honda.

'The reg plate's right, isn't it?'

Frølich nodded.

The video continued. An arm came out of the open window, the barrier rose and the car was gone.

'Rewind a bit,' Frølich said.

He rewound frame by frame.

'There,' Frølich said. 'Can you see?'

'See what?'

'The hand taking the ticket. It's dark-skinned.'

Both stared at the screen and watched the car move out of the picture.

'There are two people in that car,' Frølich said.

The young man nodded. 'If you want, you can borrow the cassettes.'

'Are there more of them?'

'They're recordings from the entrances to the tunnel in Ibsenringen and in Teatergata. But this is all the shots there are of this car. A Honda Civic with this reg plate drives into the car park from the entrance in Teatergata at 23:33 on Sunday the fourth of August.'

'And this is all you have of this car? No pics of where it's parked?'

'I'm afraid not. That zone isn't covered by cameras. But during the night some cars drive out and leave the building. If you take the cassette with you, you can check them out. In some shots you can see the reg plate very clearly.'

★ ★ ★

74

'Perhaps she's already dead,' Gunnarstranda said, watching the clip with the dark-skinned hand coming out of the window and going back in again.

There were four people in the room: Gunnarstranda, Emil Yttergjerde, Frank Frølich and Lena Stigersand. The latter had been drafted in because of the murder. She had freckles, plaited red hair and so many keys and paraphernalia on her uniform belt that she clinked whenever she moved. They sat down in front of a computer with an extra-large screen, which was attached to a video player.

'Schwenke was unable to give an exact time of death,' Gunnarstranda said. 'He only had body temperature to go on and was annoyed I couldn't tell him when she last ate.' Gunnarstranda lit his roll-up. 'But she did have a well-digested vegetarian meal in her stomach.'

Lena Stigersand zoomed in onto the windscreen.

The faces behind the glass were shadows. Lena Stigersand zoomed in again.

'The black man's driving,' Yttergjerde said.

Frølich agreed that the driver appeared to be black, but it was impossible to make out any features.

'Looks like it,' Gunnarstranda mumbled, crushing his cigarette in the ashtray. 'He has short hair and dark skin. His arm is clothed. Her clothes didn't cover her arms when she was found.'

They all stared at the screen.

'From a purely logical point of view she was killed in the car park, so she must have been sedated there too,' Gunnarstranda averred.

'But she's sitting in the car of her own free will,' Yttergjerde said, pointing to the screen, 'and her body was clothed. What was the point of knocking her out?'

'She was sedated so that the murderer could find her artery with the syringe in peace and quiet,' Frølich said.

The others turned to him, and Lena Stigersand cleared her throat pensively:

'What if the murderer drove into the car park because he wanted to have sex?' She shrugged when the others focused on her. 'It's sick of course, but . . .'

'Yes?' Yttergjerde said impatiently.

'It could be that Kristine resisted. So, he may've knocked her out with ether and to cover up the crime he killed her with heroin.'

'That's very unlikely,' Gunnarstranda said firmly. 'Schwenke found only traces of sperm in the body, and he inclined to the view that she'd most probably had sex a good while before she was killed. Forget rape or sex as motives in this case. Frølich's right. The perp used ether simply so that he could kill her in his own good time. There's something psychopathic about this whole business.'

Frølich yawned and looked outside. A woman and a small girl were balancing on a line of blocks demarcating the boundary of the park. Mother and daughter, he guessed, and was suddenly reminded of Eva-Britt. She was married now, at last — two months after meeting her husband. He and Eva-Britt had been together for eight years. And after they finished, he had barely given her a thought, until now. He was missing having someone.

He stretched out an arm and opened the window a fraction. Through the noise of cars, he could hear the girl call something to her mother before she lost balance and jumped down. The mother, however, had unusually good balance. Admiringly, Frølich watched

76

her extend a leg sideways as though she were doing a gymnastics routine on the beam.

For a second, he saw an image of Anna stretching a bare leg up the white wall of his bedroom. He shouldn't think like that, because he knew she was probably doing the same thing now, on holiday, on a hotel bed, with another man. Frølich watched the mother and the little daughter, full of contempt for his own self-pity.

'Let's start' — Gunnarstranda's voice cut through Frølich's thoughts — 'with the most logical explanation for her being found in the car park: it was the best place for the murderer to kill her. It's clear the murderer had a plan, because he tried to make his crime look like a drugs overdose. He needed a place secluded enough to carry out the two operations: sedate then inject. All the evidence suggests that he chose this car park for his crime. And here' — Gunnarstranda pointed to the picture — 'we see the two of them in the car, entering the car park. But there's still something that doesn't ring true.'

'Maybe not,' Lena Stigersand objected. 'If there are no pictures of a black man on foot in this film, it might be because he recceed the crime scene in advance, checked where the cameras are and left the place unnoticed.'

'And what about the woman on the answer machine? She begs Takeyo to hurry up,' Yttergjerde interjected.

'We don't know, as already mentioned, when she left the message,' Lena Stigersand said.

'It was probably on Sunday evening,' Gunnarstranda said. 'Mobile phone,' he explained.

They sat for a while in silence. The video played and the TV monitor showed pictures of parked cars.

Gunnarstranda turned to Frølich. 'Have we got any shots of anyone leaving the building?'

'Hm?'

'Cars leaving the building,' Lena Stigersand repeated with a smile, winking at the others: 'Frølich's got woman trouble.'

'Have I?' Frølich said serenely, looking straight at her before continuing: 'There are several exit ramps, and people and cars go out all the time, people leave and come back in to fetch their cars. Going through all the footage, registering all the visible number plates and perhaps trying to identify the cars and the people is a massive job.' He jumped up. 'Stop it there.'

Everyone turned to him.

'Rewind,' he said impatiently to Lena Stigersand. She obeyed. 'There.'

Four heads leaned toward the screen. The merest shadow in the corner of the picture. Legs and most of the upper body were hidden behind a car. The face was in profile and it belonged to a black man.

Lena Stigersand wound forward. She rewound. But there were no more shots of the man. It lasted for a fraction of a second.

'The time's 23:40,' Gunnarstranda said. 'That's seven minutes since they drove in.'

'He's killed her,' Yttergjerde stated darkly. 'In only seven minutes.'

Everyone stared, hypnotised by the quivering freeze-frame.

Gunnarstranda broke the silence. 'Evelyn Sømme and Ingunn Løvseth have to see this; we need them to confirm that the man is Takeyo.' He turned to Frølich. 'Approximately how many vehicles leave this underground car park in the relevant period of time?'

78

'The security company guy claimed around fourteen cars left between midnight and the following morning. There's less traffic at night of course. Of these fourteen, it's possible to read the reg plate of eleven, apparently. We're checking all those who used a credit card. We should be able to trace them.'

'It definitely looks as if he's escaping on foot,' Lena Stigersand said.

'But everyone knows there are CCTV cameras in multi-storey car parks. If you're going to kill someone, you don't ask the intended victim to meet you there, do you? When you know there's CCTV?'

Gunnarstranda nodded toward the picture on the screen. 'He might not have known. There aren't many hi-tech gizmos in Kenyan car parks — if indeed there are any multi-storey car parks at all in the country. Theoretically, he could've killed her anywhere, perhaps in her car. He may've just dumped the car containing the body in the car park and made his getaway.'

The others nodded in agreement.

Frølich cleared his throat. 'Does that mean we have a major lead?'

'It's a lead anyway,' Gunnarstranda said, turning to Yttergjerde and Stigersand. 'You'll have to check out all the drivers leaving the car park. I've heard we've already had a couple of calls with information. Someone with more professional expertise than we have should look at this video and see if they can give us a description of the two people sitting in the car as they drive in.'

Migratory Birds

It turned out to be a pub of the more insalubrious variety, with dim lighting and deep sofas along the walls. Jan Johansson's jazz piano streamed out of well-concealed speakers. A few regulars hung around the bar. Some elderly men had ensconced themselves on a sofa and were discussing politics and the latest royal news in loud voices. In the furthest corner sat a group of Thai-looking women whose skirts were too short and whose stares too lingering to be a gang of work colleagues out on the town.

Gunnarstranda wriggled up onto a stool by the bar. The woman behind it took an empty half-litre glass and raised an eyebrow. Gunnarstranda shook his head and asked for a cup of tea.

A thin, tired prostitute nodded to him as she stumbled through the door. He stared after her as she sat down at the table with the Thai girls. He couldn't remember ever arresting or questioning her, but he knew it had happened, more than once. That is how it is for old teachers meeting pupils from many years before, he thought. There is something familiar about the face, but God knows what their name is.

The waitress came over with his cup of tea — lukewarm water infused with a yellow bag of Lipton. She was in her thirties and could have been attractive, but the cigarette bobbing up and down from the corner of her mouth lent her a tough look, and her ultra-tight-fitting clothes made her seem ravaged and aggressive.

'Did you know Kristine Ramm?' Gunnarstranda

asked, tasting the tea.

She eyed him for a few moments and said: 'Who's asking?' She blew out cigarette smoke, like a film cliché. He had to smile.

'Oslo Police. Crime Squad.'

'What are you smiling at?'

The policeman took out his ID card and assumed a serious expression. 'Did you know her well?'

The woman left the ID card on the bar. 'Kristine worked here for about six months, but we were rarely on the same shift. I knew who she was, but I can't claim to have known her.'

'Anyone here who had more contact with her?'

'I don't know.'

'Who told you she was dead?'

She paused to think. 'That kind of thing spreads like wildfire. Might've been one of those in the corner.'

Gunnarstranda glanced over at the sofa of regular customers: men past their peak with typically ruddy complexions, who met after lunch, smoked roll-ups and told long tales over a beer.

The prostitute who had nodded to Gunnarstranda on her way in, stood up and was on her way out again. 'We've grown old, Gunnarstranda,' she mumbled. 'I hardly recognised you. You look so distinguished.'

'That's how it is,' he answered with a wink. 'Police officers, politicians and prostitutes are like wooden boats — we become old and distinguished-looking, unless we sink.' When he turned back to the bar, the woman had gone. He sat stirring his tea. After a while, a man with a stiff knee came in from a door by the bar. He was wearing sunglasses despite the dim light in the room. He wiped the bar with a cloth and limped

81

back through the door.

Gunnarstranda slid down from the stool and walked over to the group by the sofa.

He showed his ID.

The three men stared up silently when he talked about Kristine Ramm. All three of them remembered her: *Nice-looking girl, great legs and well stacked. Had any of them spoken to her? No, just 'morning' and 'good evening'.*

Gunnarstranda made a note of their names.

A crimson-faced man with thinning, blond hair asked the policeman if he had grown up in Seilduksgata.

Gunnarstranda nodded and strained to remember the man's face.

'I hung out with your brother,' the man said helpfully, raising his glass with a small grin and revealing two long front teeth.

That was all he needed. 'Squirrel Jensen,' Gunnarstranda beamed. 'Your father was a cobbler and you lived in Herslebs gate.'

The gang of pals applauded the recognition as Jensen drained his glass. He nodded to the policeman and announced to the others: 'His brother went to sea when he was sixteen. And he married a woman from New Zealand. She was a looker. So much so that people stopped in the street when they saw her. But she left, didn't she?'

'She moved back to New Zealand.'

'Why?'

'Because she was so bloody good-looking and the only woman in town with dark skin,' Gunnarstranda said. 'It's true what you say. Whenever she caught the tram, people crowded round to touch her.'

At that moment the waitress came back.

Gunnarstranda took his leave of the regulars and climbed back on the stool. 'What's the name of the man with the dicky knee who just came to inspect me?' he asked.

'Freddy? He wasn't inspecting you.'

'Freddy what?'

'Pedersen.'

'The owner?'

'More a kind of manager.'

'Could you tell Freddy I want to talk to him?'

'You can't. He's gone home.'

'He didn't walk past me.'

'There's a door at the back.' She tossed her head. 'He just left.'

Gunnarstranda rested his eyes on her without speaking.

'Yes?' she asked in a toneless voice.

'Kristine Ramm used her mobile to phone here on Sunday the fourth of August, the day before she was found dead. Do you know who answered?'

She shook her head. 'Not me at any rate. I wasn't working here then.'

'No one talk about her ringing here?'

'No.'

'Could Kristine have been working that evening?'

'No, she and I were free at the weekend. Freddy knows who was working here then.'

'And, as you know, Freddy isn't here,' Gunnarstranda said acidly, then asked: 'How did she get on with the clientele?'

'Absolutely fine. She'd been around, but you didn't realise that at first. You didn't notice until you trod on her toes.'

83

'Which means?'

'She could deal with pissed customers and gain respect at the same time. She was the type men glanced at in secret rather than trying it on face to face. But what do I know? There's nothing more to say. There are so many different people in this line of work, and Kristine did a great job.'

'Do you know who she hung out with?'

The woman shook her head.

'Boyfriends?'

'No idea.'

'Is there anyone here who knew her better than you?'

'That's not really the way we are here. We're not so close with each other, put it like that. Kristine was maybe a little more reserved, but that's the house style. We respect the fact that people are not very sociable.'

'Do you know when she was last at work?'

'The Friday before she died.'

'Do you know what time of day?'

'I relieved her at nine in the evening.'

'Did you notice if Kristine's behaviour had changed over the previous days?'

''Fraid not,' she said, taking an empty glass and pulling a beer. She had received an imperceptible wink from the gang on the sofa. 'Can't help you there.'

★ ★ ★

As Gunnarstranda was on his way out of the pub, Emil Yttergjerde rang: 'The fingerprints on the threatening letter to Stuart Takeyo match those of a guy called Egil Rasten.'

84

'Rasten?' Gunnarstranda said, staring into the air, perplexed.

'I've been doing a spot of checking. The last thing we have on Rasten is a charge of violence and damage. The owner of a pub where some Africans hang out accused him of attacking an employee. Rasten reported the owner and some guests to the police for violence and threats. The case was shelved because of lack of evidence, but what is special about this is that one of the named customers is Stuart Takeyo.'

'I see.'

'The letter in the post box is a genuine death threat,' Yttergjerde said sharply. 'I've located the man who wrote it and all you say is, 'I see'?'

Gunnarstranda moved away from the clatter of a passing tram. He raised his voice: 'We have to prioritise the woman in the car park.'

'But what do I do with Egil Rasten?' Emil Yttergjerde asked impatiently.

'Find him and ask him why he wants to kill Takeyo, see what's actually behind the reports and get a detailed account of everything he did on Saturday the third and Sunday the fourth,' Gunnarstranda said and rang off.

Family Ties

He had decided to take the prescription to the chemist and hurried across Egertorget square. Some Japanese tourists were queueing to be photographed beside the busker with the guitar and a drum on his back. Indifferent to his surroundings, he sang 'Puff, the Magic Dragon' the way he had stood and sung it for thirty years, slightly greyer in the beard and at the temple now. Gunnarstranda continued past Stortinget, the Norwegian Parliament, and crossed Eidsvolls Plass to Stortingsgaten and the Svanea chemist, where he stopped and stared in amazement. It had gone. The whole of the corner block between Rosenkrantz gate and Stortingsgaten had been demolished. He stood as if paralysed. *What shall I do now?* He trudged back to the slate flagstones in front of Stortinget, where he found a bench. *My God*, he thought, *is that all it takes to knock me off my stride?*

Two boys wearing baseball caps and baggy, drop-crotch trousers trundled past on skateboards. He watched them. They braked elegantly in front of the traffic lights, turned and jumped, their skateboards rotating in the air. Neither of them took any notice of the hole in the ground.

Gunnarstranda put his hand in his inside pocket to find the prescription, but had to flick through some pieces of paper. The first was the death threat against Stuart Takeyo.

YOU'RE A DEAD MAN, NIGGER!

Immersed in thought, he strolled back to his car and took a decision.

The traffic heading for Smestad had begun to pick up. Thirty minutes later he drove into the chaos of underground car parks in Olaf Bulls vei, where Jan Groven lived, at the end. It was a quarter to four in the afternoon when the door lock buzzed. In the hall there was a smell of dust and flowers. The sunlight angled through the windows, and every landing on the staircase was decorated with big plant pots. A young woman with many hours of sunbathing behind her waited on the top floor while Gunnarstranda fought his way, panting, up the stairs. With two floors left, he had to rest to get his breath back. He thought about the prescription in his pocket, braced himself and continued. The woman was wearing a kind of beach outfit: a short skirt and a top that revealed a lot of her stomach. She was around thirty with short, red hair combed in a boyish style.

Gunnarstranda explained who he was. 'I've come about Stuart Takeyo,' he wheezed and shook her hand.

'I'm Liv Inger Sømme,' she said, curtseying like a well-brought up little girl. 'Jan's probably around the corner . . .'

'Is it alright if I wait?'

She was clearly unsure whether this query appealed to her. Nevertheless, she maintained her mask and said casually: 'That was what I was going to suggest.' She held the door open and walked ahead with long, springy steps. 'You can sit on the terrace.'

The flat was high up; there was a view of Lake Bogstad, parts of the golf course and the factories near Fossum. The sun had begun to cast its rays onto the west-facing terrace and had drawn a yellow triangle

87

in the right-hand corner. Today's *Dagbladet* lay open on a white plastic table. It was windy and the pages were held down by a large mug containing a used tea bag.

She pulled one of the chairs from under the table and held it for him. *As though I were a pensioner on the tram*, he thought gloomily, and for a second regretted that he had come up here when he could have made an effort and found another chemist. *But why do they absolutely have to demolish buildings in this city? Can't they look after things?*

'Can I offer you anything?'

'No, thank you. Perhaps you also know Stuart Takeyo?'

'We've exchanged letters over the years.' She held on to the door frame. 'In a way we're like brother and sister.'

'Might you be the daughter of Evelyn Sømme?'

The woman nodded.

'I've already spoken to her. Is Jan Groven your father?'

'No,' she said, 'Jan and I live together.' Reading the surprise in the policeman's eyes, she added: 'Jan and I are engaged.' She coughed. 'Did my mother tell you she met Jan when she worked for the Norwegian Agency for Development Cooperation? Well, as you know, our family is not like any other.'

'Could you please sit down?' Gunnarstranda growled, all of a sudden irritated by her gauche nature.

She regarded him with surprise for two seconds, then obeyed, and perched on the edge of the chair as if to emphasise that actually she ought to be somewhere else.

'And what is your relationship with Takeyo?'

'We were pen pals when we were small, and met there too, in Africa, when I was small, but I don't remember a thing about it.' She smiled shyly and continued: 'Actually we got to know each other through letters. For me writing was pure duty, a kind of ritual that was performed for my mother's sake. Stuart wrote a lot about his belief in God and his school. And whenever I received a letter, I was jealous because he seemed so profound. I just wrote about how many fish I'd caught when I was on the island of Tjøme, the latest pop songs and that kind of thing.'

'So, it was a bit special when he came to Norway?'

'Yes.'

Gunnarstranda leaned back. A gust of wind tried to ruffle his hair, bringing with it the sounds of children bathing in the Bogstad lake.

'We've always sent Christmas and birthday presents — and received drawings and pictures. In the pictures he always looked very serious. But when he came to Norway it was like meeting quite a different person. It's hard to dislike a guy like Stuart.'

'Do you know if he has a girlfriend?'

'A girlfriend? No.'

'How come?'

She stared into the middle distance — and he had a sense that she was thinking about someone she harboured great affection for. As though she could read his mind, she looked up, almost shy at being caught doing something illegal. 'Stuart seems to prioritise work over anything else. He works day and night.'

'Has he talked about a Norwegian woman, someone called Kristine?'

She shook her head — still ruminating.

'Can you remember exactly when you saw him

last?'

'Yes, it was a Saturday before . . . it was last Saturday.'

Gunnarstranda frowned.

'What is it?'

'Last Saturday? That's when he disappeared.'

She nodded. 'Jan and I were out in a boat — Jan's skerry jeep. We were by Bestumkilen bay, and then I saw Stuart. He was being rowed to a boat by Killingen, close to the shore.

'Rowed to a boat?'

'Yes, a cabin cruiser, modern, pointy job, naff. There are lots of them around.'

'And you recognised Stuart Takeyo in a rowing boat?'

She nodded. 'Yes, a small red dinghy. We were too far away for there to be any point shouting or waving.'

'Do you know who owns this boat?'

She shook her head and coughed. 'I know it sounds a bit odd. I thought of ringing my mother or Stuart, but I didn't.'

'How can you be so sure it was Takeyo?'

'First of all, we shouldn't have been on the water that day. I mean, it was pouring down, wasn't it. It had been bright sunshine all week and on exactly that day . . . Look at the weather now as well. The sky's been blue ever since, but it bucketed down that Saturday. The whole trip was a terrible idea, in an open boat in the rain . . . And when I saw Stuart with an umbrella . . .'

She grinned. 'Stuart was in this little dinghy with an umbrella in the pouring rain. And the way he sat. You see he has a particular habit. He runs his palm across the back of his neck, feeling his hair, as it were.

It sounds strange, but it's a typical mannerism of his and I've never seen anyone else do it. Actually, it's a bit irritating because he seems a little absent when he does it, he bends his head in a rather unusual way as he strokes.'

'Was he alone?'

'No, there was a woman rowing.'

'Did you see her face?'

'Unfortunately not.'

'Would you recognise her again in a photo?'

'No, I didn't see her face.'

'How old was she?'

'She was definitely young — I noticed her legs. She was wearing an anorak, you see, with a hood, but she had a short skirt or shorts on, and, well, fabulous legs. She was definitely under forty. Probably under thirty even. I wasn't really looking at her. My jaw dropped when I saw Stuart being rowed over and climbing on board a boat like that. It didn't ring true.'

'Describe her,' Gunnarstranda said impatiently.

'The woman in shorts and an anorak? I saw her climbing up into the boat, from behind. I'm afraid I can't say much more about her, I couldn't even see what colour her hair was.' She stopped talking when she heard a key being inserted into the hallway lock. She stood up, poked her head round and called: 'Jan! We're out here.'

Gunnarstranda heard a man grunt something and clatter around in the hall.

'Was anyone else on board?'

'Yes, lots of people. There was at least one other woman too.'

'Did you see her face?'

'No, she was standing with her back to me. She was

91

talking to a man wearing a sailor's cap.'

'One man?'

'There were lots of people there, but they were sitting inside. I have no idea how many.'

'Would you recognise the man again?'

'Possibly. I'm not sure.'

'Sure about what?' a voice called from the doorway. It belonged to a slim, well-dressed man in his mid-fifties with steel-grey hair curling over his forehead and ears, like a helmet. His eyes were red and watering. 'Sorry,' he sniffled. 'It's mugwort. I'm allergic to it and it's terrible.' He blew his nose into a handkerchief with an apologetic smile and put it back in his pocket. 'There's a whole load of it outside the entrance. It should be destroyed, but I don't dare go near it.'

'And he refuses to let me,' Liv Inger Sømme smiled. 'He's frightened he might become allergic to me afterwards.'

The policeman shook hands, trying to pinpoint what was different about this face compared with the photograph on Evelyn Sømme's desk.

'What aren't you sure about?' Groven repeated with a smile.

'The boat we saw by the Bygdøy Sjøbad beach that Stuart climbed into.'

Jan Groven glanced at the policeman, who was sitting back down at the table: 'So your visit is about our friend Stuart?'

Gunnarstranda nodded and realised what the difference was. In the photograph Groven had a beard. His running eyes made the man's face like a mask, and behind it there appeared to be a very different and slightly anxious person peering out.

'How come the police are so slow with this kind of

case?' Groven asked, rolling up the sleeves of his yellow shirt. 'It's been days since the poor man vanished off the face of the earth.'

Gunnarstranda ignored the question as he lit a cigarette. 'Can you describe the man on the boat?'

Liv Inger Sømme puckered her lips.

'Have you told him about our boat trip?' Groven broke in, taking a good hold around his partner's waist and pulling her to him. 'When we got soaked?'

She nodded.

'Can you describe the man in the cabin cruiser?' Gunnarstranda repeated.

'In fact, I don't think it's possible. He looked very ordinary, and we were a long way away. I'll get us something to drink,' she said.

'Did *you* notice anything about the man?'

'Sorry,' Groven said, patting his partner's bottom as she disappeared into the kitchen with a giggle. 'He was probably my age, I imagine, and he was wearing a sailor's cap, shorts. Pretty anonymous figure, at least from where we were.'

Gunnarstranda puffed and rested his eyes thoughtfully on the other man while struggling to stifle a coughing fit. When it relented, he asked: 'Did you see the name of the boat?'

'I didn't catch the name, no.' Groven grimaced into the sun. 'There are hundreds of that type of boat, aren't there. I have no idea what they're all called. There's something American and ostentatious about them. That's where it all comes from — the USA. All our bad eating habits and our materialistic gigantomania. But the worst thing about the spread of these boats is that the owners know nothing about seamanship. They're owned by people who have a lot of dirty

93

money and no idea about coastal culture and life on a boat.'

'What kind of boat was it?'

Groven shook his head. 'It was long, white and had high decks. I don't know enough about these things. Big and expensive is probably not a very good description. Ah, you're here already,' he called, jumped up and grabbed Liv Inger Sømme as she came onto the terrace carrying a tray of drinks.

'Watch out,' she shouted, off balance, and placed the tray on the table.

Liv Inger poured the mineral water while Goven held her around the waist. Shortly afterwards, Gunnarstranda actually witnessed her sitting on his lap, like a schoolgirl.

The policeman stubbed out his cigarette. 'And there was me thinking I was close to a breakthrough.' He smiled at the two of them, her on his lap, like strangely overgrown siblings in a B-film.

'Breakthrough?'

'If Takeyo had been at sea before disappearing, he might've drowned.' Gunnarstranda poured himself some mineral water.

'But the others on board the cabin cruiser would've reported that,' Liv Inger Sømme said, horrified.

'Yes, wouldn't they.' Gunnarstranda drained his glass.

Silence engulfed them.

'Oh, my God,' Liv Inger Sømme said at length. She slipped down from her partner's lap and sat on a chair.

'Perhaps you caught a name or a number of the boat?' Gunnarstranda said to her.

Liv Inger looked down. 'No, we were too far away.'

Gunnarstranda turned and enjoyed the view over

Lake Bogstad. 'But you two have a boat, don't you. If you're on the fjord and see this cabin cruiser again — or something like it — I assume you'll tell me.'

'Naturally,' Groven said.

'When was the last time you were in contact with Takeyo?'

'It must be ten or twelve days ago. I ring him now and then to maintain contact. Last time I rang, no one was at home. That was a few days before our little boat trip in the rain. So, I reckon it's just under two weeks since we last spoke, and that was on the phone.'

'Did he feel threatened?'

'Threatened?' Jan Groven closed his eyes and sat with his mouth half open as if expecting either a huge sneeze or nothing at all.

'Haven't you taken your pill?' Liv Inger said, startled. 'I'll get you one.' She stood up and went inside.

'Did Stuart Takeyo have any reason to fear for his safety?' Gunnarstranda asked again.

'He never said anything.' The sneeze had receded. Jan Groven smiled up at the woman bringing him a foil strip of allergy tablets. He broke one off and swallowed it with a gulp of water.

'Did you know that Takeyo was involved in a racially motivated affray a few weeks ago?'

'What?'

'A man with apparent neo-Nazi sympathies harassed a doorman and some customers at a pub. Two people contacted the police. One was this so-called neo-Nazi. He reported, among others, your friend Stuart Takeyo for violence.'

Both of them looked at him in astonishment.

'Stuart would never hit anyone,' Liv Inger Sømme said with conviction.

Gunnarstranda produced the piece of paper with the death threat from his inside pocket. 'This was in Takeyo's post box.'

The two of them studied the note in silence.

'I see from your reactions that neither of you knows about this case,' Gunnarstranda said casually, reaching for the piece of paper that Groven had folded and passed to him.

'So, he didn't mention that he'd been harassed because of the colour of his skin?'

They shook their heads.

Gunnarstranda took a photograph from his inside pocket. He handed it to Liv Inger Sømme and asked: 'Could this be the woman you saw on board the boat?'

She stared at the picture, her forehead creased in thought, and shook her head. 'As I said, I didn't see a face.' She passed the photograph to Groven, who took it and studied it carefully. 'Who is this?' he asked.

'Her name's Kristine Ramm,' Gunnarstranda said. 'Have you seen her before?'

Groven shook his head and passed the photograph back.

'Have either of you heard Takeyo mention her name? Kristine Ramm.'

'But who is she?' Liv Inger Sømme asked, emotionally engaged now.

'A woman Stuart Takeyo was in touch with just before he disappeared.'

'Just before? Have you spoken to her?'

'I would've done so with pleasure,' the inspector said, readying himself to leave. 'If she'd been alive.'

Going Round in Circles

'The police again?' Evelyn Sømme folded her arms in front of her chest. 'And why hasn't your colleague come?'

'He's not so good with computers,' Frank Frølich said, and reading the expression on her face, he explained: 'We've been waiting for you to send us some emails.'

'I've had a lot on my plate,' she said with an expression that revealed she wasn't happy with this situation.

'That was what we thought, so we decided it would be better if I came here and looked at your machine and you would be spared the bother,' Frølich said in a conciliatory spirit.

'You can go upstairs. I have a patient.'

He followed her up the stairs and through a large, airy room, furnished spartanly. Her heels click-clacked on the oak parquet floor. In the corridor between the living room and the kitchen there was a fine, old, oak desk with heavy drawer sections. On the worn top, in sharp contrast, there was a white laptop between a grey telephone and a small, black modem. Frølich looked around while she leaned over her machine and logged on. The wall above the desk was decorated with three prints. Frank thought he recognised the style and colours. He bent forward to check. All three prints bore Jan Baker's signature.

'Now it should be fine,' Evelyn Sømme said, holding the chair out for him.

'I assume you know how to work it,' she said hesitantly.

He nodded reassuringly and sat down. Then he flicked down the list of titles of the saved emails and discovered she hadn't moved. 'Didn't you say you had a patient?'

'How is he . . .' she asked, unmoved, '. . . your boss?'

'Still smoking,' he answered. 'Still coughing and still going strong.'

She nodded. 'He can come here for some treatment,' she said. 'Remind him.'

Frølich nodded.

She still hesitated.

'I'm only interested in Takeyo,' he assured her.

'As you said, I have a patient,' she said, and stepped back a couple of paces.

'And I take an oath of confidentiality,' he assured her again. 'I'm exclusively interested in Takeyo.'

He watched her as she walked across the parquet and down the stairs. When she was almost at the bottom she turned and looked at him through the bars of the stairs.

He nodded reassuringly again and began to read the correspondence between her and Stuart Takeyo.

There was nothing much of interest. The two of them wrote to each other in English, and most of it was brief messages regarding dinner dates. Takeyo's contribution consisted mostly of questions about Norwegian behaviour or peculiarities he didn't understand.

He opened and read all the emails that could be related to Takeyo. After sitting for twenty minutes, he went into the deleted messages file and found one entitled 'Stuart'.

Frølich opened it, but discovered too late that it hadn't been sent to Takeyo; it was an email to Evelyn from her daughter, Liv Inger:

I know you know more than you're saying. I know you mistrust my motives whenever we speak. You have to understand you can't do anything about my feelings. But all this means nothing now. What would mean something would be for you to tell me what you know. You hold your cards so close to your chest, and that worries me, especially as the police are involved now.

'That particular email is private,' a voice said behind his shoulder. 'I didn't give you permission to read my private mail, did I.'

Frølich swivelled round on his chair. 'I didn't hear you come in,' he said, looking down at her feet. She had removed her shoes and was barefoot.

'You've gone beyond your remit,' she said starchily.

Frølich looked her straight in the eye: 'What does your daughter mean by saying you should tell her what you know?'

'You're not entitled to proceed in this way.'

The silence between them became a continuing struggle. Her fury was apparent in the two red spots on her cheeks, and her eyes were moist.

'You can leave now,' she said grittily. 'Please be so kind as to go.'

'Are you refusing to answer the question?'

She bent down and pulled the computer plug from the socket. Then she pulled out the ISDN cable, grabbed the portable laptop and marched across the floor with it under her arm. 'You do not have my permission to take print-outs of anything at all. Your little boss threatened me with a court order. Well, let him try,' she continued, ready for a fight. 'He and you can do what you like — just not here in my house. I will assume therefore that you've left my house by the time I've finished with this patient,' she said, turning her back on him and stalking down the stairs.

* * *

When Frank Frølich turned out of Bamseveien and across into Tråkka, he was thinking about going to the pub where Takeyo used to hang out. He was on his way to Majorstua when Gunnarstranda rang.

Frølich told him about the episode with Evelyn Sømme. 'Interesting lady,' he concluded. 'Hot-tempered.'

'Other news?'

'A number of messages, especially from this VG journalist, Fagernes.'

'Anything else?'

'They've finished with the car.'

'What car?'

'The car that had the body in it — the Honda owned by Sandvik. The SOC lot went through it with a fine-tooth comb without finding anything, except for a few strands of hair and a half-full packet of tampons. We'll send the hair for analysis. And, according to Yttergjerde, Rasten is nowhere to be found.'

'Rasten?'

'The man who threatened Takeyo,' Frølich explained.

'Right.'

'But the clip of the man in the car-park video was

bang on the money. It's Takeyo.' Frølich pulled in and parked before continuing: 'Lena's spoken to Kristine Ramm's neighbours in Bjerregaards gate. Not a bite except for in the video shop in Waldemar Thranes gate. A guy recognised Kristine because she used to ask for slightly unusual films: *Blow Up* and *Death in Venice* and so on — films they didn't have in stock. But he hadn't seen her for several weeks. My preliminary conclusion is that no one can tell us any more about what Kristine was doing on the Sunday in question.'

'What we know,' Gunnarstranda summed up, 'is that Marianne Sandvik says Kristine came home at six that Sunday morning, with wet hair — she had been swimming in Huk. I want us to question people living near Huk to find out if they saw anything on Saturday evening or that night — and especially on Sunday morning. If so, they can give us a description of the man she was with. What's Lena doing now?'

'She's walking round showing a picture of Kristine Ramm to the clientele in cafés around Grünerløkka. What are you doing?'

'I'm out walking in Bygdøy.'

Coastal Life

The afternoon sun pierced the canopy of leaves along the pathway and formed playful shadows on the gravel. As he walked, he met young girls on off-road bikes and young men jogging with their chests bared. When he caught a glimpse of the sea-smoothed rocks in Killingen through the foliage he found a path down to the water. Here, he loosened the knot of his tie and scanned the leafy slope. In hollows and inlets at the water's edge people were spread out, sunbathing. There was a smell of rotting seaweed and stagnant water mixed with the sweet fragrance of wild flowers. In the round bay known as Bygdøy Sjøbad the marina's pontoons were full of moored boats. Gunnarstranda was suddenly reminded of his brother. He had come out to West Oslo, here, for the rock 'n' roll festival — sometime in the fifties — from Grünerløkka, in East Oslo. Of course, it had ended in trouble. But what upset him was that this was the second reminder of his brother today. It was weeks since he had last given him a thought.

A family double-ender was chugging across from Bestumkilen as he walked between the rocks toward the car park. Once there, he stood listening for a few minutes. An echo from the fifties, he thought at first. The faint sound of music carried across the water. But the sound increased, and this wasn't rockabilly. A boat came into view, a wooden two-master propelled by a motor. The music streamed from two speakers on top of the wheelhouse. The boat slowed down, performed a manoeuvre and dropped anchor in the sea. The rattle of the chains was lost in the techno racket.

Some sunbathers craned their heads above the rocks. Some stood up to watch the people on board the boat: a few men were being served by long-legged women with flowing hair — wearing only bikinis. One of them leaned over the railing. A third woman was sunbathing topless on the foredeck.

The music died. A man yelled. Immediately an empty bottle was hurled through the air and splashed in the water. One of the women let out a piercing scream.

A man came strolling down the road. He was carrying a kayak. Gunnarstranda watched as he launched his kayak and wriggled inside. The man seemed to know the area, pushed off from the shore, turned his head and stared at Gunnarstranda. The policeman waved him over.

He paddled over with slow strokes.

'Do you come here often?' Gunnarstranda asked.

'Now and then.'

'Were you here last Saturday by any chance?'

The man nodded and squinted into the sun. His torso was tanned, his head shaven and he had a little goatee. He resembled a young, popularised version of Lenin.

Gunnarstranda introduced himself. The last word was drowned in another piercing squeal from a woman on board the boat. Then there was a splash, followed by another. The women were swimming.

The policeman and the kayaker kept an eye on what was happening. Between the rocks the sunbathers sat up and shielded their eyes to see better.

'Apparently there was a big cabin cruiser here last Saturday,' Gunnarstranda said.

'There are big boats here every day.'

'This one was supposed to have been a cabin cruiser of the really exclusive kind, and while it was here a black man, an African, climbed on board. He must've been standing around and waiting for a while before he was picked up by a young Norwegian woman rowing a small dinghy.'

The kayaker shrugged. 'Ask Arnold,' he said.

'Who's Arnold?'

The kayaker lifted his oar and pointed. The policeman turned and saw a stooped man rummaging through a rubbish bin in the car park. He took out an empty bottle and stuffed it into a big plastic bag.

The music started up again on board the two-master. A little boy collecting sea shells on the beach held his hands over his ears.

* * *

Arnold turned out to be blind in one eye. The other one squinted up at Gunnarstranda as he grimaced and revealed yellowish-brown gaps between his teeth.

Arnold asked if the inspector could help him with some change.

Gunnarstranda dug into his pockets, found two dried-up fags and a Coke top. There was a ten-krone note wedged inside it. 'Here,' he said, and asked if Arnold had seen a large, white luxury boat, which had lowered a dinghy to fetch an African waiting on the shore.

'A black fella?'

Gunnarstranda nodded.

'The *Loveliss*,' Arnold said, lifting the bag full of empty bottles. He slung the bag over his shoulder and made to go.

'What?'

'The *Loveliss*,' Arnold repeated. 'The boat's called the *Loveliss* and it's moored in Frognerkilen. The marina in the bay.'

'Do you know who owns it?' Gunnarstranda asked, excited.

Arnold shook his head. 'But the black man wasn't alone. There was a woman too.'

'So, there were three of them?'

'No, two. The woman and the black man. He'd been sitting on a rock and hanging around. The two of them chatted and then they took the little dinghy that's usually there and rowed to the boat.'

Gunnarstranda turned to the marina. 'So, it's usually there?'

Arnold squinted into the sun and pointed. 'It's usually out there, but it's not now.'

'And was this *Loveliss* here long?'

Arnold shrugged.

'Did the boat go out to sea or did it lie at anchor?'

'They left.'

'What time of day?'

Arnold looked up at the boiling-hot sun. 'Bit later than this.'

'Was it in the evening?'

'Late afternoon.'

'What time?'

'Haven't got a clue.'

Arnold wanted to go.

'Did you see them later: the boat or the African?'

Arnold stared vacantly back at him and shook his

head.

'How did she get here, the woman? Was she on foot?'

'No, she came in a car.'

'What kind?'

Arnold shrugged. 'Quite big, fairly new.'

'Do you remember what make?'

Arnold shook his head.

'Colour?'

'Dark blue, I think.'

'And the man, did he come in a car?'

'Don't know. He was sitting on a rock when I came.'

* * *

Gunnarstranda strolled back to the bend opposite the royal estate where he had parked on the edge of the road. A muscular, shiny, black horse crossed the green meadow and bounded over to the fence. It stopped and stared in disappointment after the car as it drove off, into Dronning Blancas vei and down to the path by Frognerkilen. Here, Gunnarstranda parked and got out. He stood for a few seconds scanning the marina, then slowly began to trudge over to the pier with the biggest boats. It took him ten minutes to find a boat called the *Loveliss*. Sure enough, there it was, a modern penis extension — a cross between a yacht and a cabin cruiser, with the bow plus the line of portholes constituting more than half of the boat's length. Gunnarstranda turned and walked back to what was probably some kind of office. The door of the little red building was locked. He knocked, but no one came to open the door. So, he noted down the name of the marina and various telephone numbers.

Some of the berths were owned by the local council, some were private. Afterwards he strolled back to his car and headed for the police station.

When he was driving down into the Oslo tunnel, Frank Frølich phoned and told him he was in the pub where the Africans usually hung out. 'A couple of them who work here know Takeyo. I've been given a few Norwegian names too — which I'll follow up. There are even some women.'

Gunnarstranda told him to check the marina and find out who owned a boat by the name of the *Loveliss*, and rang off.

Puzzles

'Now and then I wish we'd found a body,' Frølich sighed, getting up and walking over to the sink, where he poured away the tired contents of a coffee cup. He ran the tap.

'We've already got a body.'

'I mean the African's.' Frølich drank water from the cup.

'Well, who will get the blame for killing Kristine if Takeyo's lying dead somewhere?'

'You have to admit the job would be easier.'

'I'm not so sure.'

Frølich slumped back in his chair. 'I think we're like a blind man groping for a switch.'

Gunnarstranda chuckled. 'I'll remember that one for the next budget meeting.' He straightened up in his chair. 'But this is what it's like with missing-person cases. There's no crime scene, there's no crime; all we have is a possible victim — a hypothetical victim. You think the Stuart Takeyo case is unusual,' he continued, sticking a toothpick between his lips. 'It isn't. Missing-person cases always radiate in all directions. Has the man been killed? Has he been kidnapped by Martians? In the old days we used to believe people were swallowed by mountains. The craziest missing-person case I've ever come across happened almost thirty years ago — the Løberg case. It had the same parameters. A man vanished into thin air. He disappeared after an evening in a dance bar. The last person to see him alive was the doorman.

He saw the man get into his car and drive off. The car was found with the door wide open — abandoned in the middle of a straight road over Trysil mountain, out in the wilds. And the case went nowhere for four years. Then came the real mystery. The man's father, old Løberg, was sitting on a bench in the yard at home, under a tree. And out of the blue his son shows up. He'd been gone for four years. He walks in unannounced, wearing the same clothes he'd been wearing that night four years before, the same stained tie, and has lunch. The father was hallucinating, you might think. But no, there were others present too: his mother, siblings, farm workers. They sat and ate — seven or eight witnesses — listening to the man laughing and telling jokes as he used to do before he disappeared. He sat in the place of honour, at the end of the table, telling funny stories just as he used to. All the witnesses were agreed on one thing: it had been completely natural to see him there, just like before. Everyone had been waiting patiently for the explanation, the story, the solving of the mystery of why he had gone missing, and not least where he'd been for four whole years — and why he was wearing the same clothes: a cheap suit bought from Dressmann in Gjøvik and a white shirt with a slightly grubby collar. But Løberg talked about everything except his mysterious disappearance.' Gunnarstranda bent the toothpick and flicked it into the waste-paper basket and continued: 'After the meal they trooped out into the yard to have a cup of coffee. *Now*, they were all thinking; now he's going to tell us his secret. But then he bloody disappeared again. He strolled across the field and was gone — a figure getting smaller and smaller until he disappeared among the trees on the edge of the forest. 'When he went into the trees, I understood,' the father said in his statement. 'Anders had only come by for a short visit.' And no one's seen him since.'

Frølich stared at Gunnarstranda, who absent-mindedly exchanged the toothpick for a cigarette. The smoke curled up into the shafts of sun from the window, like a blue snake.

'The family speculated wildly,' Gunnarstranda went on, cigarette in the corner of his mouth. 'There has to be a reason, they thought, there had to be something about this day that made Løberg choose first to appear, and then disappear. They wondered if it was something to do with the air, the weather, or if there were sounds and smells on this day that were different from others.' Gunnarstranda studied the glow of his roll-up.

'That's a joke,' Frølich said.

Gunnarstranda turned to him, a faraway look in his eyes.

'A guy's gone for four years, comes back and disappears again. That is a joke,' Frølich repeated.

'Why do you think that?'

Frølich stared back. *You're a funny bugger*, he thought, and cleared his throat again. 'Liv Inger Sømme rang,' he said.

'What did she want?'

'To talk to you.'

'What about?'

'Egil Rasten.'

'Why?'

'She'd remembered that Stuart Takeyo had asked her about neo-Nazis a few weeks back. He'd asked why such organisations weren't banned in Norway and why it was a punishable offence to defend yourself against them.'

Gunnarstranda said nothing.

'Could be round about the same time as the fracas,' Frølich added.

Gunnarstranda still didn't answer.

Frølich was about to say something, but hesitated because the fax machine began to chunter. He stood up and took the piece of paper as it slowly emerged.

'Anything important?' Gunnarstranda asked.

'The name of the boat owner,' Frølich said. 'The man who owns the *Loveliss*.'

They both stood reading the fax.

Gunnarstranda walked back to his chair and sat down. Satisfied with himself, he put both hands behind his neck. 'What are you thinking about now?'

'I'm thinking about a snake,' Frølich answered.

Gunnarstranda grinned: 'Isn't that going a bit far?'

'A snake that bites its own tail,' Frølich explained. 'It's a circle, isn't it? What are *you* thinking?'

'I think it's a shame there aren't gradations of coincidence.'

'Because . . . ?'

'Because nothing is less of a coincidence than a coincidence too many.'

★ ★ ★

When, later that evening, Frølich was strolling down Schweigaards gate toward the Metro station, his mobile phone rang.

'Hello.'

'Lise Fagernes, VG.'

Frank stopped and looked around: it was a warm summer evening in Oslo. People in light clothes and light moods filled the pavements and the terraces of restaurants. Two laughing women clattered through the door of one. It had become dark enough that street lamps were succeeding in casting light; one of them shone dimly over a Turkish-looking man leaning against a street sign while fingering his prayer beads.

'Are you there?'

'Yes.' Frølich started walking. Two road workers in orange trousers and dirty T-shirts were removing the pedestrian crossing in Hollendergata. Blazing gas flames were licking at the tarmac. One of them looked up. The eyes in the bearded face with a cigarette poking from his mouth were vacant.

'I was wondering if there was any news.'

'News about what?'

He passed the unsightly entrance to a cheap hotel. At reception was a night guard, a stooped, elderly man in a white shirt with black armbands. His cheeks were sunken and his eyes watery.

'Funny man. I was wondering if you have anything to tell the public with regard to the Kristine Ramm murder.'

Frølich stopped in front of a pub window. An older couple were bent over large beers as they filled in a pools coupon. The woman was wearing a blue hat. A curly bit of black veil reminiscent of a fly net protruded from her hat and reached down to her nose. Her chubby cheeks wrinkled as she inhaled deeply from a long brown cigarette. Her husband watched closely as she put in her crosses.

'I told you last time I'm not the right person to speak to.'

'So, there's a development,' she said.

'Let's stop this conversation right now.'

'Hasn't it occurred to you that if we worked together, it might be useful? I could give you something. I'll never ever betray a source, though.'

'Have a nice evening.' He switched off his phone and put it in his pocket.

For a second, he thought his heart was going to stop. He was looking straight at Anna. But it couldn't be her.

A bell tinkled as he opened the door to the bar. She had kicked off her brown leather sandals and hooked her feet around the legs of her stool, at the bottom. Her dress was hippie-style — long and plain. One of the seams was missing a few stitches and revealed two centimetres of sun-tanned stomach. She was twisting a lock of her black hair around her fingers as she sat looking at some pictures in a catalogue. The straps of her dress bit into the skin of her round shoulders.

He slid onto the next bar stool and stole a glance. 'Hi,' he stammered.

The stool screamed as she spun round and any resemblance to Anna vanished. These eyes were violet, and searching.

'Hi,' she said at length.

'You were miles away,' he said, stretching his neck. She was supporting her chin on one hand and leafing through the catalogue with the other. There was picture after picture of beaches and hotel interiors. She was bent over in such a way that her hair fell forward like a screen, one foot slipped as she changed position.

The barman mooched over to the beer pumps and raised an eyebrow. 'A pils,' Frølich said. The beer tap spat out froth, and the man filled several glasses with white foam before the genuine article finally came.

He wiped his hands on a small, black apron he had tied around his waist.

Frølich pushed a fifty-krone note across the counter as he asked her: 'Going on holiday?'

'Are you?' she asked back, her eyes still on the catalogue.

'Nope,' he said, tasting the beer. 'Do you want anything? A pils, a glass of red wine?'

'No, thank you.'

He saw his own stupid face in the mirror behind all the bottles. *What the hell am I doing?*

She flipped over a page.

'You remind me of someone,' Frølich said.

'What's her name?'

The question made him regret everything: coming here, buying a beer, chatting. He said: 'You're not drinking anything.'

'I've just had a drink.'

'Would you like something?' he repeated, and remembered he had already asked her.

She slowly shook her head.

'You seem to be waiting for someone,' Frank said.

The mumbling of the pools players grew louder. They disagreed. The woman in the blue hat tapped a long, wrinkled forefinger repeatedly on the coupon while smoking furiously. Her husband, who had a powerful underbite, hissed his displeasure; he resembled an angry bulldog. The cloud of blue smoke above his wife's head rose toward the fan on the ceiling and was dispersed.

She followed his gaze and asked: 'What would you do if you won loads of money?'

'Buy an extremely expensive motorbike. And you?'

'I definitely wouldn't buy a motorbike.'

The barman sighed loudly and thumbed through a newspaper on the counter. A car passed outside.

'Have you ever ridden a motorbike, or pillion even?' Frank asked.

She stared down at the counter, raised her head with a suggestion of a smile on her lips and in her violet eyes. She stared at him. 'None of your business,' she said and began to fiddle with her hair again — deep in thought.

'You're sitting in a bar,' he said defensively. 'In bars you get drunk and confide in the guy behind the counter.'

'Then you're sitting on the wrong side.'

Frank stared at his drawn features again. He found her face in the mirror too. She was smiling a little condescendingly.

'I have to go,' he said at length, sliding down from the stool.

'Oh, why?'

'You're waiting for someone.'

'Yes, but we're having a nice time, don't you think?'

'Yes, I do.'

She angled her head. 'Can't you drink another beer?' As if suddenly remembering something, she added quickly: 'It makes time go a bit faster.'

He turned in the doorway. 'If you're here next time I come, let's get married.'

Skerry Dreams

When Gunnarstranda showed him into the interview room, Freddy Pedersen hesitated for a few seconds, almost as if he was weighing up the situation, before he decided to put on a good face and sat down, albeit with difficulty. 'Polio,' he wheezed, making a show of lifting his stiff leg. 'I belong to the generation who were children before the vaccine came on the scene, but I had a mother who forced the doctor to give me medicine as soon as the symptoms appeared. So, I've lived with this leg for the whole of my adult life, and I'm not that bothered, except when I have to give this little speech to every new person I meet. Happy?' he asked, straightening his trousers and brushing down his jacket.

'Of course,' Gunnarstranda answered, indifferent. When Pedersen sat like this, with his legs crossed, it was almost impossible to see that he was disabled. And he didn't look particularly hampered in his movement either. Pedersen was in his fifties; he had a tan with clear birthmarks on his neck and cheek. His auburn hair was curly around his ears and forehead.

In an overly formal way, the inspector asked: 'Name?'

A wry, sarcastic smile formed on Pedersen's thin lips. 'Freddy Pedersen.'

'Job?'

'Freelance entrepreneur.'

'What is your role with regard to the Voice of Joyce pub?'

'I'm a part owner.'

'When was the last time you saw Kristine Ramm?'

'About a week ago — at the beginning of August. Either Wednesday or Friday? I'd guess Friday.' He opened a diary and thumbed through. 'Friday,' he mumbled. 'She usually worked on Wednesdays and Fridays, and I'm not sure if I was there both days that week. Yes, I was there on Friday evening. So, I saw her on Friday the second of August. I think she left at nine. And I haven't seen her since.'

'What impression did you have of her?'

'Good-looking girl, not snobby, suitably tough. She was right for bar work. That's why we gave her a chance.'

'Did you get to know her?'

'I can't say I did, no. But she was stable, didn't come late, could hack it when it was busy, was seldom ill, and that's basically all I know about her. She was quite private.'

'What do you mean by that?'

'She rarely talked about herself — she switched off as soon as there was any topic other than beer and working hours. If you told me she was married and had two children, I wouldn't be very surprised.' Pedersen coughed and took a pastille from his jacket pocket, then carried on, making sucking noises: 'All I know about Kristine is that she was born in seventy-seven — I needed her age for tax, etc. I know she was a student and studied foreign cultures. I picked that up somewhere or other. Otherwise, I know nothing.' He gave another wry smile. 'Yes, I do. She was a vegetarian. But the most intimate thing I know about her is her account number.'

Gunnarstranda stood up, went over to the filing

cabinet beside the door, pulled out a drawer and took out a file. Concentrating on the contents of the file, he went back to Pedersen, sat down opposite him and put a photograph of Stuart Takeyo on the desk between them.

'Have you ever seen this man?'

Pedersen rested his elbows on the arm of the chair and supported his head by placing two fingers to his temples. He was thinking.

Gunnarstranda leaned back and studied his face. His shave had been thorough, not so much as a shadow of stubble could be seen on his smooth features. And he had neither dark bags nor lines under his eyes. Pedersen got enough sleep at night and was ingesting enough vitamins.

'I'm not sure, but he looks like a guy I gave a little job,' Pedersen concluded. 'The photo's like him, but I think the guy who contacted me was less straight-laced than this fella.' He picked up the photo and examined it close up.

'Less straight-laced?'

'Yes, he's cooler, more laid-back. I thought he was American, not African.'

'So, you know this man is African?'

'I read papers. This is the scientist who's gone missing, isn't it? Actually, this photo isn't much like the guy I'm thinking of.'

'Who?'

Pedersen straightened up. 'I could tell you more if you informed me where we're going with all this.'

'And what do you mean by that?'

'I don't want to give a full statement.'

'Not a full statement?'

'I'm a businessman and in some respects bound by

an oath of silence.'

'That's a new one on me.'

'I'm talking ethics here.' Pedersen leaned forward and exhaled a whiff of eucalyptus across the desk. 'Perhaps that's a foreign concept in the police service?'

'You're making this very complicated for yourself.'

'Let me worry about that side of things,' Pedersen answered flatly. 'You and I are both grown men. How about, from now on, we lay our cards on the table and part company afterwards without any hard feelings? Well, the first step is to question me, that's your job. You haven't summoned me here because Kristine Ramm worked in the bar of the Voice of Joyce. What is it about this black man that's led you to me?'

'The man in the photo is Stuart Takeyo — a university researcher, you're quite right. He's been reported missing,' Gunnarstranda confirmed. 'One witness maintains they saw him climb aboard your boat shortly before he went missing.'

Pedersen leaned back on his chair, sucking pensively at his pastille. 'The guy I have in mind,' he said at length, 'called himself something else. He claimed his name was Bobby. We met at the Voice a few days before — one evening. I think he spoke to Kristine first — as a customer — and asked if she earned a lot of money and so on. Not sure about that. At any rate, Kristine came to me in the back room and said a guy wanted to talk to me. 'Who?' I asked. 'No idea,' she said. 'But he keeps telling me he wants to talk to the boss.' OK, so I went over to the guy and asked him what he wanted. And he spoke English. That is, he knew some Norwegian, but asked if it was alright if we spoke in English. Anyway, it turned out he wanted

119

to earn some kroner. Said he had another job usually, but not what kind. What he wanted was to earn some money under the table, but I don't do that kind of thing, and so I said: 'Sorry, no, I can't help you.' Later that evening I remembered I was having a little party on the boat on Saturday. So, I caught up with the guy before he left and said he could work as a waiter on the Saturday.'

'On the boat?'

Pedersen nodded. 'I needed someone to serve food and pull beer, etc.'

'And how many days were there between his enquiry at the restaurant and the boat trip?'

'Two, maybe three, so it must've been Wednesday evening when Kristine was working and he asked me.'

'And so he joined you on the boat trip on the Saturday?'

'Yes.'

'Where did he board?'

'By Killingen, past the marina, in Bygdøy Sjøbad.'

'Why there of all places?'

Pedersen smiled. 'Why not? It was fine — as good as anywhere.'

'Yes, but you have a berth in Frognerkilen, on the other side of Bygdøy, and it would be natural for staff to board there.'

'Initially this guy got the job because it was cheaper for me than to ask people who wanted overtime and weekend rates. And it was cheaper for me to get the guy when he was needed.'

'This man's on a university scholarship. Why would he be interested in earning illicit money as a waiter?'

'You'll have to ask him that.'

'You don't think it's strange?'

'I don't think anything — at any rate, I didn't then. As far as I was concerned, he could've been a tourist or a refugee. I wasn't interested in him personally. He claimed he needed money. That was enough for me.'

'How long was he on board?'

'I dropped him off at the same place, just before midnight.'

'Why there again?'

'He wanted to get off there.'

'He didn't give a reason?'

'No. I thought he knew the way back from there or had a car nearby, or something like that.'

'Were there any others apart from him serving on board?'

'No.'

'And he only spoke basic Norwegian. Wasn't that impractical?'

'Why would it be?'

'It's always best to use staff who know the language.'

'All my guests speak English.'

'My witness says that Takeyo was rowed over to your boat by a woman.'

'That's correct. We were anchored off the bay. One of the guests rowed over to get him.'

'A guest?'

'You're not getting a name. These are people who need my discretion.'

'Ah, this ethics of yours again,' Gunnastranda said sarcastically. 'So convenient that it means your claims contradict the evidence of witnesses.'

'Are you saying I'm lying?'

'I have a witness who maintains a woman drove up in a car, untied the rope of a little dinghy on the shore and rowed Stuart Takeyo out to the boat.'

121

'Perhaps your witness should pay better attention.'

'At any rate, I can confirm a discrepancy. As you insist on holding back information about your guests, we will rely on our other witness's version of events.'

'Up to you. But you might try thinking logically: if the dinghy was first rowed to the shore and the rower picked up two people, don't you think your witness should've seen three people in the boat?'

'My witness says the dinghy is always moored in this place.'

Pedersen grinned: 'Would I keep a dinghy there? I have a berth in Frognerkilen, on the other side of Bygdøy.'

'Well,' Gunnarstranda continued. 'Then I have to ask: was Kristine on board that day?'

'Are you crazy?'

Gunnarstranda mounted a patronising smile.

'Kristine would not have fitted in well with these guests, believe me.'

'Why not?'

'Well, Kristine was great — student, not big-headed, very nice, sensitive — but these are people with a different social profile from Blindern students. They wouldn't have had much in common, if I can put it like that.'

'But a waiter who barely knows our language did fit in?'

'He waited on us.'

'So, I'm forced to conclude Kristine would've fitted in if she'd worked as a waitress?'

'Didn't I just say that someone else had the job?'

'Do you think the relationship between Kristine and Stuart Takeyo was of a romantic nature?'

'I don't think there was any kind of relationship.

I doubt she'd ever seen him before. That Wednesday evening, she seemed irritated at having to bring me in when there was so much to do at the bar.'

'Was Takeyo a good waiter on the boat?'

Freddy Pedersen shrugged. 'Absolutely fine.'

'Did he ask to be taken ashore in the dinghy to the same place in Bygdøy?'

'Yes. I rowed him ashore.'

'And that was no problem for you with your stiff leg? Getting into and out of a little dinghy?'

Pedersen's eyes narrowed. 'I've lived with my handicap for more than forty years without requiring any assistance — for anything — and even if this leg's thinner and less agile than the other, I'm nowhere near paralysed. If I'd had any problems sailing a boat, I wouldn't have bought one.'

'Can anyone confirm you dropped Takeyo off at this place?'

'I have no idea. It was late, and I didn't see anyone around on land.'

'Pedersen,' Gunnarstranda said in a low voice. 'Kristine's dead. She can't confirm or deny any of what you're saying about the relationship between you, her and Takeyo. Now Takeyo's vanished into thin air. What you're saying is that you're the last person to see him alive.'

'Is *he* dead too?'

'Some of these secret guests were perhaps still on board — some of them could've seen Takeyo going ashore.'

'There were no guests on board. This guy was the last to go.'

'Where did you put the guests ashore?'

'Round and about — Aker Brygge, Bygdøynes,

123

Dronningen . . .'

'And Takeyo went on with you from Dronningen and asked you to go to Bestumkilen?'

'I didn't say that.'

'So, what happened?'

'The last guest was dropped off in Nesodden, in Tangen; on the way back to town the guy asked me if he could go ashore where he was picked up.'

Gunnarstranda stretched his legs under the desk. 'Excuse me,' he said, 'but I can't work this out. You have a berth in Frognerkilen. It's late in the evening, you're coming back from Nesoddtangen, toward Oslo, you and this man are the only people on board. Is that right?'

Freddy Pedersen nodded.

'And so you're telling me you set a course for the west of the Bygdøy headland, toward Bestumkilen, anchored up and rowed the man ashore by Bygdøy Sjøbad, rowed back to your boat, headed across the sea, around the whole of the Bygdøy headland to moor up on the eastern side of Bygdøy — in Frognerkilen?'

'That's correct.'

'Isn't that one hell of a journey?'

'The thought never occurred to me.'

'If you'd gone from Tangen to your berth in Frognerkilen, Takeyo would've been closer to the city centre, and you'd have saved yourself a lot of faffing around.'

'That's possible too. But for all I know, he could've had a bike waiting for him where I dropped him off. I didn't give it a thought.'

'You're the last person to have seen Takeyo before he disappeared. For this to be verified, I'm going to have to ask you for the names of the guests.'

'It was a very exclusive, private party, Inspector.

124

For the time being, you'll have to regard me as the guests' representative.'

'Why didn't you contact the police when you read about Takeyo's disappearance in the papers?'

'It didn't occur to me it could be the same person. I was contacted by someone called Bobby — and the photo wasn't a great likeness.'

'Why would this man use a fake name?'

'How should I know? I don't even know if we're talking about the same person.'

The telephone on the desk between them rang. Gunnarstranda sat looking at it for a few seconds before picking up the receiver. It was Frølich and he had some important information. 'Ten minutes,' Gunnarstranda said, ringing off.

Pedersen showed his teeth in a grin.

Gunnarstranda said: 'The money Takeyo earned — was it illicit?'

'No, I didn't pay him illegally. I gave him a thousand kroner, paid into his hand. I didn't ask him for his name or any other information. This is totally above board.'

'Alright, fine. I'm more interested in the fact that you're the last person to have seen Takeyo. Accordingly, I advise you to give me a list of the guests on board.'

'If you want names, you'll have to do a bit more work.' Pedersen grinned again. 'There's no point questioning witnesses if the man you're looking for left the country ages ago.'

'You're a witness in a murder case,' Gunnarstranda snapped, banging the desk with the flat of his hand. 'Was Kristine Ramm on board your boat on the third of August?'

'She was not.'

'Has Kristine Ramm ever been on board your boat?'

'The answer is no.'

'When was the last time you saw Stuart Takeyo?'

'Assuming the man calling himself Bobby is the Stuart Takeyo you're searching for, I saw the guy on Saturday night about an hour before midnight as he was leaving my dinghy by Bygdøy Sjøbad.'

'Was he alone?'

'He was.'

'When was the last time you saw Kristine Ramm?'

'That was on Friday — the day before. She was at work and left at nine when her shift finished.'

'One witness claims that on Saturday night/Sunday morning Kristine Ramm was on the Huk headland, almost a kilometre from where you dropped Takeyo off. Have you any comment?'

'No comment, except to say that I dropped Takeyo off before midnight, which I take to mean on Saturday evening, not Sunday morning.'

'Let me ask you again: was Kristine Ramm on board your boat on Saturday evening?'

'No.'

'Kristine Ramm called quite a few people on Sunday, a few hours before she was killed. One of these calls was to the pub where she worked part-time. Did you speak to her?'

'No.'

'Do you know who answered her call?'

'No idea.'

'Have any of your employees reported getting a call?'

'This is the first I've heard of it.'

'What do you think she was ringing about?'

'Could've been anything — trying to change a shift, asking for an extra shift. For all I know the line could've been busy when she called.'

'Where were you on the evening of Sunday the fourth of August?'

'At first I was in Voice, but after nine I was at home.'

'Alone?'

'In fact, I was.'

Gunnarstranda switched off the tape recorder and smiled coolly at the interviewee: 'Thank you for making the effort to come here.'

* * *

Once Pedersen was out of the door Gunnarstranda turned to the telephone and dialled Marianne Sandvik's number. 'I'm ringing about the job Kristine had at the Voice of Joyce,' he said after their introductory pleasantries. 'Do you know if she was ever hired to work at places other than the pub; for example, on board the boat owned by her boss, a Freddy Pedersen?'

'Yes, once she was.'

'When?'

'A couple of months ago, and she thought the whole set-up stank.'

'Why was that?'

'You'll know when you meet Pedersen.'

'Could you be a bit more explicit?'

'Let me put it this way: I'd never go out with him and his friends. You know the kind: summer, scanty clothing, swimming, ageing men with a high naff factor and lots of drinks with very young women in bikinis.'

'Was she molested?'

'It was all very strange. Some of the women who work at the pub apparently thought that sort of party was great, if you know what I mean, so there was some kind of pressure on Kristine or at least it was very unpleasant for her; and she was not interested.'

'Do you remember when this was?'

'It was early summer. June, may've been Midsummer's Eve. It was just before she went home on holiday, and she usually did that around midsummer.'

'Did she feel threatened on the boat trip?'

'No, just ready to throw up, I think. We laughed quite a lot about it — my impression was it was a kind of Norwegian comedy version of Hugh Heffner at sea. Why do you ask?'

'Hm,' Gunnarstranda said to himself, staring at the door Pedersen had closed behind him. 'I suppose I'm just curious.' Then he added, 'Do you know where she boarded the boat that time?'

'Not sure . . .'

'I thought perhaps you'd driven her,' Gunnarstranda said, about to finish the conversation.

'I seem to remember she had to have the car that evening because no one knew how long it would last, and then we chatted about where she could park. I think she mentioned somewhere in Bygdøy.'

'Bygdøy?' Gunnarstranda repeated, intrigued.

'Yes, some parking spot down by the water.'

'She didn't say where?'

'No, but the crew picked her up there, from the car park. She may've said more, but I don't remember.'

'Could it have been past the marina by Bygdøy Sjøbad? Killingen?'

'Possible. I'm afraid I can't say for sure.'

128

'Do you know what Kristine was doing on the Saturday before she died?'

'As I told you last time, I was staying with Knut almost the whole of that week. I dropped in on Sunday and Monday only to change and wash clothes. When I bumped into Kristine on Sunday morning, I hadn't seen her for more than a week.'

'If you remember anything about where she parked,' Gunnarstranda said, 'please give me a ring at once.'

★ ★ ★

After noting the discrepancies between what Pedersen and Sandvik said, he strolled back to the office and went over to Frølich. 'Our boat-owner confirmed he met Takeyo on board on Saturday evening. He also lied about Kristine Ramm. Three times.'

Frølich grinned. 'So did Saint Peter the Apostle . . . lie three times.'

'The problem is that Kristine Ramm was at home on Sunday and we have proof that she was. Pedersen's lies refer to the day before. It's this jump in time that's so odd. Pedersen had contact with Takeyo on Saturday evening, but we know that both Kristine and Takeyo were in the underground car park on Sunday — one day later. I want her mobile phone checked. If we're lucky, she had it with her all day Saturday, and we'll find out if she was on board or not.'

'Then the phone call I've just received may be relevant,' Frølich said drily.

'From whom?'

'Lise Fagernes. She wanted a comment for Verdens Gang.'

'A comment on what?'

'She says she's received confirmation from a secure source that Stuart Takeyo is in a town called Kisumu in Kenya.'

Gunnarstranda, who had been rummaging through his pockets for tobacco, was suddenly still.

Neither of them spoke.

Gunnarstranda coughed and stuffed a bent roll-up between his lips.

Frølich shrugged.

'And what did you answer?'

'I said we'd get back to her, we'd ring her.'

'And what did she say to that?' Gunnarstranda's hands were trembling. He could barely find the cigarette with his match.

'She said she was ringing because *VG* was running the story on the front page tomorrow. Stuart Takeyo is alive and well at home in Africa.'

PART TWO

THE BLUE EYE

Departures

'Ah, I wanted to talk to you,' Gunnarstranda said, stopping in the corridor on his way to the office. Fredrik Sørli, also known as Chicken Brain, was standing in front of a dispenser and filling a plastic cup with Imsdal water. He was standing with straight legs and a horizontal back, performing a bow that would have gratified a king.

'Yes, I hear you're interested in Feppen,' Sørli mumbled pensively, straightened up and paused to drink the water. Sørli, who was a special investigator in the Fraud Squad, was called Chicken Brain not because he was stupid — rather the opposite, he was unusually bright — but because there was something about his eyes; they were, to put it mildly, staring, and they looked as if they could roll out any minute and drop onto the floor. His broad head was adorned with bristly, red hair, and his face tapered down to a chin that was so sunken it looked as if his mouth was in the middle of his neck. If you observed Sørli from the side, you might be reminded of a misshapen chicken, with his pouting lips like a beak, an association that he now reinforced by thoughtfully tapping the empty cup against his bottom lip.

'Feppen?'

'The guy you're after. Freddy Pedersen.'

On top of his unique appearance, Sørli had another distinguishing quirk: an unpleasant habit of grinding his teeth. Now it sounded as though someone was twisting a screwdriver in his chin area. 'We're talking

133

about a nouveau-riche investor known to his friends as Feppen,' Sørli said. 'I imagine the name rolls off your lips more easily on the golf course, after a couple of Tom Collins. It's the investor Freddy Pedersen you're interested in, isn't it?' The screwdriver was off again.

'I know he owns a cabin cruiser called the *Loveliss*.'

'That's the one. May I ask why you're interested?'

'He's turned up twice in a murder case, in the wrong place at the wrong time.'

The screwdriver went again, twice. 'You know, for a second I thought I'd found two jigsaw pieces that fitted,' Sørli said. 'I've had a *Nettavisen* journalist ring me, you see. He's trying to connect Pedersen with some hanky-panky over security bonds. Anything in particular you're after?'

'Anything relevant.'

'I'll give you a buzz then,' Sørli said as they parted.

★ ★ ★

Shortly afterwards, when Gunnarstranda turned into his office, he found the place unusually congested. Fristad, the public prosecutor, had called an extraordinary meeting and, by energetically cleaning his glasses, was making it obvious that he was displeased with Gunnarstranda's lack of punctuality. They had found seats on whatever was to hand: the public prosecutor, Frank Frølich, Emil Yttergjerde and Lena Stigersand.

After Gunnarstranda had closed the door behind him, Lena cast her eyes around and said enthusiastically: 'I've finally tracked down Egil Rasten.'

'And who might that be?' Fristad said from his

chair.

'The man who posted the threat to Takeyo,' Lena answered.

'He's no longer of any interest. At any rate, if this journalist's right in claiming that Takeyo's alive and well, and with his mother.'

'On the contrary. The threat shows he has a rational motive for leaving the country. It is, after all, a threat to his life —'

'We have to assume the journalist is telling the truth,' Gunnarstranda interrupted, a little too quickly, and had to fight to suppress a coughing fit. When he had his breath back, he raised his head to get everyone's attention.

'The story will appear in *VG* tomorrow, she says — Lise Fagernes, that is. She's the woman who found Kristine Ramm dead in the car park. It's done something to this journalist. Lots of people ring in, but she's unusually pushy. And she's managed to coax information out of our people too, not that we should focus on that side of the case now. But as they're waiting to go with their lead article tomorrow, we can establish a couple of facts: firstly, it's extremely probable that this information is correct. As this is no random news headline they're running on the Net, we have to assume they've done all the legwork and they're confident. Takeyo is in Africa. And we have to assume they have more information on tap. As far as I remember, Fagernes even had a photographer at the crime scene the day Kristine was found. But, however much they've invested in this case, I refuse to believe they can know that much more than we do — probably they know a lot less. Our starting point is simply that the case's central witness has fled

135

our investigation.'

'But we have the man's passport,' Yttergjerde objected. 'And his name isn't on any passenger list.'

'Nevertheless, my guess is that Lise Fagernes is right. As we have his passport and his name hasn't appeared on any passenger list, he must've travelled under an alias with another passport. We'll have to go through the passenger lists again.'

Frølich went to the shelf and removed one of the blue files with Takeyo's name written on the spine. He flicked through and when he found the lists put the file down.

'If Takeyo's borrowed another man's passport, I'd be very surprised if a name from our witness list didn't also appear on the passenger lists. Presumably he travelled the same day that he went missing,' Gunnarstranda continued while Frølich carried on searching. 'Nevertheless, the mystery is how Fagernes found out that the guy was alive and well in Kenya.'

'She must've had some personal contact with him,' Fristad said. 'There's only one source that can find that kind of information. The man himself — Takeyo.'

'That's not necessarily true, but you have a point. She's probably emailed him and got an answer.'

'And we haven't?' Fristad eyed Gunnarstranda with a concerned frown.

Frølich looked up from the lists and said: 'I've emailed him. But he didn't answer. For all we know, he may've opened a load of email accounts under a variety of names.' Frølich paused, and with a forefinger on the list, he shouted, 'Yep, here he is. Daniel Amolo.'

'Daniel who?'

'I know him,' Lena Stigersand said, glancing happily at Frølich. 'Amolo was reported by Rasten for attacking him. Amolo's a Kenyan and works as a doorman at the place where Rasten kicked up a fuss a few weeks ago, and it ended in a scuffle. Takeyo was also involved.'

Fristad's tics degenerated into nervous twitches. His head seemed to be attached to his shoulders by ball bearings. 'And now the man's gone to Africa?'

'No,' Frølich said emphatically. 'It says here that Amolo flew to Nairobi via Amsterdam with KLM on Monday the fifth of August. But I spoke to him yesterday.'

'And I did today,' Lena grinned.

'Do they look like each other?'

'Possible,' Frølich said, 'but I've never seen Takeyo, so I don't know.'

'Arrest Amolo and charge him with giving a false statement,' Fristad barked.

Gunnarstranda looked up. 'Why?'

'Because it's a punishable offence to obstruct a police investigation and give a false statement. If he's lent his passport to Takeyo, he must've known where Takeyo was the whole time.' Fristad rubbed his glasses angrily and his gaze moved from one to the other.

Gunnarstranda watched the public prosecutor with irritation. 'The most important thing for us to do now is to move ahead of *VG*.'

Fristad squirmed. 'How can we do that? If the journalist has direct contact with Takeyo? We're the country's legal authority. We can't bloody email suspects.'

'We have to go there,' Gunnarstranda said. 'And we have to leave this evening. When this case breaks, there's only one way to defuse the bomb: we have to

137

have a man in Africa.'

'Are you out of your mind?' Fristad barked, in shock. 'You're investigating a premeditated murder committed in Norway.'

Gunnarstranda nodded earnestly. 'And Takeyo has to be seen as our hottest lead. We know he was there — in the underground car park. He's the only person we know for certain had a real chance of killing her. If he'd been arrested in Norway today, he would have been grilled until he confessed. Only one person can confirm or deny our suspicions, and that's him. If you don't want to read about what happens in *VG*, you have to take the initiative.'

Fristad stared at him, speechless.

'I'm not intending to travel anywhere,' Gunnarstranda said, 'but I'm not the only person capable of interviewing a witness.'

Fristad followed Gunnarstranda's eyes.

'Me?' exclaimed Frølich. 'Are you looking at me?'

'Is there anything keeping you here?' Gunnarstranda asked acidly. 'Have you got married recently?'

'I'm going fishing with the lads.'

'When?'

'Saturday and Sunday.'

'The weekend's out anyway.'

'But I've never been there before.'

'Nor has anyone else.'

Frølich stuffed both hands in his pockets. 'I'm not the only person here,' he said eloquently. 'I'm not the only one here who can interview a witness.' He glanced at Lena Stigersand, who grimaced and slowly shook her head.

'But none of the others have your experience, and no one is so well versed in this case.' For Gunnarstranda, the meeting was over and the discussion concluded. He buttoned up his jacket.

'Hey, hey,' Fristad said, his arms waving in the air. 'This is going too fast. What you're suggesting involves the Norwegian Diplomatic Service, Interpol and the Kenyan police. We can forget about being there in two hours.'

'I haven't planned a thing,' Gunnarstranda broke in. 'I leave that to you.'

'To me?' Fristad's head and shoulders shook as if an electric current was going through him. His hands opened and closed. 'You forced through the autopsy, now you're leaving me to finance an operation outside Norway?' His mouth opened and closed again. 'To me?' he repeated, in apoplexy.

'Yes, to you. Kripos, the supercops in Interpol, you name it, as you always say.' Gunnarstranda ambled across the floor and stopped by the door, where he buried his hands in his pockets: 'The autopsy of Kristine Ramm revealed a premeditated murder. Such murders are one in fifty. The murder was disguised as an OD case, which may suggest a criminal organisation. That and the proven use of heroin — you can feed these juicy titbits to one of the arrivistes you chat with during your lunchbreaks.'

The two of them stood eyeball to eyeball. Fristad's lower jaw was still chewing the cud, but his gaze was inward, ruminative. 'The diplomatic service,' he mumbled in a distant voice; 'even the concept is difficult for me to grasp, but perhaps they don't need to be involved. If we're smart, we can go straight to the Kenyan police.' The public prosecutor's body had stopped quivering, and he seemed surer of himself as he looked up and thought aloud: 'The only

139

thing Norwegian officials have to do is to support local investigators interviewing Takeyo — sit nicely on a chair and listen to what the interpreter says. From a formal and tactical point of view, an interview is imperative, and press-wise a journey like this will deflate the groundless criticism that will inevitably follow the headlines. Mm, nice.' Fristad nodded introspectively and at length perched his glasses on his nose. 'Actually, we're dependent on this succeeding,' he said, and repeated Gunnarstranda's words to himself: 'We must have a man on the plane today.'

And when the public prosecutor spun round, Frank Frølich could read in his eyes that the battle was lost.

'Good,' Fristad said, as if butter wouldn't melt in his mouth, shifting his gaze from one to the next. 'I do believe we have a plan.'

Intermezzo

The flat was boiling hot although many windows had been wide open all day. Gunnarstranda peeled off his jacket and hung it over the back of a chair at the dining table, then lightly tapped on the glass bowl where Kalfatrus slowly fluttered its tail and did a quick round to say hello. In the kitchen he opened the fridge and stared down at two cans of Borg summer beer, a Coke and half a bottle of Chilean Chardonnay.

A fat bumble bee had strayed into the sitting room. It bumbled around as he unscrewed the top of the wine bottle and filled a glass.

Afterwards he strolled over to the bookshelf and played the message on his answer machine:

'Hello, this is Lise Fagernes. This is the fourth time I've left a message and, yes, I know that on principle you do not discuss cases with journalists, but whether you believe it or not, I am ringing in a private capacity. In fact, I need some supplementary information about the murder of Kristine Damm. I may remind you that I was the first to find her at the crime scene and I have a right to information to ensure my own security . . .'

Gunnarstranda smiled at Kalfatrus. 'Did you hear that?' he mumbled. 'She's ringing me in a *private capacity*.' He grabbed the little box of food and sprinkled some onto the water. The fish flicked its tail and devoured the food as Lise Fagernes left her telephone numbers and finally rang off. 'Own security,' Gunnarstranda muttered as the tape wound on:

'Hello, Marianne Sandvik here. You told me to ring

you if I had any more information. We talked about a boat picking Kristine up. I checked on the wall calendar I have here. The boat trip was on Midsummer's Day, and I've remembered something about where she parked. Not precisely where, but it was a car park in Bygdøy by the water. The point is that the cabin cruiser has quite a deep draught, so Pedersen keeps a dinghy there for people to row to the boat. There were two or three people in the dinghy going to his cabin cruiser. This has just come back to me, and it struck me that you could ask Pedersen where he keeps his dinghy. Bye.

Gunnarstranda was staring thoughtfully into the air as the tape stopped. He snapped out of his reverie when the bumble bee hit the window, fell onto the sill and started crawling around. He carefully pushed the bee onto the outside edge, where it finally orientated itself and fell a few metres before flying off.

The traffic noise from outside almost drowned the ringing of the telephone.

The answer machine cut in.

Gunnarstranda sipped at his white wine.

'This is Sørli —'

'Keep it brief,' Gunnarstranda barked after grabbing the handset.

'Ah, there you are. I've been having a look at our friend Freddy Pedersen. He grew up in Tjølling . . .'

'Brief, Sørli.'

'Well, most of the stuff we have on him concerns a bankruptcy in 1995. He ran a wine accessory shop in Gladengveien and only escaped being charged with receiving smuggled goods by a hair's breadth.'

'Wine accessories?' Gunnarstranda reached out for a pen and paper.

'Yes, wine demijohns and crown cappers, that kind

142

of thing — essences and distillery equipment. It was suspected at the time that the shop was a cover for illicit distilling and importing contraband. After the bankruptcy he became a so-called investor, living off shares, and he part owned a couple of pubs. The problem with finding information is that Feppen doesn't own anything himself. Such as a pub . . .'

'Voice of Joyce,' Gunnarstranda said, using the pen to doodle little roses on the notepad.

'Exactly. It's owned by a firm called Partykings, and the only thing that's official about Partykings is that the chairperson is Britt Lise Staw.' Sørli chuckled.

'Well?'

'Britt Lise Staw is the mother of Pedersen's partner, Lillemore Staw.'

'Mhm.' Gunnarstranda jotted that down.

'Pedersen himself has had no declared income since 1995, but lives in a villa in Snarøya, where he drives low-slung cars and eats high-class cuisine, to use their jargon. Besides which, last year he bought a beach plot in Blindleia for four or five million, demolished the shack there and built a new and bigger all-year-round house for the same sum again. Britt Lise Staw's the closest you can get to Pedersen as far as bars and restaurants are concerned. But a cold wind's going to be blowing around Feppen's ears soon.'

'Why?'

'It was something I heard from the *Nettavisen* journalist I told you about. This is a delicate matter. And even if it's clearly a complex business, it's snowballing — if I can put it like that. It involves Africa.'

'What's the name of the journalist?' Gunnarstranda asked stiffly, tearing a sheet from the notepad.

143

Movement

It hadn't occurred to him that he would meet someone he knew, and she was the last person he had thought he would run into. So, he was absolutely stunned when he saw her on the Kenya Airways flight.

It happened in Amsterdam, after boarding but before take-off. Frank Frølich had used his good arm, the one that hadn't been used for vaccinations, to stow his hand luggage above the seat. As he sat down to buckle the safety belt, he caught sight of her. She was unmistakeable. Lise Fagernes, wearing narrow glasses in black frames and a grey outfit, came confidently striding down the aisle, holding her travel bag in front of her, like in a commercial targeted at career women. She had her blonde hair gathered in a youthful ponytail.

'Long time, no see,' he said cheerfully.

She was startled for a fraction of a second as she recognised him — until she extended her mouth to form a wry smile and carried on walking without a backward glance. Only the herbal fragrance he remembered from their first meeting wafted along in her wake.

Frølich sank back into his seat, alarmed at the journalist's change of attitude. He hadn't seen anything like it since his final row with Anna. Involuntarily, he checked his watch. It was close to midnight. The morning edition of *VG* with her sensationalist spread on Stuart Takeyo's escape to Africa still hadn't gone to press. Nevertheless, she was on the same flight as

144

him. Never mind, he thought, nothing he could do about it.

About an hour later, when the plane was in the air and he had just put on headphones to watch a film, he felt a finger tap him on the shoulder. He removed the headphones and looked up into her smiling face.

'I thought only trusted members of Interpol were allowed to take jobs abroad,' she said in a provocative tone.

'What makes you think I'm not going on holiday?'

'We have our sources,' she said.

Frølich studied the face behind the black-framed designer glasses. 'And you're on your way to Nairobi?' he asked.

'I'm going further.'

'Inland perhaps, to Lake Victoria?'

'Am I wrong?' she continued, as though she hadn't heard the question. 'Because you aren't attached to Kripos or Interpol, are you?'

She was standing there, ignoring his questions, and had the cheek to keep pumping him. He replied: 'Are you travelling on as soon as we land? Or will we have time to have a beer?'

'Let's save it for a rainy day.'

He had run out of things to say and so he asked: 'Have you been to Kenya before?'

She backed between two seats as an air stewardess rattled a refreshments trolley past. She stayed there for a few more seconds as two men passed to queue outside the toilet. 'See you,' she said when the aisle was finally free again. She waved and left Frank to his own thoughts.

He began to see a thread running through her activities: first, she had written a full-page article on

145

a murder case and an important witness who had left the country. Then her plan was to talk to the individual herself: an exclusive interview with the man the Norwegian police had been hunting for days. Title: 'I Didn't Kill Her!'

Frølich felt himself getting sweaty. The gap between his and her starting position was greater than between Scott and Amundsen. Perhaps Lise Fagernes was in direct contact with Takeyo; at any rate she must have a pretty good idea where in the country he was hiding. By contrast, he had as much direction as a bingo ball in a lottery machine. For one panic-stricken second, he visualised a scene where Lise Fagernes was sitting on a sun-drenched terrace with Stuart Takeyo. The researcher was talking in a low voice while she took a pen and started making notes. Meanwhile, he was pacing up and down the corridors of the Kenyan police station, desperately trying to explain the case to some bored officers.

On the screen above the passengers' heads Bruce Willis and Billy Bob Thornton jumped into a huge digger and ploughed their way out of prison using force and horsepower. Bruce Willis, in a wig of long, grey hair, looked like Ozzy Osborne. It's all about tactics, Frølich reflected, and sent his boss a resigned thought.

* * *

He had slept for a couple of hours and had a musty taste in his mouth as he staggered out to join the queue of arrivals at Kenyatta International Airport in Nairobi.

The heat in the airport was suffocating. The air

seemed thick and stale. Frølich was stiff and sluggish after so many hours of sitting still on the plane. He stopped and waited for Lise Fagernes in the stream of people pouring through the entrance corridor. When she appeared, trundling her travel bag behind her, she seemed as cheerful as before.

They walked together past the display windows with their colourful textiles, leather work and other artisanal items. Neither of them said a word. He glanced covertly at her profile, her nose with a hint of a snub, and he wondered once again who it was she reminded him of, while trying to sense her mood: a gloomy earnestness he couldn't quite work out.

After the passport and visa control, while waiting for their suitcases on the crowded conveyor belt, he ventured to suggest that they might work together.

'What makes you think you and I are here on the same business?' she asked in a measured tone, leaning over her luggage trolley.

'Not so long ago you rang me to ask if we could work together.'

'That seems a very long time ago to me.'

'Is this how you work? Co-operation, yes, but only if it's useful for you?'

'You've taken the very words out my mouth,' she said coolly. 'In fact, though, you rejected my offer — in case you need to be reminded.' She took a green suitcase from the conveyor belt and loaded it onto her trolley. Then she glanced at her watch.

There was nothing he could say; any further attempt to meet her halfway would only have been even more humiliating. Her facial expression was as dismissive as their current communication was non-existent.

'Are you in a rush?' he asked, scanning the baggage

147

carousel for his suitcase.

She didn't answer at once. 'As I told you, I'm not staying in Nairobi,' she said at length. 'Watch out for lions and rhinoceroses. See you.' With that she spun round and pushed her trolley through customs and towards the exit. He stared after her: a long-legged woman dressed in grey, a blonde ponytail bouncing on her shoulders. Even though she dressed like a cliché, there was something professional and convincingly efficient about this slim woman's breezy tempo and the harsh sound of her heels on the tiles of the concourse. For his taste she was a bit too dolled up. But she had style. She seemed self-assured and also at home in this airport; she must have been here before. Stuffing his hands in his pockets, he continued to check the conveyor belt for his suitcase.

* * *

At the hotel reception desk there was an envelope from the embassy; Frank took it and had to push his way through the crowd of tourists, who all looked as if they had fallen out of Ernest Hemingway's wardrobe: elderly men and women with sagging bellies and thinning hair, equipped with sun cream and sunglasses, green safari jackets, green safari trousers, green safari baseball caps and sandals with advanced strap systems. They were shouting and screaming at their black driver and to each other, until, with expensive cameras and binoculars dangling from around their necks, they climbed into big lorries with tractor wheels and tarpaulins over the back. After the first group had clattered off, a new wave arrived. These were given an umbrella drink in the lobby, then some hotel employ-

148

ees hastily donned colourful costumes and performed a dance for them amid a great hullabaloo and flashing cameras.

Frank Frølich listened to music on his Discman while watching this comedy from the terrace outside his hotel room. He had just read through the papers from the embassy and understood that he wouldn't be contacted by anyone until the following day. But it was quite entertaining to see the tourists' first attempts at African hip-wiggling to the sounds of 'Brown Sugar' — the guitar riff behind Jagger's frenetic 'yeah, yeah, yeah — oooh'. After watching the third wave, he took out his suitcase, put on his blackest party shoes, walked into the street and bought himself a pile of loud Hawaiian shirts.

* * *

Later, wearing a dark suit and a Hawaiian shirt, he was eating dinner on the hotel terrace facing the street, when he caught the gaze of one of the safari-clad hotel guests near him. The man, who must have passed seventy-five quite some time ago, was sunburnt, with swellings under his eyes, and he was very drunk. Frank put his knife and fork down. The man mumbled something to him in German.

Frank pretended he didn't understand.

'Where do you come from?' the man asked finally — in English.

'Norway,' Frølich said, carrying on eating.

'Ach, Norwegen. I've lived there, a long time ago now, about fifty years. Finnmark. The most beautiful women in the world.' The man had bits of Bolognese sauce around his mouth and on his chin. He raised his glass and tried to hold it still. But he couldn't, he was three sheets to the wind. '*Skål*,' he roared, spitting tomato across the table. 'A *skål* for Norway.'

Frølich looked around. But no one seemed to be taking any notice of this man.

Frølich sipped his beer and continued eating.

After a short period of silence there was a bang behind him. The man had passed out. He was sitting with his head on his plate, his face in the spaghetti.

'Don't mind him,' said an over-made-up American woman in owl glasses at a neighbouring table. She had her hair piled on top of her head, a big double chin and a thin, sulky mouth, and was smoking a cigarette at the end of a long holder. 'It's like this every evening. Boy!' she shouted in a sharp voice to one of the waiters. 'Pick him up.'

Rendez-Vous

The following morning was chilly in Nairobi, lying, as it did, eighteen hundred metres above sea level. When he got up it was so early that the sun was casting long shadows. A few scattered puddles on the forecourt outside the hotel entrance revealed that it had rained in the night. But now the sky was blue, apart from the occasional restless cloud. An unending stream of cars filled the street.

The restaurant smelt of bacon and toast. Frølich was on his own. Presumably the green safari types liked a lie-in.

Later, strolling back to his room, he was stopped in the lobby by a uniformed policeman. The man was as tall as Frølich and held his cap tucked under his arm. The other arm was stretched out into a handshake. Frank grabbed the huge appendage and shook hands. The policeman had a head like a sea-lion, a crew cut and an angular smile displaying large front teeth.

'You are the Norwegian police officer?'

He told Frølich in a deep, hoarse voice that his name was Austin.

'I will be your travel companion to Nyanza,' Austin said, pointing to a black top-of-the-range Mercedes parked by the entrance. 'I will introduce you to colleagues in Kisumu.' He grinned and said huskily: 'But you can check out of your room first.'

Austin was a man of few words. He concentrated on driving, and Frølich's attempts to initiate a conversation produced monosyllables or silence.

151

Soon they were outside the centre of Nairobi, driving along shaded avenues next to central reservations overflowing with rubbish. Lines of marabou storks sat in the treetops guarding this feast, like vultures in the desert. From relatively affluent city districts they drove through slum-like areas where the houses seemed to have been built with tea chests and corrugated iron. They passed half-finished pedestrian bridges and abandoned industrial buildings, they passed dusty marketplaces where crowds jostled between ramshackle stalls of clothes and food, between sacks of potatoes and pyramids of tomatoes on the gravel. Some women were barbecuing corn on the cob over old paint pots filled with coal. Then they were driving through green, fertile areas with playful baboons sitting on the edge of the road, grimacing or running along the ditches.

It was only after they had been going for about half an hour that Austin broke the silence:

'What about Mr Takeyo?' he said. 'Did he kill someone?'

Frank shrugged.

'So why are you here if you don't know anything?'

Frank turned to him, alarmed by the tense undertone: 'I'd like to find out if he did,' he said.

'What's he accused of?'

'Nothing.'

'But why are Norwegian Interpol sending a man here to question him?'

Frank decided to ignore the misunderstanding about Interpol. 'Takeyo left Norway and arrived in Kenya on a false passport. No one's accused him of anything. What we're wondering is *why* he did.'

'Norway is a free country, isn't it?'

152

'Yes, it is.'

'So, what does he risk by meeting you? What is behind all this?'

'A murder, of a woman.'

'A white woman?'

Frølich nodded.

'You think he killed a white woman and then fled?'

'We don't know who killed her.'

Austin didn't ask any more questions. Instead, he put the radio on low. It played trance music, as car radios did at home in Norway.

They drove on in silence, racing through scrub until the earth and the sky suddenly opened up.

'The Great Rift,' Austin said.

The Rift Valley stretched out as far as the eye could see, green and flat, broken only by occasional volcanic-looking hills. The shadows from small puffs of cloud glided across the plain, as if in competition, while tiny villages stood out like greyish-brown scars in all the green. Austin drove down the long hills to the bottom of the valley as though the car with its silent engine was a plane, the speedometer showing 140 and rising. The cars in front of them moved aside as they approached.

'This is a good car,' Frølich said nervously.

'Yes,' Austin said in his husky voice. 'Very good.'

'Is it yours?'

Austin's head turned from side to side. 'This car — political.'

A political car, Frank thought to himself.

They were down on the flat and passed huge herds of zebu being tended by Masai wearing their traditional red shuka; they whizzed past a line of women carrying bundles of wood on their backs. Frølich stared out and for a fraction of a second had eye contact with a child crouched down and staring at the world passing them by. Zebras galloped across the plain and disappeared in clouds of dust among the umbrella-like acacia trees. Frølich alternated between looking out of the window and at the speedometer. Sitting behind the wheel, Austin seemed to have one aim above all others: to ride this horse for all it was worth with the intention of arriving as fast as possible, whatever the quality of the terrain beneath them.

Almost an hour later Austin opened his mouth again; he pointed to a lake, set beautifully in the countryside, and said: 'Lake Nakuru . . . flamingos.'

The entire southern part of the lake was pink. There were a lot of flamingos.

Then they sat in silence until Frølich's phone rang. It took him a little while to understand what was going on. He had hardly expected there to be coverage in this country.

It turned out to be Gunnarstranda, who wanted to know how it was all going.

'We'll see,' Frølich said. 'I'm sort of working with the police down here. They've delegated a man to drive me to Stuart Takeyo's hometown.'

Gunnarstranda waited.

'Lise Fagernes is here. We caught the same plane.'

'Good.'

'Good?'

Austin had noticed the intonation and glanced over at Frølich.

'It means she can't get up to anything here,' Gunnarstranda said. 'Keep it up. Talk later.'

Frank sat looking at his phone. But came to when he met the gaze of Austin, who opened the whole of his mouth in a covetous horse-dealer grin: 'I like your telephone.'

Frank Frølich smiled politely.

'You wanna swap?'

'Swap?'

Austin pulled onto the side of the road, and ten minutes later a deal was struck. Frank Frølich had a more fragile phone while Austin's personality seemed to have undergone a change. From now on the conversation flowed very easily. Austin pointed out and explained tribal society, ethnically based differences of culture, political issues and land formations. He pointed to himself and said: 'I'm a Luyia.'

After crossing the Rift Valley, they started on the ascent up the mountain. In the right-hand lane a long, almost unbroken, line of heavy juggernauts was crawling up, puffing and panting out clouds of black diesel exhaust that stank worse than burned rags. Austin raced up on the opposite side of the road. Frank sat with his heart in his mouth, braking with both feet whenever a car came toward them.

When the ascent levelled out Austin finally drove on the correct side of the road. They passed large green areas where women in colourful clothes with woven baskets on their backs were picking the leaves from bushes.

'Kericho,' Austin said with a smile as they pulled into a largish town. 'We will have tea now.'

They stopped in front of a hotel exemplifying the term 'faded grandeur'. Sitting on the terrace, they could gaze across a splendid garden from colonial times. Beyond it, tea plantations billowed over hills for as far as the eye could see. The waiter ran over with a menu for Austin, who waved him away and ordered a beer for them both.

One hour and three pints of Kenyan beer later they were ready to continue their journey. Austin was in a good mood and brushed against a tree as he was reversing out of the car park. He swore.

An Indian-looking man in a white jacket appeared in the doorway with an expression of concern. Austin jumped out of the car and rebuked him, claiming that the drive was too narrow.

When they had come down from the mountains the sun had started its quivering descent from the zenith to the western horizon. It was late afternoon as they finally entered the town called Kisumu. A rear-heavy jet plane plummeted from the sky and approached a landing strip.

'There's an airport here?'

Austin grinned. 'Yes, but you've had a nice journey, haven't you? If we had caught the plane, you would have had to get up at four in the morning. Travelling by car is comfortable when the equipment is in order.' He stretched out an arm to indicate the air conditioning and the leather seats.

Frølich felt himself sweating under his shirt. Lise Fagernes had caught the plane, of course. The ambitious journalist already had a head start on him of several hours.

Austin parked in front of a modern-looking hotel. 'You can check in now,' he said. 'I will contact you again when we have located Mr Takeyo. And Frank?'

'Yes?'

Austin coughed. 'I assume you do not mind if we do things our way? When we find Takeyo we will question him at the station here.'

'Naturally.'

Austin smiled, reassured.

Frank Frølich stood watching the car, which now had a broken right-hand rear light from the quarrel with the tree in Kericho. He mulled over what Austin had said and he wondered: *Who are 'we'? And when is 'when'?*

* * *

There was something British about the hotel. Heavy chesterfields and dark wood panelling dominated the lobby. He had been allocated a small, narrow room on the second floor. After dropping his luggage and confirming that the A/C system didn't work and that the mosquito net over the bed was full of holes, he stood still on the veranda facing the street. The noise of traffic and street-sellers penetrated the humid tropical air. Restlessness forced him to make a move. He took the lift down to the lobby, nodded to the receptionist and walked out into Kisumu. The evening was hot, but it wasn't dark yet. Some street-sellers across the way waved to him. They were selling drums and stone figures. He ignored them, found the pavement and strolled along amid a throng of people: there were well-dressed African Indians and less affluently dressed Africans. The road was a kind of main street — Oginga Odinga Boulevard — and it was broad with four lanes. The buildings on both sides were modern shops and they looked like any others in big towns: opulent window displays with modern furnishings. He passed an Internet café.

A man in rags, blind in one eye, had spread his goods out on the pavement: three biros, some old magazines and a pair of worn shoes displayed neatly

157

on a dirty cloth. The street-seller directed his one eye at Frølich and waved a biro. Frølich turned away and scanned the street and the mass of people. There were very few tourists, in fact only one white person apart from himself. Frank Frølich had spotted a figure he recognised. It was Lise Fagernes. She was more casually dressed now than at Nairobi airport: a baggy T-shirt, wide shorts, sandals on her feet, with a little cloth rucksack over her arm. Her legs shone like a Norwegian summer, as did her blonde hair. She could have been a traffic light, he reflected, and noticed she looked less surprised at seeing him than he had been at spotting her. There were fifty metres between them. She was standing in front of a kiosk and rummaging through her pockets for money. When he made a bee-line for her, she stopped what she was doing with a grin on her face.

'Well, well,' Frølich said. 'And what are you doing here?'

She turned back to the counter and received her change. 'I'm buying water.' She unscrewed the top and watched him as she drank. She had exchanged her designer glasses for a pair of black sunglasses that she had placed in her blonde hair. She was sun-tanned on her cheeks and shoulders. There's something familiar about her eyes, he thought, once again racking his memory.

'And what are *you* doing here?' she asked.

'Searching for our mutual friend,' Frank Frølich said. 'Stuart Takeyo.'

'Are you sure he's here then?'

'You're here,' Frølich grinned. 'So, the witness won't be far away. Or are you doing a report for Norwegian Church Aid?'

She didn't answer, but glanced up while fiddling with her rucksack. A camera was visible through the material.

'Are you going far?' he asked.

'You go your way and I'll go mine, Frølich. You're a Norwegian policeman and you have to lick the backsides of your corrupt colleagues in this country.'

'Whose backsides?'

'Don't think I didn't see you in that car. How many tons of medicine and how many children's schooling have to be crossed off the budget because some bent cop is going to keep it in his garage, Frølich?'

'I know nothing about that. But I am a bit flattered that you've been spying on me.'

She angled him a sharp glare. 'Unfortunately, we're at the same hotel — the Imperial.'

'Indeed. What floor?'

She smiled patronisingly.

'Perhaps we should make a schedule so that we don't meet in the lift.'

'I'd rather change hotel,' she answered, and added: 'I'm serious. You do your job and I'll do mine. That's how it has to be. I have nothing against you — you're probably decent enough — but so long as you're dependent on having a good relationship with the wrong people, I can't have anything to do with you.'

'Have you met Takeyo?'

Lise Fagernes screwed the top back.

'Have you interviewed him?'

She put the bottle in her rucksack and slung it over her shoulders.

'Can I read the interview before you email it to the newspaper?'

'Frølich. I'm the journalist here, OK?'

'Frank,' he said. 'Those who know me well, call me Frankie.'

'Frankie?' she smirked.

'Shall we skip the chat and have the beer now?'

She straightened her rucksack and tightened one of the straps. Even if the irritated frown was still between her eyes, she wore a smile that took the sting out of her words. 'Listen, I don't intend to leave a fiasco behind me here. I've come to do a job, but I also know that we've got to find a way of getting on in this town. And we should be professional enough not to fall out. So, we can say 'Morning' and 'Hi'. And that's where it ends. So, bye for now.' She turned on her heel and went.

He stood watching her and once again he noted that she was actually quite short. With a rucksack and shorts instead of high heels and short skirts, her feminine curves were hinted at rather than emphasised, which also brought out a vulnerability that contrasted sharply with the tough mask she had put on for the occasion. And as though she had felt his eyes on her back, she spun round and shouted with a little smile on her lips: 'Besides, I hate beer.'

'You probably drink white wine,' he shouted back. 'Special labels from Alsace and places like it.' He grinned and it suddenly struck him what was familiar about her eyes. But by then it was too late to tell her. She was already crossing the boulevard.

Tribal Rituals

The sun shone on the birch trunks in Birkelunden. Inspector Gunnarstranda found a parking spot, locked the car and ambled up Toftes gate. When he found the café, he remembered that this block had once housed a shoe shop. But that was a long time ago now. He opened the door. Most of the customers were eating soup or salad: young women revealing seductive tattoos on their shoulders or hips; the few men there were had meticulously shaven heads, lip or eyebrow piercings and they had studiously avoided any other shaving. Gunnarstranda slipped into this environment as smoothly as a penguin into a Freemasons' lodge, and he used the second of shocked silence that ensued when he showed himself in the doorway to make a polite bow. Then he took out the note from Lena Stigersand and walked over to the counter. A man in black with a white apron and big mutton-chop whiskers on his cheeks looked up at him enquiringly.

Gunnarstranda asked after Lotte.

'She hasn't got in yet.'

Gunnarstranda found himself a seat by the shelf-like table in the window facing the street, and turned automatically when the bell above the door rang. The young woman who came into the café could have been about eighteen and was provocatively dressed in a short skirt and tight-fitting top. On her feet she wore trainers. She waved to the man behind the counter, who indicated the policeman in the corner.

Gunnarstranda shook hands with the girl; she had slim hands and a collection of plastic bracelets jangling around her wrists.

'Are you Lotte?'

She nodded, wriggled onto the stool beside his and waved to someone she knew at the back of the café.

Gunnarstranda waited patiently. Good-looking girls have lots of friends.

'I work here, you know,' she explained.

'On Sundays too?'

She nodded again and signalled to the man behind the counter, and he brought her a bottle of mineral water and two glasses.

'As I think you know by now, we're conducting an investigation, and we've been speaking to the people who work here. I'm interested in particular in Sunday, the fourth of August, almost two weeks ago.' Gunnarstranda took a little time to take the photograph of Kristine Ramm from his inside pocket. 'I understand you were at work and serving that day?'

She nodded again.

'When I called, one of your colleagues told me you served this woman.'

He passed her the picture of Kristine Ramm.

'Yes, I did,' Lotte said. 'It's the woman who was in the paper, isn't it? But the photo in the paper looks more like her. At first, she said she didn't eat meat. But then there were problems with the salad as well. Generally, we don't have any problems. I mean, some vegetarians don't want eggs, but this one didn't want tuna, or shrimps, or eggs, nothing. And then there was a fuss.'

'Do you remember what clothes she was wearing?'

'A brown top, in some stretchy material; I noticed

162

it because it was quite stylish, though I don't like that type of thing myself, and I think she was wearing long trousers, but I'm not entirely sure. I imagine I would've noticed if she'd been wearing a skirt. I mean, she was quite cool and you see on others what you'd like yourself, right.'

'When was this?'

'Some time after twelve, but before three in the afternoon. I stop at three, you see. I'd guess . . . maybe one or two, not quite sure.'

'And she was alone?'

'Yes, that is, she was alone when she was eating, but her bloke came, and then she left — that is, both of them left.'

'Her bloke?'

'Yes. They went for it, deep-throating on the pavement outside — so it would've been a bit unusual if they hadn't been in a relationship . . .'

'Outside?'

The young woman took a deep breath. Gunnarstranda was too slow on the uptake for her. 'She left without giving a tip, and I was disappointed because she seemed pretty cool, right, but I assume it was because of all the fuss over her veggie meal. And while she was paying, she was talking on her phone, in English, she was explaining, like, where she was. She said you have to go there, take a left turn and so on. And then she went outside when her bloke came.' She pointed through the window to where the tram came and stopped to let off passengers.

'Do you remember what this man looked like?'

'Bit funky, bit rasta, sort of.'

'European?'

'Maybe. He was black, but he didn't have plaits or

dreads. His hair was short, and then he had a cool cap. And that's really all I can say. I didn't see any more. They just left.'

Gunnarstranda produced the photograph of Takeyo. 'Could that be him?'

'Possibly,' she said after studying the picture. 'But I didn't look so carefully at the guy. It was more the two of them I looked at.'

'Do you remember what he was wearing?'

'To be honest, I . . .' She shook her head. 'T-shirt anyway, and the rasta cap, bright colours, that's all I remember.'

'You didn't see where they were going?'

She smiled and shook her head.

'While she was in here, did she talk to anyone?'

'Just on the phone.'

'So, she rang several times?'

'Yes.'

'You didn't catch any of what she said, did you? Did she mention any names, for example?'

'No, it was when she began to speak English and give instructions that I listened, because she wanted to pay at the same time.'

Gunnarstranda slipped down from the stool and passed her his business card. 'Get in touch,' he said, 'if you remember anything else.'

164

South

Kisumu seemed to be a well-planned town, concentrated around a relatively small commercial centre. The building style varied from colonial houses that had seen better days, to modern shops, to poorer concrete constructions. The heroes from the war of independence against the English were honoured with street names. The centre was focused around Jomo Kenyatta Highway and Oginga Odinga Boulevard. Outside this zone were the big marketplaces. Between the centre and the lake were the railway station, the harbour warehouses and the slums. Frølich walked the streets to get to know the area.

But darkness fell quickly and swathed the town and countryside in darkness.

To begin with, he didn't give it much thought. At home he was used to daylight lasting until well into the night. That didn't happen here. Suddenly he realised he was alone, in a completely unknown place. He stopped and stood stock still. He had walked a long way and was unsure where he was. It was a long time since he had passed an illuminated shop window; it was a long time since he had seen any light.

Despite the heat and the humid air, he felt he was standing on ice, his arm and leg muscles tensed, as if he were standing rigidly on a lake after a frost and feeling the ground beneath him moving, sensing the ice could crack at any moment. It was quiet in this part of town, there were almost no cars. In the all-consuming darkness the place was teeming with people. But he couldn't see them. Mumbling voices revealed their presence, and they flitted like shadows it wasn't possible to see until they were close. The smell of sewage and open gutters that came in waves suggested that he was in a poor district. The buzzing of cicadas made the air tremble. Some cyclists pedalled past, mudguards rattling. Men talking in low voices passed in groups. Women with bundles on their heads passed so close that the whites of their eyes flashed when they looked at him. Some people had a torch. They would lift the torch and shine it in his face to see if it was someone they knew approaching. Blinded, Frølich mumbled a greeting in a thick voice.

He stared up at the stars. In a way, they seemed different, too. *In Norway, the stars are white, here they are warmer, yellow,* he thought, and as a result the sky was also able to emphasise that he was a long way from home.

I can't stay here though, he told himself, and forced his legs to carry on. The sense that he was standing on thin ice returned. It had become so dark that it wasn't possible to see where he was putting his feet. He thought about snakes, about open sewage and how no one would notice if he got a knife in the back. Why would anyone stab me in the back? He groped his way forward like a wakened sleepwalker. The only source of light was the starry sky. With his face turned to the violet cloak that filtered the yellow lustre, he continued slowly until the road curved into a bend and a huge square opened up. He stopped — surprised to see the sky reflected on the ground: straight ahead and to the right there was an endless line of bonfires, over which something was being cooked — in large pans and deep pots. Flames licked iron, casting a red

166

glare over the women working as thousands of sparks and embers tore into the night like miniature neb- ulae. To the left, down along the promenade many, more modest, flames fluttered and gleamed: women were sitting in a line with candles in front of them. They were shouting at him to buy their wares. Frølich stood admiring this interplay of red, black and orange while breathing in the fragrance of spices, the smoke from the fires, barbecued corn on the cob, dust and rancid fat mixed with the smell of fish.

But he had no idea where he was. What should he do? Hesitantly, he took out his mobile phone and keyed in the number he had been given by Austin. Immediately he put the phone to his ear he felt a chill go through him. A phone rang close by. That wouldn't have mattered much but for the ring tone: it was Car- los Santana's *Samba Pati*, personally downloaded from the internet by him a few weeks ago.

He followed the sound. The outline of the fig- ure was unmistakeable. 'Austin,' Frank Frølich said calmly. 'You have to answer the phone.'

The tune stopped when Frølich switched off his phone. Then Austin shone a light into his face. 'Well, how are you, Frank?'

A deep, husky voice. Austin's eyes glowed in the dark, and his breath smelt of alcohol. 'Everything alright?'

Frølich cleared his throat to produce some sound in his throat: 'I'd feel better if you told me why you're following me.'

Austin gave a low chuckle. 'In Africa, Frank, in Africa, anything can happen.'

Silent, they stood surrounded by darkness. Austin's silhouette seemed to merge into his surroundings. It was Austin who broke the silence between them. He asked if Frank was interested in buying anything.

Frølich shrugged. The Kenyan policeman flicked on his torch and shone it on the cloth of one woman selling her wares. Frank Frølich had to look twice. 'What is that?' he asked.

'Bones,' Austin said. 'Fish bones.'

It was fish skeletons. Frølich just stared at the strange image. This woman was selling fish with no meat on the bones.

'Who would buy fishbones?'

'People who live here.' Austin set off walking.

Frølich followed. They strode out, down between the burning fires. There were many women selling fishbones. But most of them were frying fish skeletons in big pots. Austin stopped in front of one. He shone his torch on a wooden structure the woman had built behind the fire. Hundreds of fish skeletons hung from it, their mouths wide open — a kind of crisis version of dried fish in the north of Norway, it struck Frølich. And gave up counting the number of heads with transfixed fish-eyes above slimy skeletons.

Austin pointed to the flames and said: 'The fish skin is used as fuel; the frying fat is the remnants of the fat on the fish bones. The women dry the skeletons first before they fry them and sell them in the market. The skeletons are used for fish soup. The soup bones give protein and vitamins.'

'What about the fish meat?' Frølich asked. 'What happened to that?'

Austin gave a broad grin and spoke Swahili to the woman bent over the boiling pot. She launched a tirade of unfamiliar sounds against Frølich. Both Austin and the woman grinned.

Austin grabbed Frølich's spare tyre and pinched it as he explained: 'She says the fish meat is eaten by fat Europeans like you. Filleted fish is exported to Europe, the Middle East, Japan, the USA and Canada. Whereas she, a widow with responsibility for six children, living by a lake, can't afford that kind of food. She has been to the rubbish heap outside the factory to collect fish remains. She has to feed her children on soup made from the bones she found there.'

Austin listened to the woman talking before translating: 'Fishing has become an export industry. The bones and the skin are left for ordinary people. Africans are left with the rubbish. The children in the slums of Obunga die of malnutrition. They starve on the banks of a fish-rich lake.'

Austin went up to Frølich and smiled mirthlessly: 'Welcome to Africa, Frank.'

169

The Stock Exchange

It was afternoon, but the sun was still burning down on the already well-warmed Oslo 'Pot', so-called because of the geographical shape of the city centre. Gunnarstranda was standing by a window and dreaming of a cold beer when an internet journalist called Skulberg rang and passed on Sørli's regards.

Gunnarstranda suggested they meet at Kafé Justisen. It was almost six, so he left the car in the garage and strolled across Grønlandsleiret, Youngstorget and around the bend by Venstres Hus.

The old door jangled as it closed behind him. On an afternoon made for a beer in the open, there was only one customer inside. The journalist raised a hand in the air and waved from the corner table, under the photographs of Oslo original, Peder Gunvold Hermansen.

Skulberg was approaching his thirties, had a long nose, short ginger hair and a small ring dangling from his left ear. He was wearing a narrow-striped suit, but instead of a shirt and tie underneath he wore a T-shirt with a picture of Pamela Anderson on it.

Gunnarstranda got straight to the point: 'Sørli says you know about Freddy Pedersen and his African involvement.'

'Involvement is perhaps not the right word. Pedersen has two interests in Africa. The first is money, and so is the second.'

Gunnarstranda motioned to the waitress, who was new and pleasingly forward. 'Pils,' he mouthed.

She nodded and turned to draw a beer as Skulberg continued:

'But the dream of money is realised through something as banal as medicine. Original, eh? Africa: money out, medicines in. Heard that one before?'

Gunnarstranda started rolling a cigarette.

'First, the hard facts: around the world approximately seven thousand people a day die of AIDS. There are, at a rough estimate, forty million HIV-positive cases world-wide. Imagine there's a vaccine,' Skulberg said in a lower voice. 'No,' he corrected himself. 'Imagine you're offered a chance to invest in a commercial project with the bold target of saving the world from this plague.'

Sindre Skulberg paused as the waitress brought the beer.

Gunnarstranda lit his roll-up and inhaled. Skulberg's mention of HIV made him involuntarily think about his own lung illness. So far, this was the starkest wake-up call he'd had in recent years that one day his life would end. It was a new realisation that he couldn't ignore. His work frequently dealt with death. And when his wife, Edel, had died, he'd gone into a long depression, but it had primarily been a reaction to the loneliness life represented for him without her. Now, knowing that he had an illness that was eating up his own lung tissue, it was like finally coming round a bend and discovering a sign in the road that said: *Halt. Watch out. The end is nigh.*

He leaned back against the wall, ran his eye over the run-down pub, thinking that this sleepy watering hole, where the sun's rays angled in through the windows and shone rectangles on the tables and created a cosy atmosphere of the good old days, was a place he had invariably felt at home. The fact that he could come to this realisation, he reflected, in this very place, at this arbitrary moment in time, the fact that he could experience a very normal variant of an endless series of similar situations, was in itself testimony that his present life had value. If, that is, one took the banal yet reliable cost-benefit-analysis 'morality' as one's starting point. Most people did nowadays, not generally thinking long term, either politically or altruistically. Not only was it convenient, but the zeitgeist almost demanded one defended one's own interests at every opportunity. Gunnarstranda concluded that because he wanted to be in this happy situation right now — not that he would ever describe himself as a happy person — he would try for a tiny instant to feel what a vaccine for his condition might mean to him, amid all this unremarkable, commonplace well-being. The effort, however, was wasted, in a way; this thought was alien, unfamiliar, and belonged to a way of thinking his brain and his inner core would not accept. The thought was reduced to a vague idea that slunk past a self-image that didn't want to know about it — and so it failed.

Gunnarstranda bowed his head watching the idea flee across the floorboards and disappear — while from the corner of his eye he saw the waitress distance herself — and Skulberg continued his lecture about vaccines and AIDS.

'We're talking here about HIV as a business,' Skulberg effused. 'So, we're ignoring chivalrous acts of charity and the wish to help fellow men. We're talking business and we're talking enormous profits.'

Skulberg took a swig of his beer and wiped the froth from his top lip with the back of his hand. 'Imagine a modest quantity: for example, the sale of a hundred thousand vaccines per day. If we assume there's a company with a monopoly on such a vaccine, and if we further assume it makes a profit of, let's say, one paltry krone per vaccine — and this quantity is unrealistically modest — the company with the rights would make a *hundred thousand* kroner, net, per day.' Skulberg gripped his beer glass while his eyes took on a dreamy expression. 'Imagine if the company were reputable enough to calculate the normal advance in the pharmaceutical industry — what then? If we're still unrealistically modest and up the price a zero — to ten kroner per vaccine in profit? Then we're talking a *million* kroner, straight into your pocket, net, every bloody day, and we're only working with a hundred thousand vaccines. Imagine a ten-krone profit on a million vaccines — every day. Eh? Imagine that. Only the gods know the actual size of the profit.'

Gunnarstranda flicked the ash from his roll-up. 'But I haven't heard anything about this. I haven't read anything about it. It must be a castle in the air, surely?'

Skulberg wriggled until he was comfortable on the chair and said: 'The story goes as follows: a Norwegian company — unlisted, for Christ's sake — calls itself Pharmanor. This pharmaceutical company claims they are testing HIV medicines in countries where the illness has spread widely. Thailand and some African countries.'

'Claims? Are they testing, or aren't they?'

'God knows. They might be. That isn't really the point. It's not inconceivable that they're running such projects. At the same time, they have some good friends in the right places. These lobbyists work against

173

centrally placed Norwegians in WHO, the Red Cross and the World Bank. What I'm talking about is a completely unknown little company that claims it's sitting at the end of a rainbow staring into a pot of gold. But pots of gold are only found in fairy tales, aren't they.' Skulberg tapped his forefinger on the face of Pamela Anderson. 'What do sceptics such as myself look for when we meet fiction and fairy tales? Yes, we look for the troll, the rotten apple in the basket. And we do find them.'

Skulberg leaned back with a smug grin.

Gunnarstranda studied the indefatigable journalist as he considered to what extent financial gain from others' suffering should be anything but an ethical question. *Actually, I should be up in arms, he thought. I should be morally or politically engaged when I hear such stories, but am I? This information triggers a reaction, it occupies my mind, but is that really political engagement, or ethical, or moral? Is it any kind of engagement? Isn't it the case that I'm engaged in much the same way as when I go to catch a train and discover I have to join a long queue to buy a ticket? Or if I find out the post office has closed and I have to put up with going to the supermarket to send a parcel — not to mention when a chemist disappears — that engages me to the extent that I'm getting closer* . . . He hesitated while searching for the appropriate word. *Closer to what? Ah, he thought, closer to that which has some meaning. Has some meaning?* he wondered. *For whom? For me, of course.* He decided to ignore the question that would be the result of this reasoning, the way he had for half of his life: *What has meaning for me?* He read the question, but intuitively closed the book where a possible answer might be formulated. And, in so doing, he realised that he was now observing one of the many defeats his soul had suffered. But he did it without allowing the realisation to be joined by emotions — the realisation was filed away, one image among many, as though he were a commander-in-chief in the heat of battle who, from the corner of his eye, sees another soldier fall and die. Without giving another thought to engagement and ideals, he raised his head and concentrated on Skulberg's mouth and the words pouring out of it:

'The problem with Pharmanor's HIV adventure is that their preparation wasn't thorough enough,' Skulberg said. 'They thought they had a brilliant idea, but they didn't ask themselves why no one else'd had the idea before them.'

Gunnarstranda puffed on his cigarette. It was out. He had to reluctantly accept that he not only disliked the taste of a cold cigarette, but that he was also loath to relight it. He stubbed it out in the ashtray. As he sensed that Skulberg was getting to the climax, he took the effort to articulate the obvious question the man was waiting for: why didn't anyone have the idea before them?

'The miracle medicine, this remedy that they were going to use to save the world —'

'Just a minute,' Gunnarstranda interrupted. 'Which remedy?'

'That's the whole point,' Skulberg grinned. 'Pharmanor's business plan was based on an HIV medicine that wasn't new in any way at all. A pipsqueak company like Pharmanor doesn't have the resources to develop a brilliant new vaccine against HIV. The medicine they have identified is one that has been used before for a completely different illness. One of the side-effects of this medicine, however, is that it

175

prevents HIV.'

Skulberg paused and gazed into his empty glass with an expression of profound regret.

Gunnarstranda caught the waitress's eye and held up two fingers.

'To cut a long story short,' Skulberg said, 'I'm trying to find out who's behind this Pharmanor. What I've found out so far is that the biggest shareholder is a firm called Nor-Comp. It's registered in Aruba, an island in the Caribbean and a tax haven with post-box addresses. But no one knows who owns or stands behind Nor-Comp. All I know is that the chairperson is a certain Britt Lise Staw, which should interest you.'

'Britt Lise Staw? Isn't that Freddy Pedersen's mother-in-law?'

'Yup. Britt Lise Staw is a woman who lives on an old smallholding in Stokke, with no running water. She has home care three days a week because she has something in common with ex-President Ronald Reagan — an illness known as Alzheimer's. In other words, the lady doesn't know a thing about shares or business ownership. So Nor-Comp is actually synonymous with our friend Freddy Pedersen. And life goes on. Nor-Comp and various other investors pump money into the company called Pharmanor, which will save the world, supposedly. Until a rumour starts doing the rounds that Pharmanor doesn't have a patent because someone else is sitting on the rights to the vaccine.' Skulberg took his beer and drank.

'What else?' Gunnarstranda asked impatiently.

'I'll tell you, if you can promise me some discretion until my article hits the newsstands.'

'I can't do that if what you say uncovers criminal acts.'

176

'I'll make an exception for the police. In exchange, I don't want you to tip off other journalists.'

'Agreed.'

Skulberg wiped the froth from his lips with the back of his hand again: 'The medicine, which initially was a remedy against some chronic disease or other, was withdrawn from the market in 1984 — so almost twenty years ago — many years *before* Pharmanor tried to procure the rights. In other words, the medicine is simply banned and old hat. Put another way, Pharmor's super vaccine is an example of the proverbial pig in a poke. It's the emperor's new clothes. The company doesn't have the patent and the medicine isn't usable.'

'Why was the medicine withdrawn from the market?'

'It transpired that the medicine had more than one side-effect. The positive one was that it prevented HIV. The negative one was that patients went into deep and incurable psychoses — much like schizophrenia. The medicine reduces the infection of HIV, but also creates loads of mental cases.'

'What you're telling me is that someone has speculated on a product that is basically a bubble, it's a con, but so what?'

'There's more,' Skulberg said with a fiendish grin.

'Come on then.'

'OK.' Skulberg placed both elbows on the table and leaned forward with the expression of someone who has just become a bingo millionaire: 'If we're objective, it doesn't stink quite so much. The issue of rights is something you fight about in court. Rights can be bought and sold. Medical side-effects and administrative decisions are also less important, especially for the bureaucrats who ultimately stamp papers and grant permission, if you can cough up enough good results and goodwill in WHO. The rights issue and the decision to withdraw the medicine are examples of what I would call specific structural difficulties that all firms have to cope with to a greater or lesser extent if they want to enter a market. What is legally more palpable and therefore very serious . . .' Skulberg grinned again '. . . seen through the eyes of a Norwegian legislator . . .' he added.

'Is?'

'. . . That Nor-Comp, a company you and I concluded just now was synonymous with Freddy 'Feppen' Pedersen, no longer has any shares in Pharmanor.'

Suddenly Gunnarstranda understood why Sørli and the Fraud Squad had become interested in this case.

Skulberg straightened his back. 'Apart from the salesmen in Nor-Comp, only you, Sørli and I know this medicine is fake. Nor-Comp knew that and was standing on the edge of a precipice: the likelihood of Pharmanor going bankrupt and causing the owners huge losses was enormous. But instead of plunging down the precipice, Nor-Comp sold its shares *before* anyone else found out that Pharmanor's medicine adventure was fake. As Nor-Comp is now out, there must be a group of new investors left holding the baby. When it becomes public that Pharmanor is going to market with a medicine they neither have the patent for, nor the permission to market, the value of the shares is likely to be zilch.'

'But didn't you call this 'structural difficulties'?'

'Yes, I did, but now we're talking about something

178

different — this is illegal insider trading. Some share-holders knew that shares in Pharmanor would be worthless if the blunder became public knowledge. They jumped ship in the time-honoured 'rat' fashion: they sold their shares at an absolutely criminal price without informing buyers that the medicine was unusable. The following day the shares were worthless. At police colleges and in the Justice Department, this behaviour is called fraud.'

Gunnarstranda suddenly had the feeling he was sitting in a boat with his line and lure in the middle of a shoal of fish. If there was a link between Stuart Takeyo's disappearance, Freddy Pedersen and the murder of Kristine Ramm, the odds were very high that the big fish was swimming around in the shoal that Skulberg had just identified.

Skulberg shrugged. 'The investors who earned their kroner in this way may not agree with my definition of fraud. Perhaps Sørli doesn't, either. If he considers that the sellers have done something criminal, he first has to prove some form of intent or negligence on the part of the sellers. You and I can claim that the sellers knew about the chicanery. However, it is quite another matter to prove it in a court of law. As information about the side-effects and so on isn't public, the sellers can just gesticulate wildly and act surprised when this comes out. That's the great thing about this story: the obvious confidence trick. Those who bought the pig in a poke have made the same mistake as the owners of Nor-Comp did at first. They didn't check thoroughly enough before buying. My guess is that the buyers are going to stay stumm about their blunder. I haven't read anything about it in the newspapers. I've been working on the case for months and have been using sources that aren't easily accessible. Besides — and this is perhaps the crunch — if the investors report the sellers and hope for a reaction from the Fraud Squad, Sørli will be faced with the ten-thousand-dollar question: who broke the law? Who owned the shares that these poor investors bought? The only person who can be officially linked with Nor-Comp is Britt Lise Staw, the old lady with Alzheimer's in Stokke, and by definition she isn't responsible for her actions and so will never be charged with anything.'

'The sale of the shares must be registered somewhere?' Gunnarstranda said, watching a big, greedy fish thrashing around in the foaming waters.

'Of course, all you or Fraud Squad Sørli will find if you start searching is that on both the buyer and the seller sides there are registered companies owned by other companies. Think how difficult it's been to find the truth behind the infamous Anders Jahre fortune. It's taken more than twenty years so far. And still no one's any the wiser. To be quite frank, Gunnarstranda, I think this case is a lost cause for the Norwegian authorities.'

'When did Nor-Comp sell its Pharmanor shares?' Gunnarstranda asked, deep in thought.

'Not so long ago.'

'They must've had a very good sales pitch.'

'I presume so.'

'I'd like to know when the sale was made — the date, time, everything you can dig up.'

'And what can you offer me by way of a reward?' Skulberg asked shrewdly.

'You can ask the first five questions at the press conference.'

'Which one?'
'The one we hold when we've solved the Kristine Ramm case.'

Undercover

As Frank Frølich hadn't received any calls from the Kenyan police, he phoned them. Austin had switched off his mobile. But the woman who answered his call was kindness itself. She told him that Austin was out on surveillance. Takeyo had several siblings living around the province. Austin and other police officers were on intensive undercover work to find where he could be. She promised to tell Austin to ring him.

Frølich decided to have a dip in the pool. Outside, the sun was dazzlingly bright and had turned the water a shimmering green. The surface was reflected on the bottom as a fine-meshed net, spun out of sun-threads. The tiles around the pool were boiling hot. He found himself a sunlounger. Soon he was joined by two young women. They positioned themselves strategically close. He ignored them and jumped into the pool. The water temperature was refreshingly cool. He swam back and forth in the little pool for half an hour. Afterwards, as he was rubbing sun cream down his arms, one of the women made an advance. She was around twenty years old, buxom, provocative and standing bent at the hip. Should she rub his back? He shook his head and looked away. At that moment a young boy came running across the tiles and launched himself into the water. His mother, an elegant woman in her thirties, sat down on a bench in the shade.

Frølich lay down on the sunlounger, closed his eyes and roasted in the heat. He listened to the lazy morning, heels clicking over the tiles, birds twittering in the trees above the pool, the screech of a bird of prey, and further away the drone of the traffic mixed with the sound of the little boy splashing in the water.

When he opened his eyes, the boy's mother was on the sunlounger beside his, keeping an eye on her son. She had long eyelashes and very red lips. The moment he saw her, she turned to him and whispered: 'You make me so horny.'

Frølich stared dumbfounded at his pale body, swung his legs to the side and sat up.

'Mummy,' the boy shouted. 'Mummy, look at me, Mummy.'

'He's a good boy,' she said. 'Would you mind if I sat next to you?' Without waiting for an answer, she moved over and sat on the sunlounger. She reeked of perfume. Frølich was numb with shock and just stared at her: a face with regular features, her long hair neatly piled on top of her head, a blue dress that brought out her figure, silk stockings, gold bracelets around her wrist and a chain of pearls coiled around her neck in gentle loops. She shouted to her son again, then laid a slim hand on his thigh and whispered: 'I'm gonna make you a very happy man.'

'I'm sorry,' he mumbled, helpless.

'Don't be.' She stroked his thigh. It trembled.

'I'm a policeman,' he stammered, feeling more stupid than a donkey.

She looked at him with renewed interest. 'Are you? Where from?'

'Norway.'

'Shouldn't we two just relax and enjoy ourselves?'

He had no idea what to say. He sensed that a rejection would offend her deeply — however he expressed it. But the situation was absurd.

At that moment Lise Fagernes came through the door.

The woman followed Frølich's eyes and saw Lise Fagernes, who had stopped and was staring intently at them. 'I see,' the woman whispered and removed her hand. 'You're with her? The journalist?' She stood up. With her back to Lise Fagernes, she whispered: 'Your girlfriend's no problem. Just ring me — anytime at all.' With that she bent down and pushed a business card in his sandal. Her high heels click-clacked on the tiles as she retreated.

'You're one of them, I see.' Lise Fagernes's voice was cold and sharp, like the air after a frosty night. Her fingers trembled as she took a cigarette from the packet in her rucksack.

Frølich lay back on the sunlounger, staring up as the journalist's slim silhouette obscured the sun.

The boy's mother had joined a colleague in the shade. The other woman said something, and the two of them burst into laughter.

'The big white man's club,' Lise Fagernes continued, her voice bristling with contempt.

'Actually, we were talking about you,' Frølich said. 'She knew you were a journalist.'

'And the two of you were planning to make a snowman in the garden here?'

'It's true,' he said, feebly.

'Norwegian Policeman Buys Sex Abroad,' Lise said as if quoting a *VG* headline.

'What?'

'Do you think I'm completely mad?'

Frølich wanted to protest. But at that moment the little boy had finished swimming. 'Mummy,' he shouted. 'Mummy!' The woman rose from the bench with a towel at the ready. Smiling, she rubbed the boy down, and he laughed aloud. It was the perfect idyll. Frølich glanced from the little family unit to Lise Fagernes and back again. He felt like he was a yacht picking up speed. 'I like your commitment, but you have a bit of a dirty mind,' he grinned.

'Sorry,' she intoned. She sat down on the sunlounger beside his. 'I thought she was one of the prostitutes.'

'I didn't think you wanted anything to do with me,' he said.

'I said sorry, didn't I?' Lise watched the mother and son. 'That kind of thing really gets my goat.' She stripped off and was soon in a yellow bikini. 'I'm sick of seeing aged aid-workers sitting with tarts every morning when I come down for breakfast,' she continued. 'And it's not the women that annoy me. After all, they're poor and have to support their family. It's the pathetically predictable illustration of the modern battle of the sexes that makes me angry. Now I want to swim.' She got up.

Frølich watched her — short in stature, slim, lithe and light on her feet. She stood at the end of the pool, on the edge. When she looked up it was to receive his gaze, a tenth of a second before diving in. Her ponytail floated over her back like a shiny otter.

'Have you located Takeyo?' he asked when she returned, shivering.

She looked around and wrung the water from her ponytail. 'Suddenly we're all alone,' she established and sat down on the sunlounger.

'Do you know who you look like?' Frølich asked.

'No?'

'Michelle Pfeiffer.'

'Oh, yes?' She rummaged through her rucksack.

185

'What about Takeyo?' he asked again.

She glanced up, blushing. 'Is that how you work?'

'How d'you mean?'

She shook her head dismissively and poked a cigarette between her lips. 'I'm fairly sure I'm going to meet him.'

'Where is he?'

She lit up. 'I don't know, but I can say I've made some progress. My boss doesn't need to worry — for the time being.'

'It hasn't struck you that it would be wise to have someone to discuss this case with?'

'I've got someone: my editor. We discuss the case all the time.'

'But you two are short of an important perspective.'

'Yours?' She grinned. 'Or the financial perspective that rules here?'

They were interrupted by a waiter who came over to tell Frølich there was a telephone call for him.

He strapped on his sandals and took the call at the reception desk: Inspector Gunnarstranda wanted to know what he was doing.

'Undercover work,' Frølich lied. 'What have you been doing?'

'Getting up to speed with AIDS issues and checking out Norwegian classes for our new countrymen. It turns out that all foreign scholarship students have to do a Norwegian course at Blindern, which our man did. But for some reason Stuart Takeyo wasn't given a place on the course until January this year.'

There was a silence, and Frølich wondered for a few seconds whether Gunnarstranda had rung off. 'Hello?' he said.

'Think back.'

186

'Pass,' Frølich said, gazing around.

'Kimberley,' Gunnarstranda said in a croaky voice.

* * *

'Kimberley?' Lise Fagernes repeated in surprise, shielding her eyes to see him with the sun behind his head.

'Murder,' Frølich said drily as he got dressed. 'Killer unknown. About eighteen months ago.'

She sat up. 'I think I remember that case, but what about it?'

'Kimberley was a scholarship student at the Norwegian University of Life Sciences in Ås. He came from Tanzania. He disappeared, but was found in a plastic sack on a rubbish dump in Bærum.'

'I see.'

'Have you been there?'

'I once had a boyfriend who lived in those parts. Carry on.'

'David Kimberley disappeared after a Norwegian for foreigners lesson.' Frølich buttoned up his Hawaiian shirt. 'Kimberley was researching fish breeding. It seems that government departments in countries around here are keen to breed a fish called the Nile perch. And we Norwegians know a lot about fish breeding. That's why Kimberley was in Norway.'

'So?'

'Stuart Takeyo did the same Norwegian course as Kimberley. Both vanished without trace. Both were researching the lake here.'

'Why are you telling me this?'

'You're a journalist, aren't you?'

She sat up. 'You don't give in, do you. Listen,

187

you can't sell me information. You're giving it to me because I don't want to buy it. I have nothing to give you in return.'

He sat down. 'Forget Takeyo and us for two seconds. Now I'm talking about something else. Let's call it a proposed compromise. What if I gave you the name of the company Kimberley used to get into Norway? This fish-breeding company. It's based in this district. Then you could use your press card to justify a conversation with people I can't access. Then you can put some meat on the bare bones for me. Stuart Takeyo's a separate issue.'

'Are you claiming you're no longer interested in my work on Takeyo?'

'Did I say that? The reason I've mentioned Kimberley is that I can give you information you don't already have.'

'I can get it by ringing my editor at home.'

'Ring *VG* instead then. My offer is well meant.'

They fell silent as a waiter arrived with drinks. 'I ordered for us,' Frølich said. 'Beer for me; white wine for you.'

When the uniformed waiter had served the drinks and withdrawn, she held the stem of the glass, immersed in thought. Beads of condensation ran down the sides.

'It's probably from Alsace,' he said. '*Skål.*'

She gave a nod of acknowledgement and put down the glass. 'It'll do. But I'm not sure I like your proposal.'

Frølich gave her more time to think.

'For me,' she said at length, 'it's important not to be indebted to anyone, especially not the authorities you're working with here. I don't want to find myself in a situation where I have to take special account of —'

She stopped talking as Frølich's mobile phone rang.

It was Austin. He said he was ten minutes away and wondered if Frølich was ready for some undercover work.

'Who was that?' Lise Fagernes asked, squinting into the sun.

'I have to go,' he said, scribbling down a name and an address and passing them to her. 'Inborn Fisheries Incorporated.'

When she stretched out her hand to receive the slip of paper, he stopped to meet her gaze: 'As you're not going to see Takeyo right now, the choice is really whether to lie in the sun here or do something useful. Think it over.' With that, he drank up his beer and was gone.

★ ★ ★

A few minutes later the black Mercedes braked and came to a halt in front of the entrance. Frølich jumped in.

'Ready for work?' Austin revealed his horse-teeth grin and they shook hands.

First, they drove to a café to have a light lunch. Frølich was curious to know whether Austin would mention the incident at the fish market. He didn't. While they were eating, Austin told him he had managed to locate Stuart's sister. He said she had done a number of strange things, so he had decided to confront her.

'What sort of strange things has she done?' Frølich asked as they were driving out of town and toward the village. Austin glanced over at him. 'Seen many white folks in Kisumu?' he asked with a slight smile.

'No.'

'Exactly.' Austin drove onto a smaller gravel track. And he clearly wasn't interested in elaborating. They drove alongside the lake on a track that got worse the further they went. They passed thick bushes of reeds and papyrus, earthen huts and houses built with sticks and branches, with walls of rigid clay. A few houses were made of brick. After a while they reached some small houses and a little shed that functioned as a shop before driving into a kind of market square in a village by the lake — Dunga. Austin parked the car in the shade of a tree. They got out. Frølich put on a peaked cap and sunglasses and looked around. A few narrow wooden boats had been pulled up onto the shore. Line after line of low brick houses lay in the shadow of the trees where the forest finished and the beach started. Between and behind the houses the vegetation was green and lush, and the wind that came in off the lake was fresh and cool in the baking heat.

Stuart Takeyo's sister was waiting for them outside one of the houses. She was around thirty, with a nice figure, clean-cut features and a very serious expression. Her hair was long and black, and woven into neat braids. She was wearing faded jeans and a yellow T-shirt. On her feet she wore plastic sandals.

Austin and she talked in the local language. She sent Frølich cold, hostile glares.

After a while Austin introduced him in English: a Norwegian policeman from Interpol searching for her brother. She turned her back on Frølich without saying anything. Then she took them with her, down to

190

the beach and into the shade of a large tree with long grey fruits hanging like salamis from the branches. There were some stools around and Stuart's sister motioned for them to sit down.

Some distance away, by a modern-looking pavilion with a concrete floor and a corrugated-iron roof, a few elderly men were watching them. The men nodded and raised their arms in welcome. Some children ran over and sat down with them under the tree. In one of the houses a curtain moved to the side of the doorway, and an elderly woman appeared. The fresh breeze caught her wide skirt as she came over to the tree with a rolling gait. She was carrying a tray with glasses and a jug of squash.

After pouring their drinks, she left them. The children, who also wanted squash, hung on her skirt. Only one of them didn't follow her. A little girl in a checked summer dress, with short hair woven into braids across her head, sat on the pebbles down by the water's edge, uninterested in what was going on.

Stuart's sister raised her glass as a sign they should drink. The squash was very sweet. On the edge of the beach, behind the little girl, some big black birds were hopping from rock to rock. Their heads were shaped like hammers. Behind the rocks grew impenetrable beds of reeds. Frølich scanned the lake. Some small, white eggs were bobbing up and down on the horizon; they were the wind-filled sails of distant boats. He cleared his throat, pointed and asked if the boats were coming in with the day's catch.

'My husband's boat,' Stuart's sister said, nodding across the water.

Austin coughed and clapped his hands. 'We'd like you to tell us where your brother is.'

'He's in Europe,' she said. 'He's in Norway.'

Frølich and Austin exchanged glances. Austin started to grin.

Frølich could read the woman's expression: she knew where her brother was, but she would never reveal his location to them.

Austin changed over to the local language. From the discussion Frølich only understood one thing: the woman was angry and Austin was, too. It was developing into a row.

Frølich got up and walked down to the beach. The little girl was kneeling and running her hands through the pebbles while mumbling to herself. She was singing a tune. The notes mingled with the roar of the waves breaking on the shore. Frølich pricked up his ears and crouched down. He recognised the song she was singing. 'Hello, little girl,' he said to her.

She didn't react. Her body just continued to rock, and she dug her fingers into the pebbles while singing the song Frølich recognised from Norway. The words she mumbled to the tune were unintelligible, but she managed the refrain well enough: *bom bommeli bom . . .*

Then he realised. The girl was blind. 'You've got a good voice,' he whispered to her.

She went quiet and lifted her head.

'What's the name of the song?'

She stood up. Her dress flew up as she bent down for something on the ground. She had been sitting on a little battery-driven cassette player. Now she fumbled with the buttons. Soon the same tune, more metallic, came out of the loudspeaker. But it was sung by a man. And he was singing in broken Norwegian: '*Lille prinsesse, gi meg dog ditt hjerte, lille prinsesse . . .*' — 'Little princess, give me your heart, little princess . . .'

Something was happening under the tree. Takeyo's sister strode down to the beach like a crazed Fury. 'You leave her alone!' she yelled, took the cassette player and switched it off. She seized the girl's hand and dragged her back to the house where the old woman reappeared in the doorway.

Austin and Frølich exchanged glances.

A man singing in broken Norwegian. The song about the little drummer boy who got the princess because he had three small boats in the harbour. And the man singing it must have been Takeyo. Frølich watched Takeyo's sister as she handed over the little girl to the old woman and then strolled back to Austin without dignifying Frølich with a glance.

'Ask her who the girl got the tape from,' he shouted.

'She says you know,' the Kenyan policeman translated. 'She says Stuart Takeyo sent her the cassette from Norway a long time ago.'

'Ask her who the girl is.'

'She says it's none of your business.'

Frølich walked back to the edge of the beach and stared across the lake. A couple of small boys came running over. Frølich recognised the older of them from the gang who followed the grandmother for squash. He stepped forward and said: 'I know where he is.'

Frølich glanced over at Austin. He and the sister had started to quarrel again. The boy followed his gaze and said: 'Her brother. I can go in the Mercedes and show you where he is.'

'I want to go in the Mercedes too,' the other boy whimpered.

Frølich looked down hesitantly at the two heads. The older boy seemed to know what he was thinking

193

and said: 'It's true. I know where he is. For me it's not important to go in the Mercedes. I'll write the address down for you for ten dollars.'

Ten dollars, he thought, this boy had business sense — he was avoiding the local currency. But ten dollars was a month's wages in this country. He cast another glance at Austin and the woman under the tree. Austin was gesticulating. The woman was gesticulating.

'Five dollars,' he said. 'But I'll be back. And if you're bluffing, you'll be in deep trouble.'

Where There's A Will

After Frølich had gone, Lise Fagernes lay in the sun with her wine glass balanced on her stomach. She was mulling over what he had said. She concluded she liked the sudden change of heart. After being rejected, he had met her head on and made a concrete offer in a bid to secure her co-operation. One favour for another. And with that he had, in a way, floated a little boat on the moat she had dug around her integrity. Could she actually afford to decline such an outstretched hand? He was serving her the case on a silver platter, with a very clear subtext: she was to discuss her results with him later. And that was what she was considering now, while occasionally gripping the stem of the glass and sipping the wine: would it be tactically judicious to take the bait he had served her? What was the risk for her? *Well,* she thought, *I am first and foremost a journalist. And that role has two sides: to have a nose for a scoop and to retain your own integrity.* And while she was lying in the sun, feeling its rays tan her stomach, thighs and forehead, she knew that in reality the decision had already been taken.

She checked her watch, sat up and started to get dressed.

Half an hour later she was in a taxi. It was a rusty, ancient Mazda with no other fixtures apart from the driver's seat. It looked like a dented farm vehicle from deepest Østfold. It smelt like an old carpet and she had to sit on a rough-hewn wooden plank behind the driver.

As the taxi set off, she felt her scepticism return: *Why am I doing this? Is it that I haven't got enough to do, or am I just being kind?*

The journey took longer than she had expected. They left the busy part of town behind them. They drove past the slums and alongside the lake toward the weathered mountains in the west. They looked like a giants' romping ground; huge rocks piled up on one another like traditional sculptures in XXXL format. She knew the local populus indulged folk tales about how the huge rocks had got there — myths about magic and punishment rites.

The landscape was becoming more and more rural: mango and papaya trees grew along the road, forming a kind of hedge behind which acacias and fever trees spread across the plain. *But,* she told herself, *a fish-breeding business doesn't necessarily have to be in a town.* After a while the driver turned into a narrow, dusty gravel track leading between the rocks. Finally, they stopped in front of a solitary brick building.

She asked the driver to wait, clambered out and stood looking sceptically at the building. The yellow paint had faded, there were grey stains on the plaster and bits of boarding nailed to most of the windows. No company signs, no people going in and coming out of the open door. Only the stained letters under the cornice told her that inside there was a business bearing the name Frank Frølich had written on the scrap of paper: Inborn Fisheries Inc.

An elderly man stood leaning against one of the pillars in front of the entrance. He was wearing a worn suit jacket and a black hat with a peak. He had the typically erect Maasai figure and a bony, expressionless face with pierced and stretched earlobes, making his ears resemble two knots on either side of his head. He had to be a watchman. She walked closer and asked politely if he knew the area. But the man continued to chew on a piece of grass and stare straight ahead, as though he hadn't heard. His eyes were half closed, and grey, nigh-on colourless, irises flickered restlessly through the slits. The man didn't seem to be aware of her, even though she was quite close. Perhaps he was deaf or in a trance, she thought, sneaking past him. In the doorway she glanced over her shoulder. The straight-backed Maasai was standing on the same spot, with his back turned to her, the wind ruffling his trousers.

She hesitated for a few seconds. At length, she took her press card from her rucksack and continued through the doorway. She came into a dark, narrow corridor smelling of dust and urine. *Turn back*, she told herself. *It's crazy to stay here.* But there was something else in her head, a voice saying: *This is Africa; this is how they do things. What's scaring you is your old, familiar weakness, your fear that you won't be able to crawl back out of the snow cave.*

A bare light bulb hung from a piece of flex in the ceiling. A staircase with a concrete balustrade led to the floors above. She coughed. It echoed as if she had coughed inside a basement room. But the building was as quiet as before. As if to gain time, she rummaged for the piece of paper with the name and address on. Warily, she raised one foot and placed it on the next step. *What would anyone else do? A man? The experienced editor who was sitting at home in Norway right now, waiting for her to send him an exotic, punchy article from central Africa?*

She felt goosebumps form on her skin and her

197

mouth go dry. She gulped, coughed, then swallowed again. A glance over her shoulder told her the Maasai hadn't moved, he was still facing the taxi. The dust had settled outside. The taxi driver was drumming his hand on the door as though bored. This was a normal working day, and she was carrying out investigative journalism.

So, she forced herself to go up the dark staircase that led to a landing and then continued. Someone had thrown a bundle of clothes in the corner. The stench of urine was becoming stronger. She stepped over the rags and went on up.

The staircase ended in another landing, where she walked through an opening in the wall and came into a long, dark, narrow corridor which continued left for about ten metres. Where the corridor turned there was another bare light bulb dangling from the ceiling. *People must be here.* Someone has switched on the light.

'Can I help you?'

She gave a start and spun round.

Where had this man sprung from? He was standing right behind her — a short man, fifty to sixty years old. He was a little plump with an Indian appearance, grey combed-back hair and square glasses with a heavy frame.

'I'm a journalist,' she stammered, surprised that her voice even carried. 'From Norway.'

'And may I help you?' the man repeated in the same flat tone. It was impossible to see his eyes. The glare from the bulb made his glasses impenetrable.

'Inborn Fisheries Incorporated?' she asked.

'There is no such company,' the man assured her in a monotone.

'But you have a sign outside on the wall. I'd like to talk to a representative of Inborn Fisheries.'

'Please leave this building.'

This wasn't going well. She reached inside her rucksack for her tape recorder. 'May I have your name?'

The man didn't move. The silence continued. And it didn't seem like a good idea to fiddle around with the tape recorder. The man said: 'Why are you interested in Inborn Fisheries?'

She had no answer to that question. This initiative was a shot in the dark. But she thought: *I'm the journalist here*. And asked: 'What's your job in this company?'

The bespectacled man answered in a monotone again: 'There is no such company.'

Lise cleared her throat. She felt a touch of dizziness and was unable to think clearly. The dark corridor, the dreadful stench, the man's impenetrability. She felt the forces of her surroundings impacting on her. Her brow was sweating, and she could feel beads of sweat running down her spine.

'I must ask you to leave this place at once,' the man said, stepping aside to let her by. The message was unambiguous. She wriggled past him and walked back to the stairs. He followed her. Seeing the doorway and freedom outside, she felt her legs come back to life. Halfway down the stairs, she stopped and turned. The man was a large silhouette in the opening in the rough wall. 'Do you know the name David Kimberley?' she asked.

The silhouette was motionless, silent. *I've hit a nerve there*. She said: 'Do you know the name Stuart Takeyo?'

The man shouted something in a foreign language. There was a sudden movement in the sparse light.

A shadow appeared at the bottom of the stairs. It was the Maasai with the black uniform hat. In one hand he was holding the traditional club. Now he was standing with his head raised. And she could almost feel his gaze through the sombre hallway. 'I can take a hint,' she said in Norwegian. 'I'm going.'

She hurried down the stairs, past the Maasai and out onto the road. She stumbled toward the taxi and tore open the door. 'Drive back,' she said and jumped in, slamming the door after her.

The driver stared at her through drowsy eyes.

Lise looked at the yellow building. A moment later the old Maasai glided out of the doorway. As he continued through the porch toward the car, he picked up his bow and a quiver that had been on the ground.

'Drive,' she shouted.

The driver turned. He was grinning disdainfully, shook his head and laughed.

'Drive,' she repeated in desperation.

The old Maasai came closer. He crouched down and stared through the car window. A wrinkled, hollow-cheeked face with lifeless, grey eyes.

'Please,' she implored, 'drive back now.'

'He's just fooling with you,' the driver grinned and started the engine.

That man is not playing games. 'Drive!' she shouted, almost hysterically.

The driver laughed again. The old man outside grabbed the car door. She flicked the lock.

'You didn't say where to,' the driver said, still grinning.

'Away from here.'

The driver accelerated and while he was driving, he

laughed to himself and shook his head.

Lise Fagernes was shaking. She had cramp in her fingers.

★ ★ ★

Half an hour later, she stumbled into her hotel room and took a shower to wash off the sweat and stench of the strange building. *Whatever that place was, I don't want to go there again,* she thought, as she dried her hair.

Afterwards, she sat naked in front of the open veranda door to log on to the Net and write. She was oblivious of time and place, feeling only a tiny current of air from the veranda door on her stomach as she worked. The light had faded over the afternoon. She stretched and could feel she was hungry.

Then the telephone rang.

She got up from her laptop and went into the alcove where her bed was. She lifted the receiver. 'Hello?'

Not a sound.

She raised her head and looked at herself in the mirror. The caller hadn't put down the receiver. All she could hear was a quiet crackling noise.

The door isn't locked. She lowered her arm and cradled the receiver. Staring down at her arm and stomach. Goosepimples. *Could it have been Frankie? But, if so, why didn't he talk to her?'*

Call reception. They can trace the call. She looked at her hand. It picked up the telephone again. The forefinger of her left hand dialled the number for reception. It rang and rang, but no one answered. She stood listening to the dialling tone. A chill spread from her arms and stomach to her back. She didn't

201

notice herself replace the receiver. The most important thing to do now was to check the door. Slowly,
without making a sound, she turned and stared at the
brown door. Should she go to reception and ask them
who it was that rang? *Get dressed. Why are you standing
here without a stitch on?*

The telephone rang again.

The goosepimples spread down her thighs. She shiv-
ered, cast another glance at the mirror beside her bed,
at herself, naked in front of the bed and the telephone
ringing so loudly it was vibrating. An image from a
nightmare. The ringing drowned the noise of the A/C
system, pounded in her eardrums, and although the
shrill tone was unbearable, she couldn't bring herself
to lift the receiver. In the end, she saw her hand grip
it, remove it from the cradle and place it against her
ear. She heard it very clearly. Someone had rung off.

What is this? Telephone in hand, she scanned the
walls, then the open veranda door and outside, where
she saw a huge treetop. At the same time, she heard
the flapping of a thousand pairs of wings as a flock
of white birds took off from the treetop. She saw the
reflected image of the bedroom door in the window.
She thought: *The door isn't locked and I'm not wearing
any clothes.*

In four long strides she was by the door and had
twisted the key.

She leaned back against the door. The sun was
going down. Lise Fagernes gasped for air.

* * *

When Austin drove up to the hotel entrance to drop
him off, it was late.

202

'It was her daughter,' Austin said.

'Do you know that?'

'I know she has a daughter who is going blind. And that girl is our trump card.'

'How come?'

'Takeyo is going to take her to Nairobi to be operated on. I will post a man outside the village. You can relax. All we have to do is wait. Takeyo will swim straight into our net. At any moment.' Austin grinned.

Frølich held the door handle, but didn't open the door.

'Yes?'

'A net's not necessary. Takeyo's here,' Frølich said.

'Of course.'

'Some boys claimed he was here, in Kisumu.'

Austin grinned. 'And did they want some money? Well, the money will not hurt them, but leave this to us, Frank. This town is so open. And Takeyo will never let the girl in Dunga down. You and I will be talking to him in a couple of days, I am sure.'

'You don't understand,' Frank said with warmth. 'I have his address. They gave me the address.'

Austin looked up at him, resigned. 'It is you who do not understand. You have been cheated.'

'Surely it's worth a check?'

'OK, let me see,' Austin sighed, reading the note. Then he smiled at the Norwegian. 'Stuart Takeyo is supposed to be hiding here?' He chuckled.

'What's so funny?'

'Nothing.' He shook his head. 'We can go there tomorrow. But you have been cheated, I can promise you that.'

They parted company and Frølich got out. After Austin drove off, he saw two boys shuffling nervously by the entrance. They were standing by a white van, a safari type with a pop-top roof.

Frølich stopped and stared at them.

At that moment he saw Lise Fagernes come out of the hotel door.

The engine of the van roared and one of the boys ran over and grabbed her arm. The other shoved the sliding door open.

'Let go!' she screamed as the boy tried to drag her into the van.

Frølich was by the van in three strides. He grabbed the boy by his neck and right arm. The boy let go of the woman and kicked out with his legs as Frølich lifted him up, swung him round and slammed his squirming body against the side of the van. The second boy at first stared passively at what was happening. A second later he threw himself through the open side door. The vehicle roared off. Frølich let go of the boy. The lean figure fell headlong, crawled up onto all fours and sprinted off after the van like a hare. With equal ease he scrambled head first into the moving vehicle. His long legs stuck out the side as the van rounded the band and was lost from view.

Frølich turned. 'Are you hurt?' he asked Lise Fagernes, who struggled to her feet with difficulty. Her knee was grazed. 'Just a flesh wound,' she smiled wanly. 'Otherwise, nothing apart from stomach ache.'

'What happened?' he asked.

'Where I come from, it's called common assault.'

'But why?'

'I have no idea.' She brushed down her clothes. 'Is it now I should apologise for all the bad things I've said? Or is 'thanks for your help' enough?'

He looked around. Everything seemed normal.

Some hotel guests strolled past and carried on blithely through the doors. No one had taken any notice of the incident, which had been over in seconds.

'Seen them before?'

'Not the two boys.'

'The driver?'

'Not sure. But he was wearing an unusual peaked hat.' With that, she started to tell Frølich about her visit to the yellow building.

'What did you find out?' he asked.

'It's pretty common for businesses to use Maasai as watchmen,' she said. 'But this guy was spooky. At any rate, there's something dodgy about this company.'

'Are you frightened?'

She gave a strained grin. 'Is it a long way home to Norway?' she said wearily. 'Frightened? Yes, of course I am.'

'I'll talk to one of my corrupt colleagues about the matter,' he said, stuffing his hands in his pockets. 'They could probably have a chat with this so-called watchman.'

'I think I'm a bit dizzy,' she said suddenly, leaning back against the wall.

'You've had a shock,' he said. 'What were you going to do so late?'

She stared back in surprise. 'Me? I was going to buy some water. Before I went to bed.'

'But you can get water at the reception desk.'

He shouldn't have said that. Her eyes narrowed: 'Can I? That's true. I'd forgotten.'

'Were you going to meet Takeyo?' he asked suspiciously.

'No,' she snapped. 'And what I do or don't do has nothing to do with you. Goodnight.'

She turned on her heel and went back in, while Frølich stood lost in thought. She was definitely in shock. But it bothered him that they couldn't establish a tone for their conversations. One minute she was open, the next closed and annoyed. That wasn't good. She ought to see that, especially now. She should have given herself the time and space to discuss what had happened.

★ ★ ★

He lay wide awake under the mosquito net for several hours. The heat was unbearable and his brain was churning — about Lise Fagernes. He wondered if she was in danger. How had she got into this and why? He wondered whether she could see the gravity of the situation. Why did she seem so dismissive? Was there something she was trying to prove? The whole time he could see the naked expression of shock on her face as she was struggling to her feet. Was this dynamic persona of hers only a mask?

Later, he thought about the blind girl sitting on the beach, trying to sing a Norwegian children's song. And he thought about Austin. The policeman who was mysterious and unapproachable one minute; jovial and open the next.

He lay like this, his eyes burning in the dark, determined to think about other matters. Just as his lids finally began to droop, he woke with a start, roused by the irritating whine of a mosquito that had managed to sneak in under the net.

Cause And Effect

After waiting in vain all morning for a telephone call from Austin, Frank Frølich strolled down to the lobby. Rounding the corner on the stairs, he spotted the same mother who had made him the offer by the pool the previous day. She was standing in reception and talking on a mobile phone. When she saw him, she turned away — as though she had been caught red-handed. Without showing a reaction, he continued down the stairs and over to the sofa and chairs by the big windows facing the street. He sat down and kept an eye on her in the glass panes. After a while she finished talking. She turned and was about to leave, but hesitated when she noticed him. She stood for a few seconds in two minds, then rushed past him and out. Again, he was struck by how affluent she seemed as she waited by the kerb — pretending to study her nails, Italian sunglasses in her hair, wearing clothes that had associations with London or Paris — until a dark-blue BMW with tinted windows pulled in next to her. She click-clacked in her stilettos around the car and got in. Tyres screaming, the car sped off.

He thought about the strange conversation they had had. She had known about Lise Fagernes, had known she was a journalist. From there his mind went to the kidnap attempt he had witnessed the previous evening. He stood up, walked through the broad doors and looked for the BMW, which had headed north, to the area known as Backlands. He took her business card and his mobile phone from his pocket and called her.

'Yes,' said the deep voice he recognised instantly. There was interference on the line, so she was still in the car. 'Who is calling?'

'Frank, the Norwegian policeman.' That was as much as he was able to say. She rang off at once.

He walked on, into the street and north. But instead of going into the town, filled with curiosity, he strolled to the same residential district he had seen the dark-blue car heading toward, Backlands. He passed house after house, each more beautiful and exclusive than the last. The contrast between the poor district of Obunga and this opulent suburb was striking. Here, the houses resembled the immense detached houses in Beverley Hills, here there was no open sewage, no running gutters, here you could promenade under shady trees bursting with flower tendrils, amid the chlorine perfume from garden swimming pools, here parabolic antennae grew from rooftops, here shards of glass were cemented on top of the high walls surrounding the gardens, and here CCTV hummed quietly above house entrances. This district matched the style of the car that had picked her up.

He mooched on aimlessly, turning right and left, until he came to an abandoned high-rise building in an overgrown, fenced-in wilderness. It was enormous. He gave up trying to count how many floors there were with empty windows. Instead, he wondered if this could be a multi-storey car park, a forgotten film set or just one of the many unfinished aid-project constructions scattered around the African continent. A soldier with a cocked machine gun slowly emerged from a shadow behind the fence. Frølich greeted him, the soldier greeted back, and his serious face split into a smile. He was a slim young man and despite the heat he didn't seem to be affected by his thick uniform or heavy-duty boots.

'Is this a multi-storey car park?'

The soldier shook his head. 'It's a public building. It's going to house the local police authorities,' he said. 'It's just not finished yet.'

Behind the fence, and where, a long time ago, there had been a garden laid out, now bushes and small trees grew. The bush was reconquering the plot. 'This will probably be the highest building in town,' Frølich said politely.

'Maybe,' the soldier said. 'Work on it stopped ages ago.'

'How long?'

'Ten years perhaps. I don't remember. Maybe fifteen.'

'When will work start again?' Frølich asked.

'No one knows,' said the soldier, turning towards the gaping windows. 'No one knows. Come in and have a look. There is a wonderful view from the roof.'

The soldier said his name was Jackton. They walked through the hole in the concrete wall that someone planned would be a door one day. The lift shafts were empty. They had to use the staircase. There were a lot of steps. All that was missing was window panes, tables, chairs, filing cabinets, lifts and working people.

The soldier was right. From the roof it was possible to see the whole town and far beyond. There was a fresh wind blowing. Lake Victoria stretched endlessly to the horizon in the west, broken only by some bluish-grey mountain tops on a spit of land far away. He turned, scanned the town for buildings and places he had been. He sought out the smoke from the fish skeleton pots in Obunga, and found the exclusive properties in Backlands and the hotel where he was staying. Somewhere down below was Stuart Takeyo. Perhaps he was one of the people walking down the high street at this moment. Frølich thought about Austin. He had offered to check the address he had bought from the boys in Dunga. Frølich suddenly felt irritated that Austin hadn't got in touch yet.

'How do you pass the time here?' he asked Jackton. 'Isn't it lonely patrolling the site?'

'Not at all. There are eight of us working in shifts.'

'Eight armed guards?' Frølich had to smile. 'But nothing can be stolen from a deserted high-rise.'

Jackton stared back intensely. 'Hard to know,' he mumbled. 'You can never tell.'

Frølich glanced toward the hotel again, uneasy. A white figure was hurrying into the main entrance. It had to be Lise Fagernes. She had been out, on her own. And yesterday she had said she had hopes of meeting Takeyo. Frølich checked his watch in frustration. Austin could be absolutely anywhere. But not far from the hotel he saw a line of taxis.

'Nice building to patrol,' he said to the soldier, 'but I have to be going.'

* * *

He was unsure what to do. On the one hand, he was an advocate of openness; on the other, he was tired of her stubborn refusal to share information and leads. He strode quickly to the hotel. He was only a few hundred metres away from the entrance when Lise Fagernes came running through the door and got into a waiting Peugeot. Frølich was no longer unsure

210

what to do. He sprinted across the street to a free taxi and got in. 'Follow that car,' he said, pointing.

'No problem.' The young driver turned the ignition key, once, then a second time.

The car with Lise Fagernes in was nowhere to be seen.

At the third or fourth attempt the engine began to splutter.

'No problem,' the driver mumbled nervously.

The exhaust pipe backfired as the car finally set off down Oginga Odinga Boulevard. The traffic was heavy. Everywhere cars, with their horns sounding, packed the streets, while newspaper vendors, banana sellers and beggars nonchalantly trudged between them. Frølich lifted his water flask to his mouth. The water had become lukewarm and it smelt. The taximeter clicked slowly. They were stuck in a queue, an endless line of vans and rusty, brown, dented estate cars, most of them Peugeots. But where was Lise Fagernes? The driver glanced over his shoulder and saw how stressed his passenger was becoming. So, he began to hoot his horn. Then he mounted the pavement. People jumped to both sides as he ploughed through, but two men talking stood their ground. The car came to an abrupt halt. A pedestrian shook his fist. Soon the pavement was a wall of gesticulating men and women. One woman in a green sari banged her fist on the car bonnet. The driver swung the wheel left, back onto the road. Even if they had advanced quite a distance, they were now stationary again. A man stuck his head through the car window trying to sell mobile-phone cases and key rings with a whistle attached. Frølich stared out, through the window on the opposite side. The seller didn't give up, tapped him on the shoulder and demonstrated the whistles. Frølich intently studied the back seats of the surrounding cars, searching for Lise's blonde hair — without success.

Finally, the driver managed to snake his way through to the roundabout and branched off down to the lake. The feeling of being in motion dispelled the worst unease. 'Do you know which car she's in?' Frølich asked, leaning forward in his seat as the red dust from the gravel road hung like a flapping cape between the cars, reducing visibility to almost zero.

'I think so, yes. No problem.' The driver accelerated. They caught up with a brown estate car, the driver accelerated again and they came alongside.

Wrong car. There was an Indian-looking woman in the rear seat. The driver gestured, both slowed down, stopped and discussed something or other. After a while the other car started up and drove on. 'Well?' Frølich said excitedly as the driver turned round.

'He hadn't seen any taxis with a blonde woman in the back. But he would keep an eye open. No problem,' the driver said. 'We'll wait here until she comes back and then we can follow her.'

Frølich had to laugh. The driver did, too. 'Like I said, no problem.'

Frølich paid and got out of the car. He walked alongside some big warehouses and made a bee-line for a street with more traffic. Soon he was among shops, busy people, crowded pavements, four lanes of stationary vehicles, Chinese-looking bicycles, donkey carts and overladen, rusty, run-down vehicles mixed with some more modern-looking mini-buses.

'Hey mister, please, mister.'

Frølich came out of his reverie to see one of three small ragamuffins peering up at him with outstretched hands. He searched his pockets. Shit, no coins. Instead, he found the scrap of paper with Takeyo's address on and a scrunched-up banknote. One solitary crumpled banknote.

'Please, mister, you, Mzee, give me some money.' The two nearest boys were older than the one at the back sucking a finger. The boy's modesty appealed to Frølich and he gave him the note. He snatched it and shot across the street like a bullet fired from a gun. A lorry screeched to a halt and hooted its horn. Frølich thought his heart had stopped beating. But the boy had sensed the danger and veered to the right. He ran off with his pals close behind. His two friends cursed and swore as aggressively as the lorry driver. Frølich felt giddy. An old man in rags, ravaged with leprosy, came toward him with the stumps of his fingers out-stretched. Frølich about-turned and quickly made off up the street.

★ ★ ★

I have one last chance, he thought, searching for the address he had been given by the two boys on the beach in Dunga. But when, minutes later, he turned into the pavement of Oginga Odinga Boulevard, the traffic was as stationary as before. Frølich looked around and immediately saw the solution to the problem.

'Free?' he asked the group of men sitting on the pavement and smoking. They had bicycle taxis, known as *boda bodas*.

'Sure.'

A strong man jumped up and walked over to one of the glossy pedal cycles leaning against the wall. The

213

frame was heavy and solid, painted a gleaming metallic red. The handlebars were decorated with small flags from a variety of countries. Two sets of round, shiny mirrors protruded on both sides. And instead of a bell he had mounted an advanced horn with a rubber bulb. The luggage rack was covered with a large, stuffed plush cushion.

Frølich produced the address.

The boda-boda man cast a glance at the note and demanded five hundred shillings. 'You big man,' he explained. The guys on the pavement grinned.

And he didn't want to know about how Norwegians rode pillion. Frølich had to sit side-saddle. But the position was quite comfortable because there was a foot rest attached to the rear wheel hub. The boda-boda man wove his way through the traffic jam like a needle through knitting. They were maintaining a good speed. The boda-boda man was pedalling hard, his upper torso bent over the handlebars. Frølich slipped into a semi-doze as he gazed idly at the ramshackle facades on the opposite side of the street. The traffic became lighter, the soundscape changed from the strident hooting of horns to almost silence, broken only by the creaking pedals of the bike.

'There. You see?' said the man in front of him, glancing over his shoulder and pointing to a street sign.

Frølich recognised the name of the liberation hero: Mboya. They came closer. The street was deserted apart from a solitary pedestrian walking ahead of them. Frølich turned his head when he heard a familiar sound. They were overtaken by an ageing motorbike with the roar of a genuine BSA. A thin young man, bare-headed with a flapping shirt, raced past so close

214

that the boda-boda man was forced to veer to the side. They started to wobble. Frølich jumped off. The bike fell. Frølich was about to straighten it up, but the boda-boda man was standing with rigid, bent knees. Automatically, Frølich followed his gaze. The motorbike had stopped. The rider was supporting the bike with one foot on the ground. The pedestrian had also stopped. They exchanged a few words. The motorbike rider pulled something from his belt. Slowly, he raised his right arm. Frølich saw what he was holding. 'Duck!' he shouted and threw himself behind a parked car. At that moment the first shot went off. A fraction of a second later came the next. When Frølich hit the ground there was a deafening salvo of three or four shots. The echo rang around the walls and was followed by silence. The same silence that reigned after a goods train had thundered past, he thought, as he glanced over his shoulder. The boda-boda man was rooted to the spot, a leg on each side of the fallen bike.

The motorbike rider revved up and was gone. A man lay on the ground.

Frølich ran. But he wasn't alone. A scabious stray dog loped across the street to the man on the pavement. His upper body was resting against the wall — his legs splayed. His chin was resting against his chest. Frølich knelt down. 'Are you alright?' The young man lifted his chin. At that moment he opened his mouth and both eyes. For a brief instant, he stared into the sky, before his life left him. The dead man rolled over onto his side. The blood stains on the wall were like a number on a dice. The dog lapped up the blood running into the dust. The dog met Frølich's gaze. It bared its teeth and growled.

He still had cotton wool in his ears. Got to his feet.

A car drove toward him in slow motion. It was moving more and more slowly. When it passed, he saw Lise Fagernes sitting on the back seat. Frølich stared after the car as it disappeared. When she craned her neck to see him through the rear window, her hair fell in the same way, in slow motion.

* * *

He was driven back to his hotel by a uniformed officer. But not twenty minutes later the telephone rang.

'How are you, Austin?' he asked wearily. 'We should've gone there last night.'

'Hindsight is just another word for stupidity,' Austin said coolly.

'But this should never have happened.'

Austin sighed. 'You may have heard the adage: in Africa anything can happen?'

It was Frølich's turn to take a deep breath. 'That's the second time you've said it.'

'You still believe I was following you last night?'

'I believe as little as possible.'

'Well, I would very much like to ask you a few questions.'

'Ask away.'

'We would like to have a proper chat with you.'

'We?'

'About the shooting incident and Miss Lise.'

'Miss Lise?' Frølich said, his eyes on the TV, where CNN was struggling in vain against a snow screen.

'Yeah, a Norwegian woman who claims she is a journalist.'

Cod

Tove had prepared the cod the Norwegian way: tomatoes, chilli, potatoes, onion and garlic in layers with salt cod and olive oil. It had all boiled for so long that Gunnarstranda recognised the smell immediately he opened the door to the stairwell. 'Sorry for finishing off the bottle of aquavit,' she had said. But that wasn't completely true. The bottle was still unopened, a gentle, northern Norwegian variant that tasted more of fennel and oak barrel than caraway.

They talked about food and other trivialities. He noticed in her gaze that she wasn't happy. But he didn't notice that she had fallen quiet. Until he glanced up.

'You're down in the dumps,' she said.

'I'm just full.'

'They say cod is best in the autumn and winter,' she said.

'Rubbish.'

She lit a cigarette and sat staring at the spiral of blue smoke rising from the glow. 'What are you thinking about?'

'Apart from nothing?'

'What *you* call nothing.'

'Would you believe me if I said I was thinking about my grandparents?' He pulled one of the chairs from under the dining table and rested a leg on it.

'Why them?'

'You wouldn't be interested.'

She looked away from the coil of smoke. 'Do you want me to chuck you out?'

'Well . . .' He poured himself a bit more aquavit while searching for the right words. 'I was very small. They must've been seventy-five, maybe seventy-eight, at any rate under eighty — so I was probably ten. I remember sitting on the floor and looking up at them thinking, it's quite an event to turn eighty. It's not often that people become so old, and these two were almost eighty. So they must've had an awareness of death, I thought — a kind of clarity gained over a long life. I should add that they once lost a child. A boy, a cot death after a few weeks — and on the wall behind them hung this picture of the boy, photographed dead, in the coffin. I'd looked at the picture many times and thought to myself that he was sleeping, this uncle I'd never known. And while I was sitting like that, on the floor, ten years old, I realised the boy in the picture was dead. Well, I was thinking about that just now, while you were getting irritated that I was as distant as usual. It wasn't just that the two of them were familiar with death after a long life — they'd had a positive and active relationship with death for many years, and I was thinking I lacked some of their perspective. I was thinking that our culture's deficient or unhealthy attitude to death in general was impoverishing me in a way that they hadn't been impoverished.'

Tove frowned at the latter formulation.

'I mean,' he expatiated, 'in the old days, life and death were regarded to a greater extent as two sides of the same coin. Chinese emperors were buried with terracotta soldiers, Egyptian pharaohs were buried with their servants, the sarcophaguses were adorned with symbols of life — sexual symbols and conception rites, and the Vikings yearned to die in battle.' He concentrated in order to choose the right words.

218

'Today, there are Muslims who blow themselves up,' she interjected. 'In holy wars, death's an important weapon, which must imply a view of life and death as inseparable sides of the same coin.'

He nodded. 'It bothers me that our modern attitude to death is a distortion. I remember a formulation I once read: there are only two moments when humans are reduced to objects, in birth and death. Otherwise, we ourselves experience life, whereas in the moment of birth and death it is we who are experienced as we are transported from one state to another. But if death really is beautiful, then humanity's turned it into something ugly because we keep death at a distance from life, because we never talk about it. We connect death with cruelty, dark powers and our own fears. And if this distortion's wrong, I think, then . . .'

'Then what?' she asked sharply when he fell silent.

'Then it bothers me that I can't do anything about my own way of thinking or that I myself am unable to change or turn around this perception. For half of my life my relationship with death has been based on murder cases. For me, death has been something sinister, the result of an assault and acts of evil.' He smiled self-deprecatingly. 'And now I'm trying to get out of this one-way street — or moderate this perception — by thinking about an image I have of me sitting on the floor looking up at my grandparents. Because I think that was the first time I'd reflected on death. I thought the two of them must've come to terms with death over a long life. They must've known that their lives would end soon. And something else that strikes me now is that if death was so clearly in my consciousness as a child, then it's taken me a lifetime to distance myself from this perspective.' He glanced up and was quiet.

'What is it that's bothering you?' she asked insistently.

He tilted his head. 'Apart from the fact that life would have been more boring without cod and aquavit?'

'And sex, good books, conversations with good friends and so on. Actually, what is it that's got under your skin?'

'I'm ill,' he answered in a sombre voice.

Common Denominators

Four hours had passed since Austin had phoned him at the hotel. It was late evening now. He was sitting beside Lise Fagernes in the back of a taxi — a veteran version of the English variety, with folding seats and a glass partition between the driver and the passengers. They were driving with the windows open and in silence. The streets were desolate in the darkness, and when the taxi finally pulled up outside Hotel Imperial they staggered out — her first and then him; he paid the driver. When he turned to the front entrance she was standing on the same spot, blocking his way, her fists clenched, her eyes spoiling for a fight. They stared at each other, silent, until she wobbled and grabbed a road sign for support.

'And the moral of this story is . . .' he said in a conciliatory tone. 'Don't go anywhere without a press card.'

'I never go anywhere without a press card.'

The grey taxi drove off, its engine rattling. Frølich watched it go. The rear lights weren't working.

'You have to use it,' he said softly.

'And I did,' she answered, equally obdurately, 'but I'm a woman, blonde, and I didn't have any cash on me. The shit who locked me up made some absolutely repugnant suggestions.'

He didn't answer.

Lise Fagernes glared at him. She was so furious that she had tears in her eyes. 'Sometimes I don't know how blokes like you can bear to be a man,' she

221

snarled.

He felt like being sarcastic, but held his counsel.

'Come on,' she said.

'Come on what?'

'Tell me what happened. Why was I arrested in the middle of the street?'

Frølich took a deep breath.

'Come on,' she shouted aggressively. 'Tell me!'

He could feel his temper rising. 'Don't stand there bleating. Haven't you been stupid enough already? Didn't I ask you if you would kindly take things a bit easier? Eh? If you could be a bit more open? But, oh, no, you're so bloody clever, aren't you. You had to meet Takeyo alone, didn't you.'

'The bloody police stopped me meeting him. And you're trying to kid me you weren't behind this? Don't you think I saw your pathetic little attempt to follow me today? And when you failed, you got your fascist friends to stop me instead. What did you hope to achieve by having me arrested? By not letting me meet Stuart Takeyo? What was in it for you?'

She was leaning forward, her hands half open, as if ready to claw him. She took a step, tripped and almost lost her balance. This woman was no longer behaving like an experienced journalist; she was just very angry and very frightened.

Frølich tried to stifle a grin, but couldn't.

'Are you laughing at me?' Her eyes brimmed over. 'Do you know how bloody filthy and hot and wet it is in their prisons? Do you know how many beetles and creepy crawlies I had to flick off my legs in there? What's so funny?'

'Listen, please.' Frølich was suddenly serious. 'Could you calm down? That screechy voice doesn't suit you. And as you haven't understood a thing, I'll have to spoon-feed you: you will never meet Takeyo.'

'That's what *you* think. But you think wrong.'

'Don't you remember driving past me just before reaching the street where Takeyo was supposed to be hiding? Don't you remember a dead man lying on the ground?'

'Dead?'

'Yes. He'd been shot. Do you know why you were arrested? Because that poor man's dead. Stuart Takeyo was shot in the street two minutes before you passed me.'

Lise Fagernes stood up straight. 'What are you saying?'

'You heard me correctly. You were on your way to see him, weren't you? At the disused brewery? I wanted to take the police there last night, but they just laughed at me. But quite a few people must've known about his hiding place. Because he was shot when he was leaving it. He was on the run again. Why do you think? Could it have been because someone was going round town asking questions and stirring things up? But that's none of my business. What annoys me is that the bloody ethics you're always quoting meant that neither I nor any of the police you despise got to talk to the guy or prevent him from winding up as dead as a dodo.'

Lise Fagernes didn't say a word.

'And now I have to travel home without exchanging a single word with the main suspect in a murder case. But you, being so bloody clever, can profit from this. Shall I dictate the headline for you? 'Norwegian Police Fiasco in Africa. Main Witness Shot Dead In Front of Oslo Officer'.'

'What are you saying?' Lise Fagernes whispered again, ashen-faced.

'I'm saying my plane takes off from Nairobi tomorrow afternoon. My advice to you is: go on holiday, get togged up in safari clothes, travel to Maasai Mara game reserve and do something you understand. Use your camera. Goodnight.' With that, he pushed her aside and went in.

The man at the reception desk, who had been following the row with a slightly concerned expression on his face, sent Frølich a reassured nod.

'You can't just go. Wait a minute,' she said.

Frølich ignored her and marched through the lobby and into the open lift. As the doors were about to close, she was there, forcing them open with her hand and sliding inside. 'OK,' she stammered, 'Takeyo's dead. And I had no idea, alright? God have mercy on his soul. But neither you nor I knew him. I'm sorry I was so angry and I'm sorry I had a go at you. But I was stuck in a filthy hole for more than three hours without knowing why. I was in a foul mood, but I'm not now. Now I'm over it. Let's put this behind us. Tell me what happened. Who did it?'

Frølich pressed the button for the second floor again. 'A guy on a motor bike, a BSA, judging by the noise. Takeyo came out of the disused brewery. I didn't know it was him, I only saw someone walking down the street. All of a sudden, this guy roars up, an arrogant bastard, he stops and coldly and coolly pulls out a gun and shoots him. I didn't even know it was Takeyo. The police told me, and if my boda-boda man hadn't been there, it could well have been me sitting in clink. These guys are no shrinking violets.'

The lift stopped on the second floor, and the doors

opened. 'Are you going up?'

She nodded.

Frølich breathed in and held a hand in front of the photoelectric sensor. 'It's so sad that he's died. I never met Takeyo, but I'm upset for him, for his family, for everyone who loved him and not least for this country, which has a crying need for clever people like him. The police say the criminal fraternity here stick out like a sore thumb; the killer's only chance is to go on the run if he's to escape detection. And I think these officers are competent enough to know. The reason they nabbed you is that during the police surveillance I initiated they saw you with Takeyo's sister — and she couldn't explain who you were or what your intentions were. Accordingly, you were seen as a suspect and they arrested you at once.'

'How is she — his sister? Is she in trouble?'

'I'd assume they're grieving.'

'They?'

'The sister, her children, her husband.'

'Why did it take so long? Why did I have to sit in that dump for hours?'

'Your role in this had to be explained.'

'My role?'

'A rich, white woman appears in the poorest corner of the world, asks questions and searches for a man who is found dead shortly afterwards. My job was to convince the police you had nothing to do with the murder.' He turned and was about to walk away.

She held him back.

He stared at her hand until she let go. 'Don't be annoyed,' she said quickly. 'I feel a need to talk about this. Have you got the time?'

'Afterwards. After I've packed.'

When she came out of the lift, he was sitting in the lounge overlooking the swimming pool and had almost finished a can of beer. She was wearing a tight red dress and headed straight for the bar. She ordered something. A cocktail. And it was served in African fashion: a small bottle of tonic and a quarter of a litre of gin in a bottle. The men looked up and followed her with their eyes as she crossed the lobby. 'They don't sit at the bar here,' she said, sitting down and mixing her drink. Her hair still seemed to be wet from the shower.

'The air's cooler outside,' he said, studying her as she drank her first glass in one go.

'Sorry,' she said. 'I'm not used to this.' She poured more gin and the rest of the tonic. 'Murder, arrests, etc. I have to calm down.' She took another swig, but without emptying the whole glass. As she put it down, they eyed each other.

In a way, it felt as if they had already become closer. But he knew nothing about her — her family, friends, where she came from, where she had studied. But in this place, at this moment, she was totally familiar to him.

After a few seconds, they both averted their eyes, simultaneously.

'Right now, I'd like to talk about something else, apart from murder and arrests,' she said.

He didn't answer.

'Being here like this reminds me of Karen Blixen,' she continued.

'I've never read anything by Blixen.'

'You've seen the film though? *Out of Africa*?'

226

'No, I'm afraid not.'

'What was the last novel you read?'

'Don't remember.'

'Don't you read novels?'

'Not much.'

'Do you read non-fiction?'

He nodded. 'But it's even harder to pick out favourites from them.'

'I've co-written a book.'

'Not bad. What's it called?'

'*Mantra.*'

She beamed at his expression. 'This is where you have to ask me what it's about.'

'OK. What's it about?'

'It's about saying yes to yourself.'

He nodded pensively. 'Did it sell well?'

She grinned. 'Shall we try to talk about music?'

'Fine. What would you like to listen to now?'

'Robbie Williams.'

'Is that what you're like?' Frølich said with mock disdain.

'So, we can't speak about books or music,' she established, semi-jocularly. Through the open glass doors, the tones of a band playing African rhythms wafted in.

'Do you watch a lot of films?' he asked.

'Yes and no.'

'What's the best film you've seen?'

'*Shakespeare in Love.*'

'Why that one?'

She mulled over his question. 'It's romantic, sexy, funny and it's based around classic literature. What about you?'

'An old film with Orson Welles — *A Touch of Evil.*'

She nodded. 'I've seen it. Why that one?'

'Because I can watch it lots of times without ever getting sick of it. And it's related to my own reality.' He made quotation marks with his fingers. 'The hunt for truth. Orson Welles plays a cop . . .'

'And so that makes you feel secure, I suppose,' she said.

'Secure?'

'Yes, it's about murder and mystery and sexual fear in cartoon format. That kind of story would never touch the vulnerable in you.'

'Why wouldn't it?'

'Fine,' she said. 'Tell me how the film touches your vulnerable side.'

He reflected, but ended up saying resignedly: 'You have a point. However, are you claiming that *Shakespeare in Love* affected you in that way?'

'At least it dwells on something important in everyone's life: what is possible and what is impossible in love.' She stared vacantly into the distance. 'And I've used up a lot of energy finding that out.'

She thought of events and people he knew nothing about.

'But the original,' he coughed, 'the original deals with love much better. Shakespeare's own work.'

'Sure. But we were talking about films. I haven't seen a film of *Romeo and Juliet*.'

They fell back into silence.

When he was about to say something, they both spoke at once and burst into laughter. 'You first,' he said gallantly.

'I'm wondering if this is a general thing with men,' she said. 'Men can only be entertained by action films and thrillers because they're incapable of letting emo-

228

tion touch them. What were you going to say?'

'I was going to suggest we changed the topic.'

'To what?'

'You choose.'

'Let's try music again. What's your favourite music?'

'It varies.'

'What's top of your list at this particular point in time?'

'If we ignore the classics like Tom Waits and Dylan — well, then, for example, I like the old double live album by Colosseum.'

'I don't understand that,' she said. 'Listening to boring guitar riffs and pretentious drum solos from years ago. Most of it's just crap.'

'Do you know what I think?' he said, with a wink. 'I think people like me will never get past seventies rock. I think we're actually listening for something to touch the vulnerable parts of us.'

Her laughter rippled into the room. It was the kind of laughter that made men and women turn to see the source and then smile to one another. She didn't notice. But her glass was empty.

He motioned to the waiter. 'Another G and T please.'

'I was thinking of inviting you to a real cognac,' she said. 'On my veranda, not here. I bought a bottle at Gardermoen airport, and I have a fantastic view.'

* * *

They had to stand close in the crowded elevator, which seemed much smaller than on the previous occasion. He watched the luminous numbers appear on the display.

229

The thick carpet muffled the sound of their foot-steps. She fidgeted nervously with the keys as she unlocked the door. The A/C unit hummed in the cool room. There was a smell of perfume and sweet sham-poo. Her room was a kind of suite equipped with a lounge and a desk. An opening in the wall led to an alcove with a bed. The mosquito net above it was drawn up and hung like a ribbon from the ceiling. There was a laptop on the desk.

'Huge,' he said, looking around. The suite looked out onto a veranda on both sides.

'I always take up a lot of space,' she replied, drop-ping the key on a table.

He said he envied her the pleasant temperature. 'My room's baking hot. The A/C doesn't work.'

'Shall we sit outside?'

Frølich nodded, opened one veranda door and walked out into the warm, humid evening. The view she had praised so highly had disappeared in the darkness. The singing of the cicadas in the trees was deafening. Lake Victoria was just visible under the starry sky with the moon, black and endless. He leaned over the railing and looked out. Muffled voices and music came from below.

'Doubt you would've believed,' he called into her, 'when you found Kristine Ramm in the car that time, that you'd end up on a veranda in Africa, with a cop, eh?'

'I've never believed that I'd end up on a veranda with a cop anywhere,' she said. 'Do you mind if I smoke?' She came out with a bottle of Renault in her right hand.

'It'll deter the mosquitoes,' he said.

'What's yours?' she called.

230

'My what?'

'Weakness. You probably don't have any?' Her face was briefly illuminated by the match.

'There are so many it's hard to choose one.'

A warm wind rustled the leaves in the garden. The rustling was barely heard over the buzzing of the cicadas. The odd stray tone from the dance music rose and blended with the other sounds. In the sky the crescent moon cast a pale light that dimly lit up her shoulders.

'This reminds me of when I was small and listened to the adults having a party below,' she said, pouring cognac into two plastic beakers from the bathroom. 'These bother you?'

'Best cognac I've ever tasted was in a plastic glass in a hotel room,' he reassured her.

They sat with their backs to the window. It struck Frølich that they could equally well have been in a spaceship thousands of miles away from home, yet still bound to each other.

Her blonde hair shone white in the darkness. The cigarette glow lit up her small hand. When she lifted the cigarette to her lips and sucked, the glow was reflected in her eyes. 'You can't image the difference between this place and where I've just been,' she said, kicking off her sandals, lifting her legs and resting her feet on the railing. The moon cast a pillar of light over the leaves on the trees and continued up both her calves. 'But I refuse to believe that Takeyo killed Kristine Ramm,' she continued. 'And it's absolutely crazy that he should be shot and killed here.'

'There can be many reasons. We didn't know him.'

'But he wanted me to interview him. I emailed him, he answered and asked me to come. He wanted to clear his name. But if he didn't kill Kristine Ramm . . . My God, it's so awful to think that the dead woman had a name, a reality around her.'

They fell silent.

'It can't be chance,' she said at length.

'What can't?'

'That he's dead. That he was murdered.'

'Following clues after a murder is like gathering the fragments of a dream. It's all about finding pieces of some surrealistic act and trying to make them fit into a comprehensible picture. We've been trained to ask: who benefits from this? But every time I'm close to answering this question, I have to rub my eyes, and I think: is this possible? Is this body lying here, cold and dead, because he or she was in someone's way, because someone had a particular plan or some short-term or imagined state of happiness? And then I think that, in that moment, in the seconds before the fatal blow is struck, there's some form of unreality about the situation that gives meaning to the irrational, it's the same state we are in when we dream.'

'What do you mean by 'imagined state of happiness'?'

'The murder will always be associated with the murderer's intention, whether he or she's caught or not.'

'*Verdens Gang* ordered me home,' she said, 'the minute I told them about the incident in front of the entrance last night. Now that Takeyo's dead there's even less reason to stay here.'

'When are you going?'

'Don't know. It depends on the ticket. Besides, I'd like to discuss the case at least one more time with the chief editor.'

Neither of them spoke for a long while. Her face glowed red every time she inhaled smoke. The tobacco smelt sweet.

'I don't know whether I want to just clear off home. In a way, it feels as if I'm in the middle of something.' She stubbed out her cigarette in the ashtray and stared down at her lap.

They looked up at the same time.

She laid a hand on the table, between their glasses. It was a slim hand, long fingers with red nails, filed round, shining like little hearts against the table. He took her hand. It was firm, warm.

After a few moments he felt her thumb gently stroking the back of his hand, to and fro. 'Here we are then,' she said in the dark, 'just you and me, and we have nothing to hide behind.'

When he stood up, she did the same, and when he felt her lips on his, he closed both eyes. They went in. Neither of them said a word. There was a rustle, like a still wind in the treetops, as the large mosquito net fell and unfolded around the bed.

Nothing mattered, not time, not the darkness, not until she opened both eyes; the pale light of the moon shone through her eyelashes and filled both irises with a soothing gleam, as tender as the beating of two hearts slowly finding the same rhythm — in time and accelerating, separated only by two layers of bare skin.

Sea Shanties

The alarm clock on Gunnarstranda's bedside table rang a little before six o'clock. As usual, he had woken up and managed to roll a little store of cigarettes before it rang. But today he had decided to try the deferring technique.

When he got into his car at six-thirty, he had managed to resist the roll-ups, but felt a little unwell. He drove along the E18, against the rush-hour traffic, accompanied only by German motorhomes and the occasional bus.

At precisely nine o'clock he turned into Strandpromenaden in Sandefjord. He drove up the little hill, parked in front of the Park Hotel and surveyed the large, well-kept park while he took a few longed-for drags on the day's first cigarette.

The magnificent hotel appeared uninhabited and abandoned; it reminded him of a museum, with marble steps, colossal mirrors and wall hangings. There was no one to be seen anywhere. The restaurant was also completely empty, but a group of helpful waiters ran toward him as soon as he showed his face in the door.

'I've got an appointment with Løding,' he said, looking at his watch and confirming that he was no more than five minutes late. At that moment some activity was heard coming from the lobby below. Gunnarstranda turned. A man in his forties came running up the marble steps.

'Ah, you must be the police officer from Oslo?' The

234

man greeted him jovially and introduced himself as shipowner Nils Johan Løding, then waved away the waiters and took Gunnarstranda to a table by the window, with a view of the marina and the park. As they were sitting down, Løding's mobile phone rang. The man half turned away to talk, and Gunnarstranda looked out. A young man was strolling down the lawn. Baggy shorts flapped around his knees, as though he were wearing a pleated skirt. His jumper was long and his hands weren't visible at the end of the sleeves. He had pulled a strange knitted hat down over his ears, and it seemed to be heavy, because his long body was stooped as though he were staggering under the weight of a sack of flour.

'I assume Skulberg's informed you that I'm not going to discuss business in the course of our little conversation,' Løding said, putting away his phone. 'Even if you are a policeman,' he added. 'We both know that in business we in Sandefjord have been well trained to keep on the right side of the law.'

Gunnarstranda smiled politely at the joke.

Løding continued: 'Regardless of what the cops and the press might think about the case and regardless of what we might earn or lose on our investments.'

A waiter came to the table with two glasses and two small bottles of mineral water on a tray. Gunnarstranda stared at the bottles and wondered if it was a sign from above that waiters always offered him water — unbidden.

'Anything to eat?'

'No, thank you.' Gunnarstranda took a roll-up from his pocket. After the waiter had finished pouring the water, he got down to brass tacks: 'I'd like to talk about Saturday, the third of August, when you apparently boarded a boat belonging to a certain Freddy Pedersen, popularly known as Feppen.' He flicked his lighter a few times before it lit and he did his best not to singe his eyelashes. 'This is about the takeover of a pharmaceutical company,' he added.

Nils Johan Løding, who had been fidgeting with a serviette while Gunnarstranda had been talking, stared down at the table for a few seconds. Gunnarstranda liked the cut of his jib. Løding was the kind of man who gave the impression of nobility without displaying the arrogance or effeminacy that often accompanies people of his type. The impression he gave was of strength and at the same time a lack of affectation: slightly curly, unruly hair that was allowed to lead its own life, a marked, honest face with a hooked nose. His shirt was rumpled and bore the signs of having survived many skirmishes in the washing machine. He had slim hands with long fingers adorned only by a very plain wedding ring. When the man looked up, he met the policeman's eyes with a firm gaze and total composure. 'That's quite right.'

'Was this woman on board?' Gunnarstranda asked, placing the photograph of Kristine Ramm between them on the table.

'Yes,' Løding said equally firmly, and took the picture. 'Good-looking woman, served drinks and tapas, but this photo isn't a good likeness. She was wearing a uniform that day. You know — white blouse, black skirt — and she had her hair tied up in a bun.'

'But you're sure it's the same person?'

'I chatted to her a bit. It was raining that day, and there wasn't much space on board. She said she came from Bud, outside Molde. I've been there a few times, and we talked a bit about the place. While my

236

father was alive, I was a sailor on one of our boats, and the captain came from Bud.' Løding smirked. 'Real bear of a man with bright-red hair and a beard. Once I saw him knock back a bottle of rum in one swig — in Kingston, Jamaica — but that's years ago and another, rather special, story. Anyway, I was curious to know if the man was still alive — even though that is unlikely — but she couldn't tell me.'

'Could you give me the names of anyone else on board?'

'Not without first asking for their consent.'

Gunnarstranda produced the photograph of Stuart Takeyo. 'This man was also on board.'

Løding glanced down at the picture. 'Old whale catchers don't talk business, Gunnarstranda.'

'But you realised he was on board?'

'Will you be able to use my testimony later without mentioning my business connections with Freddy Pedersen?' Lødig asked, eyeing him sharply.

'I'll try.'

'I'm not sure that answer's good enough.'

The inspector inhaled. 'There's no way back,' he said. 'You're already involved.'

'How?'

Gunnarstranda lifted the photograph of the deceased woman and said: 'Her name's Kristine Ramm, and she was killed about twenty-four hours after the boat trip we're talking about.' Gunnarstranda held a palm in the air when he saw the expression on Løding's face change. 'I'll be absolutely honest with you. I'm not in the slightest bit interested in Nor-Comp, Pharmanor, shareholders' interests, share prices, how much you or any others have lost buying shares in Pharmanor — or anything at all to do with shares.

I'm only interested in the murder of Kristine Ramm.'
He put the photograph of Kristine Ramm down and
tapped a finger on the one of Stuart Takeyo. 'Was this
man on board Pedersen's boat?'

'He was.'

'What was he doing there?'

Nils Johan Løding stared him straight in the eye.
'Has he been killed too?'

'For the moment he's only disappeared.'

Løding picked up the photograph of Takeyo and
said: 'If anyone should be shot, it's this man. Personally, I hold him responsible for the loss of ten million
kroner.'

Sunday Excursion

She was lying on her side. Her round bottom was touching his stomach. The mosquito net had come open and ridden up over their legs, making their feet easy prey for mosquitoes. But he didn't bother; he carried on dozing, aware of her light touch. Her shoulder stood out against the window, black. It was still dark outside and she was breathing noiselessly. He realised something must have woken him, so he tried to concentrate on sounds, without initially hearing anything apart from the monotonous hum of the air conditioning. But then he heard it again: there was someone whispering in the corridor.

She gave such a start she almost rolled onto the floor at the banging on the door.

'What's that?' she mumbled incoherently.

'The police.' He crawled out from under the net and grabbed his clothes. 'Only the police have been taught to knock on doors like that.'

★ ★ ★

Half an hour later Frølich was sitting in the same Mercedes that had brought him here earlier. But now he had been relegated to the rear seat. There were four serious men in the vehicle. Frølich and Austin sat in the back. The driver was a thin young man in a green boiler suit. He held the steering wheel as if he were reading a book. The man in the passenger seat was very powerfully built and wearing an Italian designer suit. His bull neck spilled over the blue collar. He spoke Swahili into a flashy mobile phone the whole time. As soon as one conversation was over, the phone rang again. If it didn't, he tapped in another number himself. And he rebuked the driver in a low voice whenever a bump in the road made it difficult for him to make a call. Over his lap he had spread a newspaper, on which there were two automatic pistols. Austin had a service weapon on his belt.

After crossing a railway line, where they saw men of all ages trudging along, the grey light slowly mutating into sunrise and day, the driver turned off the tarmac road onto a gravel track in a poor state of repair. The morning sun shone on the faces of a line of women coming toward them, all carrying loads on their heads, on their way to the market. The driver accelerated and overtook other vehicles, braked in front of a deep ditch that a tropical rainstorm had harrowed out and that almost divided the road into two. Slowly, the driver manoeuvred the car over this fissure, and a series of wet holes and deep wheel ruts, until the road straightened, and the man had his foot hard down on the floor again. Their Mercedes caught up with a slow lorry, bumping along. The driver turned off the road and into the countryside and hurtled between the bushes. Tufts of grass and brushwood rustled and cracked beneath the car. Bullneck stopped tapping in numbers until the terrain levelled out into a track of some kind, a new carriageway created by cars wanting to avoid the bumps in the makeshift road, which in places was no more than two ruts.

Frølich cleared his throat and asked: 'Where are we going?'

'Wichlum,' Austin grunted, and added: 'A fishing

240

village.'

Frølich looked out at the countryside: flat bush-
land; only isolated acacia trees and bushes broke
the monotony of the topography. Apart from people
walking, they passed a number of men on bikes; most
were taxis where the passenger sat on the luggage rack
with their feet on a stirrup while holding a briefcase
or a shopping basket. And there were cargo bikes: one
man, pedalling away, had tied a metre-high pile of
beer crates on the luggage rack — yellow cans with
an elephant logo; the next cyclist was transporting a
pile of loaves; another was carrying great bundles of
kitchen utensils. They raced past a cyclist carrying a
coffin. Frølich turned and watched the cyclist pedalling hard with the coffin sideways across the luggage
rack. None of the other men in the Mercedes reacted.
Many pick-up trucks functioned as buses — *matu-
tas*. These, too, were packed to the gunwales; young
men with their shirt-tails flapping in the wind hung
on tight to the vehicles that tore along wherever the
terrain allowed. They passed isolated mud huts in the
bush, tethered donkeys, goats roaming free between
the bushes, and zebus with their hunched backs in
muddy water holes beneath swarms of insects. In a
field there were two mud huts with a hotel sign over
the entrances.

They were approaching the lake, but this time from
the south, and as they drove along the mountain
ridge, green, fertile land opened up in front of them,
rolling down to the water, which reflected the cloudless sky. Gradually the occasional buildings became
built-up areas. They reached a hilltop, and the young
man behind the wheel pulled in and stopped. They
got out. A crowd of young men and small boys had

241

gathered in the middle of the road beside some grey buildings. They shouted to the policemen and pointed down to the lake. The driver grabbed one of the automatic weapons and jogged ahead of the others. A determined-looking man joined the little group and showed them the way.

Frølich was unsure what to do, but stayed close to them. He did as they did, crouched down and ran, a white man in a Hawaiian shirt, shorts and sandals. Austin stopped and raised a hand as a sign to the others. Someone from the crowd on the road let out a shout. The group scattered in every direction amid the pandemonium. Then a shot rang out. Frølich threw himself to the ground. The three police officers had a quick confab. Then they disappeared into the bushes beside the road.

A live exercise. Frølich stared down at himself. No helmet, no bulletproof vest, no weapon. He could feel the sun baking his legs and forearms as he met the gaze of two small boys grinning broadly at him. One wriggled his way across the road like a snake and joined him. He could only have been seven or so. He whispered 'Bang, bang,' and giggled. Then there was another shot. Followed by a long salvo. The boy rolled his eyes and giggled again. He was wearing tatty shorts and a ragged T-shirt. He was barefoot and the dust up and down his thin arms and legs was grey. Frølich attempted a smile, but it felt more like a grimace. The little boy sat up and peeped over the bush with a serious expression. Shouts and screams came from the town. 'Come on,' whispered the little boy, crawling between two bushes. Frølich followed him. His knees ached, the sun burned down on his back, and he was sweating so much his shirt stuck to his body. They rounded a rock where the terrain began to descend.

They stood up. Frølich brushed the dust from his legs and saw that fishing nets had been spread over the slope, which shone like silver. Millions of small sardines and shrimps were drying on the nets. Below the slope, on the beach, there were rows and rows of small, colourful boats. Frølich had seen this panorama before, but couldn't remember where. The little boy ran over to a tree where some women and a couple of men were sitting in the shade. Everyone was looking across at the village. Frølich went over to them, craned his neck and stared.

The village was idyllically situated: scattered houses above a wonderful white beach arcing round. Along this beach more small, colourful sailing boats had been pulled ashore. Between the houses two police officers patrolled like soldiers. Austin held his right arm out straight, service weapon in hand. He shouted to the driver in the green overall. The sight of the man in the car with the mobile phone reminded Frølich that he still hadn't rung his boss about Takeyo's murder. Bit late, he thought, watching people slowly emerge from the shadows of trees and house-fronts. Everyone was heading for a little shed by the beach. A dead man lay on the ground. Outside the shed entrance. Arms and legs were pointing at impossibly acute angles, as though the man was a crushed insect. It was when he saw the dead man that he remembered where he had seen the picture of this beach and the boats. It was a photograph in the *Playboy* magazine that had been on Stuart Takeyo's desk in Oslo.

★ ★ ★

243

'His name's Ibrahim Suleiman,' Austin said. 'He's a crook.'

'He *was* a crook.' Frølich turned away from the corpse. The waves washed onto the white sand, between the colourful boats, which were gliding ashore. The fishermen on board rolled up the sails attached to the loose boom at the top of the mast. Men jumped out of the boats and unloaded boxes of fish onto the concrete platform where buyers dressed in suits and nice shoes waited with biros in their top pockets. They had driven here in white flatbed trucks bearing huge refrigerated containers. The vehicles were parked in the shade while negotiations went on in the brick pavilion. The police officer with the mobile phone was sitting on a stool and drinking beer with the driver. Some fishermen were crossing the square, licking their fingers and counting the greasy banknotes they had received for their catches. The buyers clambered into their containers and shovelled ice over the fish they had bought. Some fishermen were cleaning their nets on the beach. Amid shouting and gesticulating. No one except Austin seemed interested in the body.

'Do you recognise him?' Austin asked.

Frølich shrugged.

'Is this the motorcyclist that killed your friend, Stuart Takeyo?'

'Takeyo wasn't my pal,' Frølich said. 'And I only caught a glimpse of the motorcyclist.'

'The boda-boda man had seen him before,' Austin said, taking the Norwegian with him. They rounded the corner of the little house. A BSA motorbike leaned against the wall. 'Last night Suleiman took the chairman of the fishermen's association hostage.' Austin

244

nodded toward a serious-looking man with a monocle standing in the background. Austin weighed a paper bag in his hand. The contours of a short-barrelled revolver were visible. 'This baby is going to the ballistics lab,' he said.

The serious-looking man came closer and tapped Frølich on the shoulder. He was wearing a striped suit and carrying a large ledger under his arm. His hair stuck up in all directions, and his monocle was attached to a waistcoat button with blue cord.

Frølich shook his hand and said hello.

The man explained the town was honoured to have a guest from Norway and it was time to sign the protocol.

'Protocol?' Frølich stared enquiringly at Austin, who nodded formally and motioned to the other two policemen, who joined them. Then they all stepped over the body and into the office of the man with the monocle. Everyone signed the visitors' protocol. It was Frank Frølich's turn. He sat down at the desk. The pen didn't want to work at first. He raised his head and looked through the door at the dead man. The pebbles under the dead man's neck and head were sticky with blood. He looked down at his wristwatch. His plane would be taking off in three hours. And he was still five hundred kilometres away from the airport.

Old Friends

It was afternoon. He found Lise Fagernes in the lobby. She was waiting by the lift. In the crook of her arm, she was carrying a bouquet of flowers.

'I've changed my flight to tomorrow,' Frølich said.

'And I've been sent some flowers.' She asked the woman in reception to put them in water. As they strolled out of the lobby and toward the taxis, she told him the bouquet came with respect and many apologies from a company called Inborn Fisheries Incorporated. 'It seems your friend Austin has paid them a visit.'

He opened a door for her, walked around the car and got in.

'They claim they'd lost a mobile phone and apparently suspected me of having stolen it.'

'Creative,' Frølich said.

'It's the most stupid excuse I've ever heard. And then three of them showed up to frisk me — without even asking if I had it first.'

'The flowers confirm at least that the firm exists. What does *VG* say about your journey home now?'

'As Takeyo has been shot, and as I can give the story a personal angle, I can extend my stay by a couple of days.'

At that moment the driver made a sharp turn. Lise fell against him. It was an odd situation. They clung to each other. He felt confused and read the same insecurity in her eyes. She straightened up, quickly, almost as a reflex. Shortly afterwards, they exchanged glances again. A second later he felt her lips brush his cheek. Frølich turned to her. But the moment was gone. She was staring straight ahead.

The driver braked in front of a flimsy-looking bridge. It consisted of two pairs of six-inch-wide planks. The driver coaxed the car forward and onto the bridge. It held.

'I can recommend the man who helped me to find Takeyo down here,' she said suddenly and delved into her rucksack. 'His name's Robert and he's a journalist. An absolutely great guy. I think you'll like each other.' She passed him a business card with a newspaper logo — the *Daily Nation* — and a name: Robert Otien. Frølich put the card in his breast pocket.

Soon after, they arrived at Dunga beach — the village where Takeyo's sister lived.

She was waiting for them in the same place she had stood the last time Frølich was here. But his current travel companion seemed to have higher status than police officer Austin. The two women embraced as though they were two sisters meeting at a funeral. Frølich waited patiently until they released each other. Then he offered his condolences on behalf of the Norwegian police. Afterwards he had no idea what to say, so he told her he had witnessed the shooting. She listened to him in silence.

After he had finished, she replied in a polite but measured tone that she and the rest of her family would now pray to God every day for their future. It had all looked so positive with Stuart earning money abroad. Now they would have to cope on their own.

They sat down under the tree with the strange fruit. Silence reigned until Stuart's sister suddenly turned to Frølich, inhaled and demanded accusatorily: 'What is it you want? What do you want from me — from us?'

The aggressive tone took him aback. When he finally managed to collect himself and answer, he avoided the question, and instead asked if she knew why Stuart had come home from Norway — all of a sudden.

'That was how God wished it,' she said seriously. 'Stuart was going to die, and God brought him home so that he could die here. In Africa.'

He cleared his throat and asked: 'He didn't give a reason himself — as to why he came?'

Instead of answering, she glared at him dismissively.

The silence persisted. Just the rhythmic beating of the waves as they washed ashore could be heard. Frølich was unsure how to continue, but he didn't have to. The silence was broken. A metallic man's voice started to sing a well-known Norwegian children's song. Three pairs of eyes turned to the papyrus bush, where the little girl was standing with the cassette player hanging from one hand. The wind was pressing her dress back against her lean body.

'Miriam.'

But the little girl didn't hear her mother's call. Her sightless eyes stared rigidly above their heads. Stuart Takeyo's sister was startled and stood up. Lise Fagernes cleared her throat, ill at ease. 'That man,' she said in Norwegian.

'Him?' Frølich motioned toward an elderly man standing by the corner of a little shed. He was a tall, lean figure with a furrowed face. Wearing sunglasses and a peaked cap on his head.

'That's the Maasai I talked about. The one driving the white van,' Lise Fagernes said in a low voice.

'*That* white van?'

This was a bizarre situation. A grating, metallic

248

children's song, along with the sound of crashing waves, wafted through the air. Four people eyeing a figure fifty metres away — almost as though he were a lion or a leopard that had graciously dignified its prey with a sight of himself.

Frølich turned to Takeyo's sister. 'Have you seen that man before?'

She didn't seem to hear the question.

'Has he threatened you?' Frølich asked in a low voice. 'Is he threatening you now?'

'I don't want to talk anymore,' she said. 'You have to go.' She walked quickly toward her daughter.

'Why?' Frølich called after her. He looked for the man again. But he had disappeared. 'Did you see where he went?' he asked Lise.

'No.'

The tune stopped playing when the girl's mother switched off the cassette player. Frølich ran over to the ramshackle shed where the man had been standing. Behind it there were just rushes. The man was nowhere to be seen. Frølich forced a path through the rushes and around the house without finding the man anywhere. He pushed the brown wooden door, but it was locked with a padlock. Slowly he wandered back to the tree. 'Ask her again if that man's been threatening her,' he said to Lise.

The woman was standing with the blind child in her arms and shook her head. 'Go now,' she said. 'Please.'

'Was that why Stuart came back here? To protect you against him?'

She shook her head again. 'Go,' she repeated angrily. 'Leave me and my family in peace.'

'So much for the bouquet,' Lise Fagernes sighed nervously.

249

Frølich didn't want to let the woman go. He said: 'One of the police's theories is that Ibrahim Suleiman had a score to settle with your brother. They think Stuart may have owed Ibrahim money for drugs, or they'd quarrelled over a girlfriend. And that's why Suleiman killed your brother.'

'Nonsense,' the woman answered absent-mindedly. She still seemed ill at ease. 'My brother never touched drugs.'

'Austin, the policeman who talked to you last time we were here, thinks there's a chance that Suleiman belongs to the Mungiki sect. A gang of extremists who practise black magic and have been in court for violence.'

The woman put the girl down and said: 'I don't want to talk anymore.' She turned her back on them and took her daughter with her.

At that moment Frølich's mobile rang.

He lifted it distractedly and took the call.

'I have to speak to you.' It was a woman's voice, speaking Norwegian.

'Who is it?' He walked back to the shed again to look for the man with the hat and the glasses.

'This is Evelyn Sømme. I apologise for the little misunderstanding we had when you were looking at my computer. But something's happened. I have to speak to you.'

'Right now?'

'Yes, can you come here?'

'Can't we do this over the phone?'

'No. I have to speak to you personally.'

'What would you like to talk about?'

'Can't you just come here?'

Frølich stared across Lake Victoria and said with

a hint of jocularity in his voice: 'It's a bit tricky right now. Can't you speak to Gunnarstranda?'

'Why? Is it the rain that's bothering you?'

'No.'

'Then come on over.'

'I'm rather a long way away.'

'Where?'

'Dunga beach, outside Kisumu in Kenya. I'm interviewing Takeyo's sister.'

Frølich looked at the telephone display. Evelyn Sømme had rung off.

Further away, Lise was talking to Takeyo's sister. She turned, answered and gesticulated excitedly. He left them in peace.

A mole built with rocks stretched out into the water in front of him. Beyond it there were lots of water hyacinths — the plant that Takeyo had been studying. It resembled seaweed. A pelican was resting on a pole at the end of the pier. It was standing on one leg and had drawn the other underneath it. As though it had sensed his gaze, it flapped its wings and flew off. It floated low over the water until it had air under its wings and rose into the sky. Frølich watched it go. Then he discovered many more. There must have been hundreds of them, just floating, spiralling upward, higher and higher — they were like drifting clouds. There had to be unusual thermals above the water. Far above, the flocks of birds seemed to thicken, as if a hole in the heavens was spewing out small snowflakes that immediately morphed into living pelicans. A bit further away hovered another flock, circling round and round, and forming a huge cylinder, then a cone, which became a balloon, to form a face, that turned back into a cylinder. Frølich looked from the birds down to the two women and the little girl. She was staring at him now — through her lifeless eyes.

He gestured to Lise. 'Let's not hold them up any longer, shall we?'

When they got into the back seat of the car, the little girl and her mother were standing hand in hand. They were motionless, as though all they wanted was to make sure the taxi with its two passengers was gone for ever.

Frølich sent a text to Gunnarstranda:

Evelyn Sømme rang, wanting to say something in confidence. Check her out. She knows something. F

Up North

Between the million-dollar houses in Backlands, on the valley side, sloping down to the lake, with a view of the west and the sunset, stood the Sunset Hotel. The building was reminiscent of a tower block in a Norwegian satellite town, with sharp angles and a tendency to functionalism — or it would have, had it not been for the construction of open balconies on every floor and external staircases encased in airy, shadowy brick shafts.

Steps led up to the lobby. Frølich nodded politely to the woman at the reception desk, but continued up a staircase and came into a bar where a whole wall of glass doors led out onto a tiled terrace with scattered tables. A tall, slim, sinewy man wearing dark trousers and a white shirt, the image culminating in a pair of wrap-around sunglasses, was leaning against a pillar.

'Robert Otien?'

The man had both hands thrust into his back pockets. He nodded.

They walked down a little path and sat at a table in the shade of a small thorn tree. Otien fidgeted with a broad, metal watch bracelet, clicking it against his skin. 'Lise Fagernes is a beautiful woman,' he started.

'Sure,' Frølich answered.

'Warm-hearted,' Otien said. 'Sensitive.'

Frølich felt his smile freeze. He turned away and gazed across the water. The silence was oppressive. But he tried not to let it show. On the opposite side of the bay he spotted a large factory.

'That's where the fish are filleted,' said the journalist, who had followed his gaze. 'There you can see one of the country's most important modern industries — beaten only by coffee and tea production.'

'Oh, yes?' Frølich said, relieved that the conversation was developing in a less personal direction.

A waiter came with two beers on a tray.

'It was different in the old days,' Otien said, and went quiet as the waiter poured. 'Before, the fishermen used to bring home enough tilapia and omena for themselves and their families, and enough to sell so that they could buy other things they needed. It was the women's job in those days — to take care of the fish that were brought ashore and then sell on the market and buy whatever the family needed. The fishing industry employed predominantly women on land. And fed the whole population around here. At the end of the seventies the fishermen were catching more and more giant Nile perch, fish that could weigh up to several hundred kilos. It was a big event. But that was before the international finance imperialists got a sniff of the resources here.'

'I've been to Obunga. I've seen the fish bones and the frying.'

'So, you've seen with your own eyes what development aid has led to.'

A hawk-like bird swooped down to one of the trees in the garden. It watched them with a rigid, earnest eye.

'Is that an eagle?' Frølich nodded toward the bird.

Otien twisted on his chair, looked up and examined the bird. 'That's an eagle alright,' he said.

Both of them watched the bird as it took off and flew away.

'The Nile perch provided the basis for much of the development aid from the imperialist powers,' Robert Otien continued, raising his glass to drink. 'The English set it up in the fifties.' It was clear the man pumped iron in his free-time. Sinews and arteries wound around his forearm like roots clinging to cliffs. The watch bracelet jangled again.

'I've heard many strange names for the country I come from, but imperialist power sounds rather dogmatic.'

Otien studied his glass before putting it down. 'Do you think I'm impolite? Do you know we place a lot of emphasis on courtesy on this continent of ours? And we have unswerving faith in fate. It marks us. For example, both of my brothers and three of their children died of AIDS. But, of course, I wouldn't blame our nice friends up north for that reason. This is fate. Two of my brother's children are still in hospital, but the impotence and fury I feel at them not having medicines I should direct against my government, shouldn't I? The truth, however, as formulated by the rich countries, is that the earth doesn't have the resources for us living in the poor part of the globe to become as rich as you in the north. It would be just a waste of breath to blame the rich for spending money on liposuction and plastic surgery when HIV threatens to decimate the population in parts of Africa. Besides, it would be discourteous, wouldn't it.'

'Point taken.'

Otien smiled with the same cool composure. 'Back to fisheries? Well, the governments in the countries around the lake — Uganda, Tanzania and Kenya — have been very busy converting the lake's

255

resources into money. Especially when the quantity of Nile perch exploded in the eighties and nineties, people thought we had struck gold. Big filleting factories for Nile perch were built around the lake. *Someone* invested money in the factories to reap the fishery rewards. This *someone* organised the distribution of the fish. *Someone* had refrigerated lorries come to collect the fish from the villages. They don't have electricity, so the fish can't be stored there. So, the fishermen can't negotiate a price; they have to act quickly to sell their fresh goods and are forced to accept what buyers offer — which, of course, isn't much. In this way *fate* determines that fishermen remain poor. Fish are put in cold storage and transported to factories like that one.' Otien nodded across the bay. 'The factories work to ISO 9000 standards. Fish become an export industry because fish are defined as a national resource, injecting life into the national economy. And so the prospect of earning more money materialised, for *someone* who was willing to put trawlers on the lake. The catch quotas rose and rose in the nineties while the fish brought up from the lake became smaller and smaller. The women previously employed in the distribution process lost their jobs. The price of fish began to rise in the towns around the lake. Fish was no longer food that normal people could afford to buy. Children began to go hungry. The best fishing grounds began to run low on stocks.'

Otien fell silent. They stared at the factory in the distance. Frølich thought about Lise Fagernes. Otien had been to bed with her. He sensed it. The truth was in the air he inhaled. And Otien presumably felt it too — it must have been the same feeling that made him so measured and arrogant. Why had Lise arranged this meeting? To tell him something she didn't want to express in her own words?

'You keep stressing the word *someone*. Who is it exactly?'

'The point is,' Otien continued, as though he hadn't heard the question, 'that progress has upset a harmonious system. The lake has been overfished, a few owners are earning a lot of money, and some Africans have been offered work in the factories. But this reliable source, this lake, the blue eye of Africa, is out of balance. A little world in microcosm is suffocating — in the same way as our own.'

'This ecological imbalance is interesting,' Frølich conceded. 'There are similar examples of ecological imbalance in my homeland. But time's passing quickly. I suggest we talk about Ibrahim Suleiman's murder of Stuart Takeyo.'

Robert eyed him. 'You are not what I expected,' he said out of the blue.

'Thank you, and the same to you,' Frølich said, tongue-tied. For a second, he saw Lise's body in the semi-darkness under the mosquito net, felt the pressure from her calves on his shoulders, the smell of sweat, of her sex. The image rendered him speechless because it was almost real, as though he had jumped back in time and was there, in bed with her. He had to look up and away.

The silence between them persisted. Otien fidgeted with his pack of cigarettes. 'You think Stuart Takeyo fled from Norway, don't you.' He lit up.

'Didn't he?'

Robert picked a beer cap from the floor under the table and held it up. 'Do you know what this is?'

'A bottle top.'

257

The journalist placed the cap on the table and used it for the ash from his cigarette. 'No,' he said. 'It might be an ashtray or a bit of rubbish. But it definitely is not a bottle top.'

Frølich heaved a deep sigh.

'What I'm trying to say is that you base how you see Takeyo's motives on your own assumptions,' Otien said quickly. 'You see him through your post-colonial eyes, as you see this country, as you see me. That's just how it is.'

'OK,' Frølich said condescendingly. 'I'm rich, white and a bastard. Does that make you feel any better?'

Otien continued to smoke with a wry grin on his lips: 'Takeyo may have come here because he had to,' he said at length. 'Perhaps Takeyo had something to do here, something urgent.'

'What would he have to do here?'

'Maybe protect his family.'

'Is his family in danger?'

'Not any longer. Not after Ibrahim Suleiman shot Takeyo on the orders of *someone* here in Backlands, Kisumu.'

'On whose orders?'

Robert Otien gave a broad grin: 'You asked me *who* makes the big bucks from this industry. Shouldn't we ask where they are?'

'You tell me.'

'Some of them live in Europe, and a few live here in Backlands. The ones living here use African Indians as straw men. I don't know why Takeyo was murdered, but I do know something. In Backlands there is a special house. It is big, one of the biggest. A woman I know works in this special house. She does the washing. She saw a car — a dark-blue BMW — about to drive off, so she ran out and told the driver to wait so that she could go with him to the bus stop. From there she can catch a matatu to her home town, Bondo, and visit her mother. This is fairly normal; if someone is driving to town, others on the staff can always have a lift. But, no, the driver just drove off without her. While she was standing on the road and watching where the car went, her brother came along in his little pick-up and took her. He dropped her off by Kibuye market, and there she saw the same driver talking to the man she recognised as Ibrahim Suleiman. The driver handed him a wad of cash in an envelope.'

'Fine,' Frølich said. 'How did she know there was money in the envelope?'

'Because Suleiman opened it and counted the cash. It was a lot of money, and Suleiman came over to the woman and said he would pay her if she went to bed with him. She refused, but Suleiman would not take no for an answer. She told him to clear off; she was not the kind to sleep with men for money. Then he began to boast, showed her a revolver and told her to read the paper the following day. When she met him next, she should consider what might happen to her if she continued to refuse.'

'When was this?' Frølich asked.

'A few hours before Stuart Takeyo was shot and killed by this same Suleiman.'

'That could be a coincidence.'

'Coincidences are like drops of water. Insignificant on their own, but together they can mobilise enough force to wash the ground from under your feet.'

Frølich began to count on his fingers: 'One, the driver wanted to be on his own. Two, your girlfriend saw him with Suleiman in the market. Three, she saw

259

him hand something to Suleiman, which suggests there's a return favour. Four, Suleiman drops a hint that he's about to commit a brutal act that will be in the papers. Five, Takeyo is murdered by Suleiman shortly afterwards. Do five drops constitute a glass of water?'

'And number six,' Robert said. 'Lise Fagernes told me a woman spoke to you by the swimming pool at Hotel Imperial on one of the first days you arrived. A dark, elegant woman with a boy, right?'

Frølich felt a chill run down his back. 'Yes,' he said.

'Lise Fagernes thought the woman was a prostitute. Well, I can tell you that I know who she is. She isn't a prostitute. She lives in the same house.'

'As who?'

'As the driver who gave Suleiman the cash. Why would this woman act like a prostitute with you? She doesn't even have any children. It was a set-up, Frank. My guess is she was told to find out who you were because you are white and in touch with the police here in town.'

Robert Otien had a point. The woman had known that Lise Fagernes was a journalist, even though Lise had never seen her before.

'Who'd told her?'

'I don't know. But I know she is in cahoots with the guy who gave Suleiman the hit-man job. And for some reason Takeyo was killed after she had kept tabs on you.'

Frølich mulled over this new information. It was strong stuff. He asked: 'Who is this woman?'

'She runs the house I've been talking about.'

'Runs it? Who owns the house?'

Otien shrugged before answering: '*Someone*.'

'You don't know?'

Robert Otien shook his head dolefully and grimaced as if deep in thought, then flicked the ash from his cigarette. 'Let's examine what we actually know. We can add a seventh coincidence: Suleiman is a former child soldier and a refugee from Somalia. He is a pariah in this district, a crook who steals, who smokes *bhang*. No one, at any rate not the bodyguards of a factory-owner in Backlands, would talk to him without having quite specific, shady, reasons. And number eight: this driver we are talking about is on the security pay-roll at the factory in this district.'

'Do you, or don't you, know who owns this house?'

'I have no idea who owns it. But I do know one thing — coincidence number nine, which I consider actually clinches the whole thing: the security guard works at the only factory here in Nyanza with a connection to your country — Norway.'

Frølich was silent.

Robert Otien rose to his feet. 'Thank you for the beer,' he said. 'Say hello to Lise and tell her I am looking forward to meeting her again.'

'Just a moment.'

Otien turned and waited.

'Is it possible . . . ?' Frølich wondered aloud. 'Is it possible to find out who owns this house you've been talking about?'

Joining The Dots

Gunnarstranda raised a hand to knock on the door; he saw his shadow in the rectangle of sun on the tiled floor, and lowered his hand again. He sighed, annoyed. He should go through the usual protocols, he supposed, and marched down to reception and asked the woman wearing the switchboard headset to call Fristad.

'You have a visitor,' she said into the handset, arching her eyebrows at Gunnarstranda. 'Name?'

The public prosecutor met him in the doorway, his glasses hanging from a cord over his chest. 'I believe this is the first time you've come here unbidden.'

'Pedersen's our man,' Gunnarstranda said as they sat down at Fristad's solid conference table.

'Because . . . ?'

'Among other things, because he's lying. He denies that Kristine Ramm was on board his boat on the infamous Saturday in question.'

'One mendacity does not a murderer make,' Fristad smiled smugly. 'Did you hear that? I'm a poet.'

Gunnarstranda waited until Fristad had finished laughing at his own wit. 'The first lie was to deny he had a dinghy anchored off Bygdøy Sjøbad. It was there all summer, but it isn't there anymore. On top of that, he's served up a tissue of lies in order to cover over the clues linking Kristine Ramm to his boat.'

'Are you still pursuing this conspiracy theory?' Fristad suddenly seemed irritated. 'In fact, I'm of a mind to shelve the whole case.'

'Shelve the case?' Gunnarstranda was taken aback. 'Now?'

'Conveniently, this Takeyo is dead, isn't he. We know he drove the car to the crime scene. We know he was in the car park — alone — a few minutes after. We don't have anyone else who witnessed the crime. Everything points to Stuart Takeyo as our man. So, we're shelving the case. It's simpler and cheaper than to follow your wild conspiracy theories.'

'But you haven't heard what the theory's based on.'

Fristad scoffed. 'OK, I can accept that Pedersen's not to be trusted — if he lies about the boat trip on the Saturday evening. But why would he wait a whole day before killing the woman, and furthermore, in a car park?'

'He always lies through his teeth. He's lying about Takeyo, for example. Pedersen maintains Takeyo was on board to serve the guests. That's not true. Kristine Ramm was serving the food. On the Saturday in question Takeyo was brought in to appear as an HIV researcher. But Takeyo knew nothing about medicine. He was, however, a genuine scientific researcher. He came from a country in East Africa and had first-hand knowledge about the place where the medicine was supposed to be working miracles. His number was to talk to a group of investors about how utterly fantastic the new medicine was. The arrangement was a sales promotion of an unofficial share issue using the time-share sales pitch: take it now or you'll regret it. The issue was presented as the best and most secret scoop of the year. With the figures that Takeyo put forward the purchase of shares in Pharmanor was supposed to be a gilt-edged investment. And people took advantage of the offer; deals were struck for large sums of

263

money.'

'I see, so we have a witness who lies and in addition finagles money. So far, this might be a case for the Fraud Squad.'

'If you could just let me finish,' Gunnarstranda said, with irritation in his voice. 'There's an important point related to this share issue. Even if these investors sign to buy shares, there's no immediate formal transaction. The money changes hands a few days later. This deal's arranged on Saturday evening. To have the deal officially registered, these people have to use a broker who's certified by the Central Securities Depository as a financial administrator. But the system is closed on Saturdays and Sundays. It's open from seven o'clock in the morning on weekdays. However, even then, when the shares are recorded, it is still not certain that the money has moved into the seller's account. Stay with me now. I have a statement showing that registration on the CSD for the Pharmanor shares took place on Monday the seventh of August at 07:00.'

'So?'

'Time is everything. I've spoken to the CSD. Even if their system opens at seven, they don't know any administrators who work before eight. So, this broker had been instructed to register the transactions as fast as he could — as soon as the CSD opened on Monday morning. Let's go back to Saturday though. Pedersen dropped off Kristine and Takeyo in Bygdøy on Saturday evening. They were undoubtedly dropped off at the same time. Kristine had her car there. That evening Pedersen was happy and content. He had achieved his aim and got signatures on various bits of paper. All that remained was to wait and

264

keep the façade smooth and blemish-free until the money had changed hands and was in his account. While Pedersen drives home and goes to sleep, Kristine and Takeyo are developing warmer feelings for each other. They were kindled on the boat. And now they're alone. It's a summer's night and warm; the town is deserted. It's stopped raining and it isn't dark until four in the morning. They walk together, they walk and talk without sleeping, and of course what happens is that Takeyo tells her the truth. He tells her he works at Blindern, at the university, that he knows a lot about flowers and bees and numbers and statistics, but he knows zilch about HIV. And Kristine Ramm's a social anthropologist and probably fired up about the inequalities of the world. She reacts as all young people and idealists do. She's upset and angry. And what does she do when she's angry? Yes, she decides to contact Freddy Pedersen and tell him she doesn't want any bloody part of it.'

Fristad squinted at him with a sceptical expression.

'We've got her mobile phone,' Gunnarstranda added. 'She rang Pedersen — that is, she rang the pub. I thought, at first, she rang to ask for a shift or something like that, but it was a Sunday, she was free, why would she ring the pub? None of her colleagues knew anything about her private life, and none of them can remember talking to her that day. Yet Kristine rang the pub and talked to someone that Sunday. Who? Of course, she spoke to Pedersen. And what does he do? Yes, he panics and asks to meet her to talk some sense into her. Don't forget, Kristine Ramm was on board that Saturday. She mingled with the guests. She had a long conversation with Løding, the shipowner. In fact, Kristine Ramm could scupper the whole deal. If she contacts Løding, for example, and tells him what she knows, Løding will block his account and warn the others. And the entire multi-million deal will go up in smoke. Pedersen has to silence her. He says: Fine, let's meet and talk these difficult things through. Kristine takes Takeyo along as a witness. Perhaps she's the one who asks to meet in the underground car park, simply because it's a public place. At any rate, she drives there with Takeyo. Kristine is killed there and Takeyo flees.'

Fristad sat engrossed in thought. 'That was a nice story,' he said at length. 'So, let's say you're right. Kristine and Takeyo agreed to meet Pedersen in the car park. They drove in and parked. What happened next?'

'That's what I want to ask Pedersen.'

'I thought you had a theory.'

'I do.'

'But if Pedersen croaked Kristine Ramm, why was she killed and not Takeyo? He must've witnessed the whole scene. Sorry, Gunnarstranda. This isn't a theory; it's wishful thinking.'

'I'm only asking to be allowed to interview Pedersen.'

'Why? What's the point?'

'The point is to find the answers to the questions you just asked.'

'Well,' Fristad said. 'It's much easier to ask me. I'm an expert in such conspiracies. You see, I've read all the editions of *Detektivmagasinet*. Takeyo and Kristine drive into the car park. You postulate a third man on the scene — Pedersen, the perpetrator. If you're right, Takeyo must've got out of the car, leaving Kristine alone. OK, Pedersen waits until Takeyo's out of sight.

Then he gets in the car, covers her mouth and nose with an ether-filled cloth. She falls unconscious within seconds. Then he sticks the syringe into her and leaves. The whole scenario takes less than a minute. In the meantime, Takeyo wanders around and goes back to the car, sees the body and realises all hell's been let loose and runs to Daniel Amolo's to get a passport and leave the country as fast as humanly possible.' Fristad beamed. 'It must've happened like that — if your theory holds water. It's just a shame that, in my role as prosecuting counsel, I will never be able to find any evidence that Pedersen was there — and could have committed the murder.'

'Pedersen has a motive. Takeyo didn't have one.'

'But Takeyo's the one with the opportunity. And the CCTV footage proves he was there — at the crime scene.'

'He was there and had the opportunity. But it's a long way from there to proving he killed Kristine.'

'That's precisely why we're shelving the case, with a good conscience.'

Gunnarstranda stood up. 'But we lose nothing by interviewing Pedersen. Because in the very marrow of my bones I know his motive: the woman was killed because she threatened to ruin his confidence trick. But — if you refuse to accept such a theory, then there's still something which is just as important to find out: why did Takeyo decide to play the role of AIDS scientist on the boat? This question's perhaps the most important of those we can't answer. Now that Takeyo's dead, only Pedersen can give us that answer. Another issue is why Takeyo ran to Amolo's for his passport — why didn't he go back to his digs and take his own?'

'The answer to that one's obvious. Fleeing under a false name is quite convenient — especially if you've killed someone.'

'OK,' Gunnarstranda said wearily. 'Let's make a deal. If Freddy Pedersen can give a satisfactory explanation of a single one of the lies he's served up, I'll give up — whatever.'

Fristad sat cleaning his glasses. 'If we're going to charge anyone in this case, you're going to have to come up with some proof. Proof, not circumstantial evidence. But as long as Frølich continues to cost money in Kenya, it would be logical to wait for whatever comes out of the reports. In the meantime, Pedersen deserves to be grilled good and hard. And I assume he's in the best hands, isn't he?'

Marine Life

It was two o'clock in the morning when two youths, on board a Shetland GH fourteen-foot open boat, with a 25 hp Yamaha engine going flat out, realised there was something wrong with the vessel drifting in the strait between Husbergøya island and the Skjærholm islets at the end of Oslo fjord. They were both seventeen years old and holiday-cabin neighbours on the eastern side of Nesodden peninsula. They were on their way there when the boy sitting in the bow, with his long hair fluttering in the wind, shouted over the noise of the engine to his pal and pointed. They probably wouldn't have done anything, had it not been for the engine. As soon as his pal, sitting lost in his own thoughts on the rear thwart, let go of the accelerator and went into neutral in order to hear better, the engine cut out. With that, their focus was directed on the boat drifting on the starboard side.

Both the boys dreamt of owning big, expensive boats. Both knew what sort of cabin cruiser was drifting in front of them: a forty-foot Fairline Targa, which cost upward of a million kroner. Neither of them knew what this one cost, only that it was extremely expensive.

There is something sinister about lifeless, abandoned objects that are usually under control, such as empty streets or abandoned houses, but perhaps especially boats drifting around at night, inert. There was an eerie aura about this cabin cruiser. The two boys bobbed up and down in the waves as they stared at the *Loveliss*, thinking that it might have slipped its moorings from a marina somewhere. But how could it have drifted so far from land without anyone reacting? Perhaps the people on board were asleep? But why had the skipper of the boat not dropped anchor? It was cold sitting in an open boat on the sea. But the two friends hadn't felt the cold until now.

The surface of the sea was as black as the night sky. A breeze was blowing that went right through their clothes. Both of them were wearing shorts — because it was summer, because neither of them had thought they would be out so late, and, besides, at first the trip was only meant as a quick dash home. But with the chill wind slowly biting through their jumpers they were beginning to feel the cold. They sat shivering and staring at the boat for maybe five or six minutes. The sea showed with all possible clarity how out of control the *Loveliss* was: the low waves beat against the side, making the bow first point to land, then in the opposite direction, until the boat slowly turned round again on its own axis. Eventually the boy on the rear thwart twisted the ignition switch. The Yamaha engine started at first attempt, strangely enough, and the boy with the long hair sent his pal a nervous glance, when he steered the tiller and pointed the bow of the GH at the drifting vessel. In these seconds, with the GH resolutely approaching the cabin cruiser, the same resolution seemed to rub off on the two friends. The one in the bow grabbed the boat hook from beside the oars. He lifted it as they got closer and searched for a chunk of rope to fasten the hook to. Both boys had now forgotten the eeriness that had hovered over the cabin cruiser. They were in the process of performing a piece of classic seamanship. They were recovering

270

a drifting boat. If they were thinking about anything, it was to do with this adventure, a demonstration of strength of body and mind; a brief thought about money and a reward might have flitted through their minds. But this could not be detected in their faces. They were two determined boys working together to approach the drifting boat in the most efficient way possible. It was the boy with the boat hook who spotted a rope end under the surface of the water. He grabbed the end and felt the weight as he pulled. And it was him who let go as though he had been burned a few seconds later.

'What's up?' yelled his pal.

'Bloody hell,' came the answer. 'Jesus.'

Insomnia

It was night, and hot. Frølich, eyes wide open, lay staring into the darkness. The A/C unit was as dead as before, and the bedsheet was soaked in sweat. Lying on his back, he thought about travelling home. He thought about Lise, thought about Robert Otien, but stopped there. The thoughts that would ensue from this combination did not on the face of it seem uplifting. Besides, she hadn't been around earlier in the evening.

He re-ran his conversation with Otien and assessed the possibility of a connection between an employer here in Kenya and someone in Norway. At first, he reacted negatively to this idea. Acknowledging such a hypothesis meant accepting the existence of plots, which again suggested a form of paranoia. Paranoid conclusions are always susceptible to attacks. But what did such a hypothesis boil down to in purely concrete terms? Was there a company with financial interests in two different countries? Such as Inborn Fisheries Inc? And so what? Was there a link between Takeyo and this company in the same way as there had been a link between the company and Kimberley? The crazy old man with the bus-conductor hat who had turned up in Dunga upset the logic of this pattern. What was his part in all this, if indeed he was involved at all? Frølich felt a strong need to discuss these things with someone.

In the end, he sat up in bed and switched on the television. The screen was just snow. He looked across at the telephone. Should he ring Gunnarstranda? No. It was the middle of the night. The man would have a heart attack. Should he ring Lise? No. She was probably asleep. And what if she wasn't alone?

He got up, opened the door to the balcony and walked naked into the darkness, trying to avoid thinking about how many mosquito bites he would get standing like this. But the fear of itchy unpleasantness was less important than the cool breeze slowly cooling down his body to its normal temperature. He held the railing, stared into nothing and listened to the sounds of the night: buzzing cicadas and rustling leaves. Suddenly he felt something light touch him. A pink petal was resting on the back of his hand. It lay there like a little feather, barely moving until an almost imperceptible breath of wind began to ruffle it. But the little petal was caught between two black hairs, holding it back. The struggle between the hairs and the wind lasted a few seconds until it picked up in strength and the little petal was gone. He stroked his hand where the petal had been and discovered two more petals fluttering down in front of his eyes. One flipped over, spiralled and fell. The second fluttered slowly from side to side. Soon he saw more. He peered down and saw the pink and white specks dancing around the lights further down — like snowflakes, he thought, and peered upward. Straight into a shower of rose petals and what had to be her hair and head, five or six metres above him.

'Hi,' he whispered.

'My God you're slow on the uptake,' she answered, tearing up another rose petal.

'Can't you sleep?'

'Can you?' she grinned through myriad fluttering

273

rose petals.

'What does one do about that?'

She rested her chin in her hands and asked: 'Actually that was what I wanted to ask you. Have you any suggestions?'

Sins Of Omission

The sun had scarcely risen when the telephone on Gunnarstranda's bedside table rang.

It took him twenty minutes to have a quick shave and a cup of coffee. Then it took him thirteen minutes by car to reach Shed 30 on Akershus quay. There was almost no traffic. The entrances to the Vålerenga tunnel gaped open like dark nostrils in the mountainside.

The *Loveliss* was moored at the Harbour Police quay. Gunnarstranda ran down the steps. The corpse was already packed into a body bag on a stretcher the paramedics were loading into an ambulance.

'No external injuries,' said the uniformed policeman who met him. 'A long rope had got caught in the propellers and snarled them up. No wonder the boat was adrift.' He pointed down into the water. Both propellers were knotted in an entangled mass of blue rope. 'The question is how the man fell in the water, but I have a theory.'

'Oh, yes?' Gunnarstranda looked up at him.

'The body was fully dressed, but the flies on his trousers were open and that's usually how we find them,' the officer said quickly. 'I mean the men who drown when they've had too much to drink. I reckon the engine was barely ticking over, the guy was off his face and he went to the railing to have a piss, it's only two steps, and then a wave hit the boat and he lost his balance. As he fell, he managed to grab hold of a coil of rope and he was left hanging and the loose end got caught in the propellers, which wrapped the rope around his body until the props came to a halt and the engine died.'

Gunnarstranda looked at him. 'And then?'

'And then he drowned. He wouldn't have been able to move an arm with the rope wrapped around him.'

Gunnarstranda turned and watched the ambulance disappear up the hill to Mosseveien. 'And there were no external injuries?'

'Not as far as I could see.'

'He was fully dressed?'

'Trousers, shirt and jacket anyway. And trainers. Nice boat,' said the officer, climbing over the railing after Gunnarstranda.

'Who cut him loose?'

'The paramedics.'

'Why?'

'They wanted to try to resuscitate him.'

'A man who'd been submerged in the water for several hours?'

'They *are* doctors.'

Gunnarstranda peered through the windows.

'Has anyone been inside?'

'No one.'

'And the boys who found the boat?'

'They were sitting dutifully in their boat until we came.'

'Good,' Inspector Gunnarstranda said and proceeded to call for forensic assistance.

PART THREE

THE SECURE SOURCE

Sifting The Evidence

On returning home, Lise always had a sense that she had been away for a long time. It must be to do with the total change, she thought, the way she adapted all her senses, her body, her mind to a different type of reality — a journey like this one had taken her out of her everyday world and so she was forced to re-adapt when she came back. It was always strange to meet people who hadn't been through the same metamorphosis, those who behaved in exactly the same way they had done before she set off.

Opening the glass doors, walking into the reception area of the *Verdens Gang* building, she nodded to the woman behind the desk and experienced the same feeling in her stomach. She hurried over to the lift door that had just released two people she didn't know. She slipped inside. The doors closed and the glass lift took her slowly up through the floors. It was afternoon now and eight hours since she had landed at Gardermoen Airport. She gazed through the glass side of the lift and looked down on the people in reception. They were becoming smaller and smaller. When the lift stopped, she hesitated for a few seconds before pressing the button and continuing all the way up to the cafeteria, which was empty in the summer heat. The terrace doors were wide open. She walked over and leaned against the railings as she scanned the rooftops and spotted the Freia clock in Egertorget. She lit a cigarette, thinking she should have stayed in Africa much longer.

A little later, when she went into the editorial office, struggling to hold a boiling hot cup of tea, Federica stood up and waved her telephone. Lise hurried between the lines of desks. It felt like the egg and spoon race at school. She nodded left and right as her tea slopped over and ran down her forefinger. 'Ow,' she whispered, put down the cup and licked her finger before taking a seat. Federica had put down the receiver on her pad. Lise took it and placed it under her chin. 'Oh, hi,' she said. 'I was just going to ring you, but I need a cup of something hot first.' She swivelled round in the chair and grabbed the cup of tea, which was bubbling unappetisingly around the brim. She blew carefully and took a sip while listening to the voice in the receiver and loftily waving her free hand to Federica, who pointed to her cheeks and gestured how jealous she was of her tan.

'If you've read what I've written, you know about as much as I do,' she said, putting down the cup. 'There isn't much to add. Takeyo was shot by a Somali refugee from a motorbike. This man, Ibrahim something or other, was shot and killed the day afterwards by the Kenyan police during a hostage shoot-out. One of the Kenyan police's theories is that Takeyo was killed as part of a drugs vendetta. But the Norwegian police officer I met is convinced Takeyo's murder was on orders from Norway.'

She pressed the receiver harder against her cheek and took the mouse from beside the keyboard. 'No idea, myself,' she said. 'That's the Norwegian policeman's opinion. I'm a journalist and only report what the police say.'

She listened again. 'I assume he bases his opinions on the outcomes of investigations back home. That's

280

why I didn't write anything about it. I don't know . . .'

She had received a lot of emails and absent-mindedly opened them while listening to the voice on the telephone. 'For me as a journalist this story is interesting,' she said. 'And my boss is up for it. I'm going to follow the case. The interesting bit is how a murder in Kenya can be organised from Norway. Is it even possible? My guess is we're going to run this angle pretty hard.'

She listened again and rolled her eyes to Federica. Some conversations could be so tedious. She said: 'Why do the police think as they do? No idea. All I know is that they're interested in one company called Inborn Fisheries and one called Kisumu Grand Fisheries. Do the names mean anything to you?'

She skimmed her emails with the receiver under her chin. Why was she plagued with all this spam? Lotteries for a Green Card in the USA. 'Housewife finds $10,000 in closet'. 'Sexy chicks showing it all' . . . She started to delete unread messages. Where did they get her name from?

'The first company deals with breeding, the second the export of filleted fish. Thanks for calling, by the way,' she said distractedly. 'I'll keep in touch. Sorry this is so messy, but my job now is just to keep my nose in front of the police.'

'Hectic transition from safari-land?' Federica asked sympathetically after Lise had put the phone down.

'That was a source,' Lise mumbled. 'Actually, it was pretty good, but sometimes a bit manic.'

At that moment, her computer pinged. It was an email from Robert Otien.

For a few seconds she was taken aback, then she opened it.

The message was unusually brief for him. No flowery phrases about yearning or moonlit nights. Only a short note, which he asked her to pass on to her Norwegian policeman friend. Poor Robert, she thought, and read:

The house is owned by Kisumu Grand Fisheries.

★ ★ ★

She started trawling the net. One hit was the Norwatch website — a page owned by *The Future in Our Hands*, which set as its goal a critical examination of Norwegian involvement in southern European countries. Getting warm, she thought, and kept clicking. She tried a search engine with keywords such as 'fisheries' and 'Nile perch', but didn't find anything until she tried 'Lake Victoria'. Reports appeared about an imbalance in the distribution of fish resources, and she read about Norway. The company UNITOR had been involved in the building of a series of filleting factories some years ago — with considerable support from the Norwegian Agency for Development Co-operation, NORAD in Norwegian.

She sat thinking: this was pure Norwegian politics. NORAD organises financial support for private businesses to establish commercial activity in the south. What stood out here was the coincidence. UNITOR's activity had been in Uganda. Robert Otien had tipped Frank Frølich off about the series of factories being built with Norwegian aid money. Takeyo studied at Makerere University in Uganda's capital, Kampala. This was perhaps what police would call a lead, but should she contact Frank? Presumably he had already read the same as her. Nevertheless, she picked up the

282

telephone.

A woman answered Frølich's telephone and said he wasn't in.

So, she copied Norwatch's website address and added it to the brief note from Robert Otien in an email. Should she do anymore?

She knew nothing about Frank Frølich except that she liked him. In which case, what should she write? Something to express that fact? Should she write: Hi, thanks for everything, we had a pretty good time, but I don't know you, you don't know me and I don't know if I dare take the risk — well, I'm not sure I have the energy to find out more. I'd rather have dozens of vacuous one-night stands because that's less commitment and I have no interest in giving more of myself to men who . . . who . . .

She shook off her sentimentality and wrote:

Hi Frank (ie), here's a note from Robert. Afterwards, I searched the Net and found a bit about Norwegian involvement in establishing the fishing industry around Lake Victoria a few years ago. I'm following this lead. I'll call you one of these days. Check out the website, Lise.

She sent the email and looked for NORAD's telephone number.

Indian

Gunnarstranda had collected all the papers on the David Kimberley case. As far as he could see, there was nothing that matched the Kristine Ramm case. But there were a lot of files — and this was actually what computers were for, he thought, writing a note to Lena Stigersand, in which he asked her to run a match on the two cases.

Afterwards, it felt quite natural to light up. Defer it, he thought, staring at the cigarette for a few seconds. Irritated, he stuck it in his mouth and lit up. With it in the corner of his mouth, he grabbed the telephone and dialled Sørli's number. He fidgeted with his Zippo lighter while it rang. He had taken the cigarette instinctively. Out of habit: pick up the phone and a fag. An automatic action — like riding a bike. He inhaled, flicked the lighter and ran a finger through the flame, then brought down the lid and extinguished it. The cigarette tasted of nothing. Yet he inhaled again. 'I need more material on Pedersen,' he said when Sørli finally answered.

'You did ask me for the short version,' Sørli answered, to the point.

'Yeah, yeah, but now he's dead and deserves a bit more attention.'

'What do you think?' Sørli asked, curious. 'Was it an accident?'

'It was bloody convenient anyway. The interior of the boat was as clean as a cancer lab. Hard to believe any people had been in there.'

'No fingerprints that shouldn't have been there?'

'Barely any of Pedersen's, so now it's up to the autopsy.'

'But what do you think they'll find? Apart from water in his lungs?'

'Guess,' Gunnarstranda said dreamily.

'I'm not so well up on your case,' Sørli answered dispassionately. 'Pass.'

'If they find alcohol in his blood, the case is probably lost as far as I'm concerned. But I hope they'll find traces of ether or chloroform — like in the girl's body. If not, Freddy Pedersen will end up as a statistic. Norwegian men of around fifty who drown in a boating incident.'

'I see.' Sørli rotated a screwdriver in his jaws and continued: 'As Pedersen was disabled, it'll be difficult for you to prove he wasn't washed overboard by a rough sea.' The screwdriver rotated again.

'Exactly,' Gunnarstranda said sombrely. 'The two boys who found the boat are the only ones who acted correctly. They towed the boat ashore to Akershus quay. But down there some bright spark cut the body loose, so no one can know how the guy was trussed up.'

'Shit happens. It's hard to blame them for that. They couldn't know the body was someone you had your claws in.'

'Well,' Gunnarstranda said to get to the point. 'With regard to the details surrounding Pedersen, what I'm wondering about is the transition from wine-shop owner — wasn't that what he was? — to stockbroker. Seems like a rather big step, and so sudden.'

'I haven't got all the data off the top of my head, but I believe Pedersen was part of the IT boom in the mid-nineties. It was all tied up with the Internet.

Think his wine business went bust in 1995. The Internet was pretty new then. It was a time when only a very few newspapers were on the Net and only a small number of Norwegian businesses had started using it. That is, it was beginning to take off: Telenor was investing hard in the private customer department they'd set up, and subscriptions were selling well. Microsoft had launched a new user interface in ninety-five and soon afterwards they had their own Windows browser.'

'So, growth exploded around 1997?'

'About then, yes. And Freddy Pedersen's stock-exchange interests started with the Internet. You know, he was in fact a trained engineer.'

'Trondheim University?'

'No, what we called an EPA engineer in the seventies. A technical high school in Gothenburg.'

'But did he make any use of this training?'

'Yes, he did before he went freelance, let's put it like that. And after his wine business went down the tube, he started at the stock exchange with the first IT companies. And I would guess he sold up in time. The computer bubble on the stock exchange burst a few years ago. If he hadn't sold up with a profit, he wouldn't have had a base from which to do what he did afterwards. The problem is that it's absolutely impossible to find out what he owned when he died. It wouldn't surprise me if he used straw men and bogus companies even when he went food shopping.'

'And this file of his, is it big?'

'Files,' Sørli corrected. 'Collected works in six volumes. I'll send you the most salient bits.'

'There's one more thing.'

'Yes?'

286

'If I want to examine people's finances —'

'Forget it.'

'But this case is about big sums of money.'

'Talk with me or . . .'

'Or?'

'Well, there are companies that specialise in credit assessment. But it's not cheap. And from what I've heard, you should keep an eye on your budget.'

★ ★ ★

That afternoon, Gunnarstranda studied the files the Fraud Squad had on Freddy Pedersen. He assiduously went through all the enclosed documents and had prepared for a long evening. He, therefore, frowned in surprise when there was a ring at the door. Automatically he glanced over at the goldfish. But Kalfatrus wasn't particularly interested in this breach of the evening's routines.

Gunnarstranda trudged into the hallway, holding a hand over his aching back. He had been sitting still for too long. It was Tove. She was wearing the blue dress he loved.

'Hi,' she said, sailing past him and inside. A fragrance of perfume followed in her wake.

'You don't need to say a word,' she said. 'I know this isn't convenient.'

He smiled weakly, closed the door and followed her into the sitting room.

'Anything to drink?' he asked.

'With some food?'

'If you're happy with a fried egg or a cheese sandwich.'

'We'll go out another time then,' she said, rummaging through her bag. 'Here,' she said, holding out a little package.

'And it is?'

'Open it,' Tove said.

'For me?'

'Yes.'

He opened the little package and looked down. 'Have you been to the chemist to fetch my medicine?'

She nodded. 'You're not going to tell me you would've collected it yourself, are you?'

'And the prescription?'

'Have you missed it?'

He shook his head. 'I was looking for it, off and on.'

'Come on,' she said, nodding toward the packet. 'Don't try and sneak out of it. There are numbers on the side that show how many doses you have left at any one time.'

She turned to the desk while he fumbled with the packet. While he read the instructions, she stood with her back to him. She tapped the glass goldfish bowl with a finger. 'Actually, I think you two are quite similar.'

'Two who?'

'You and the goldfish. Well, I know you are,' she added with a smile: 'The advantage of having a fish is that you don't have to take them for a walk and you can occasionally forget to feed them without suffering remorse. But there's one disadvantage: you never really get close to them.'

He strolled into the bathroom and closed the door behind him. Inside, he stood weighing the green thingy in his hand, for some time. His eyes in the mirror blinked once and then again. Slowly, he placed the inhaler against his mouth and breathed in. The pain, the twinge that signalled a bout of coughing, was the same. But there was no cough. His eyes in the mirror were as dry as before. There was a little twinge in his lungs, but he didn't have to cough. He stared down at the green object. The act of breathing in this powder that the doctor called medicine, was it an expression of anything but following the advice of someone paid to evaluate his general health? Was the act really the result of an urge he himself tried to control, to restrain? But what was that urge? A desire to be well. Normal? Immortal? Or was the act just the outcome of blind obedience?

When he closed the bathroom door behind him, she was sitting with her nose in a newspaper. She didn't ask.

'Would you want to?' he asked.

'What?'

'Cuddle a fish.'

She smiled archly, but said nothing.

'Where would you like to go?'

'Go?' she asked, with the newspaper in her lap now.

'Where would you like to eat?'

'It looks like you're working,' she said.

'One does have to eat now and then,' he said, picking up the jacket hanging over the chair.

'I think I'd like an Indian meal,' she said as they walked down the stairs and out.

'It worked,' he said as they stepped onto the pavement.

'Hm?'

'The medicine. I think it works.'

She said nothing. He glanced across. She noticed his gaze and looked up. 'I'm glad,' she said. 'Is Indian OK with you?'

Goodwill

After opening the door, Evelyn Sømme stood eyeing Frølich in silence.

'My condolences,' he said, feeling a little stupid and uncomfortable as he always did when he said this word.

She didn't answer; she just stared at him.

He cleared his throat impatiently.

'Is that why you've come?' she asked.

'Not only for that reason.'

'What's the real reason?'

'What did you want to talk about when you called me?'

'When?'

'You called my mobile and rang off when I said I was interviewing Stuart Takeyo's sister.'

'Nothing important,' she said, clinging to the door frame.

'What did you want to talk to me about?' he repeated.

She closed her eyes and sighed. 'Something that happened before he left. Stuart was worried. He came to ask me for advice.'

'When?'

'Shortly before he fled. I suppose it must've been the Thursday or the Friday before.'

'What kind of advice?'

Evelyn Sømme coughed. 'Have you ever heard of Mungiki?'

'The word has come up.'

'I thought you might've read about it when you

were there. It's a kind of sect. People who work to resurrect African tribal culture, rites, magic and circumcision of women.' She paused.

Frølich shifted his feet on the doormat, but sensed he shouldn't push, and waited quietly.

'It's quite extreme. These people seem to have connections at the heart of political circles, they try to control channels of communication, so they can earn money from the corruption that's rife there. But the worst is that they aren't shy of resorting to violence and murder to achieve their aims. They don't have much formal power, but they're brutal. People are frightened of them. When they strike, it's done the African way: arson and murder, and traditional weapons like the spear, bow and arrows, clubs — at night. I don't know much more than that. Stuart, he —'

'Yes?' Frølich interrupted impatiently.

'He was convinced someone from this milieu was threatening his home in Kenya.'

'Are you telling me Stuart Takeyo disappeared and went to Africa to protect his family?'

'No, or rather I'm not sure . . .'

Frølich stayed silent.

'He had a little niece, Miriam . . .'

'Mhm?'

'He had some idea of providing her with a future — in the same way that he'd been given an education and . . . well . . . this girl has a serious eye condition.'

Frølich waited, but she wasn't forthcoming. 'I understand that. But what advice did he want from you, fru Sømme?'

'Someone here in Norway was pressurising him.'

'What kind of pressure?'

'He was being forced to do something he didn't

291

want to do.'

'What was that?'

'He wouldn't say. You see, he came here, I think it was the Friday before he disappeared. That was why I was worried when he didn't show up on the Monday. When he came here, he was very upset. And he told me that his family, his sister — Miriam's mother — had been threatened by these people.'

'This sect?'

'Yes, and he'd been assured that the threats would stop if he did something — I'm not sure what — did someone a favour here, in this country. And then he asked me what my advice would be.' She sighed. 'If you only knew how much thought I've given this.'

'What did you advise him to do?'

'I said he mustn't let himself be forced into doing anything. Once you give way, these people would just demand more and more. And two days later he travelled home, only to end up being shot dead.'

Frølich breathed in. 'You think he was killed because he didn't give in to the pressure?'

'I haven't had any peace. I keep thinking if only I —'

'That's wrong. You couldn't have done anything either way. Takeyo succumbed to the pressure.'

'What?'

Frølich nodded. 'Takeyo did something he didn't want to do, something he shouldn't have done.' He coughed and took a couple of paces backward, making a move to leave.

'Wait.'

'Yes?' he said, turning.

She shook her head and looked down. 'Nothing.'

He watched her. 'In Norway, these sects aren't so

dangerous,' he said at length. 'It's people who keep their mouths shut about what they know who are dangerous. Bye.' He left.

'Wait,' she called after him. 'Tell me what you mean.'

Frølich carried on to the wrought-iron gate and opened it. Evelyn Sømme was standing in the same place, motionless in the doorway.

'These mumbo-jumbo types might want to have women circumcised, who knows,' he said, 'but what I do know is that a couple of them are part of a company that sent a student to the Norwegian University of Life Sciences last year, and that in some mysterious way this student was murdered, here in Norway.' Frølich gestured with his arm. 'Here, fru Sømme. He was killed here, in Norway. Just imagine if you'd told us about Takeyo's problems before anyone got the idea of having him suffer the same fate as the student.'

Evelyn Sømme hadn't moved. Her face was distorted, and her lips were trembling. 'What are you talking about?'

'David Kimberley. He was a student at NULS last year and was murdered. What —'

Frølich stopped speaking. Sømme had closed the door and gone back in, without letting him finish what he was saying.

Feeling the fury rising in him, he walked back to the door and rang the bell. But there was no reaction. He knocked on the door. 'If you know something,' he shouted, 'then learn from your previous mistakes. Make sure you tell someone.'

Not a sound. Frølich, breathing hard, turned and went back to the car.

Another Piece In The Jigsaw

Hip-shaking Elvis, bought at a bazaar in Delhi two years previously, hung from the rear-view mirror and rocked to the beat of 'Have You Ever Seen the Rain?' by Creedence Clearwater Revival. The song smacked of the seventies and cowboy boots. It made Lise Fagernes think about Frankie Frølich. When she slowed down in Prinsens gate to turn right, Elvis lost the beat, but found it again down Karl Johan. She parked outside the Grand Hotel, where actually there was a No Parking sign. But she only wanted to buy a yoghurt. Surely errands of this kind were allowed under the rules of continuous loading and unloading in the briefest possible time?

Afterwards, she sat with the window open, key in the ignition and phone buds in her ears while watching people drinking beer or white wine in the chairs the Grand Café had put out on the pavement.

Finally, someone answered.

'The name's Lise Fagernes,' she said, tearing off the top of the yoghurt cup. 'I'm a journalist and I'd like to know if there's anyone there who can answer questions about UNITOR's government-sponsored involvement in Uganda about ten years ago.'

She stirred the yoghurt while she was transferred to the first person.

'Yes,' she said quickly as a man answered. 'My name's Lise Fagernes . . .'

She delivered her spiel again. The man told her to ring UNITOR.

'I already have done . . .'

The man suggested the Ministry of Foreign Affairs. She had spoken to them too. The man chatted away. She closed her eyes and enjoyed the taste of yoghurt and melon on her tongue before swallowing. 'I understand of course, but you also have to understand that it's really unsatisfactory to speak to whoever's on the switchboard all the time. I actually thought that your branch of work was relatively open. And people who have been working on aid over the years know each other. Surely you could give me the name of someone with experience and competence, someone who could give me a tip on how to proceed?'

She listened and felt a chill run down her back.

'Really?' she said in a faraway voice. 'Is only one person responsible for the financing of industrial projects in East Africa?'

What was happening outside the car window suddenly seemed like a scene on a TV screen. Little people moving in a silent movie — meaningless activity performed for reasons she didn't know. The plastic yoghurt cup slipped from her grasp and down onto the passenger seat. She stared at the white milky mass spilling onto the seat cover. She let it spill. Her fingers wouldn't obey, not at this moment. All she heard was the voice of the man talking on the telephone.

'Hello,' the man said impatiently. 'Are you there?'

'Yes,' she said with a cough. 'I'm here.'

The man wanted to give her this person's telephone number and address.

'No,' she said. 'That's not necessary. In fact, the name's on my list.'

Night Life

After pulling into the bus lay-by, Frølich leaned over and opened the passenger door. Gunnarstranda got into the car.

They glanced at each other. 'You're tanned,' Gunnarstranda said.

Frølich cut a mistrustful grimace. 'What's the matter now?'

Gunnarstranda shrugged. 'I just wanted to congratulate you on your tan.' He wriggled until he found a comfortable position on the seat. 'While you were down south, Lena interviewed the man who had lent his passport to Takeyo. A hard nut, this Amolo, but he loosened up when Stigersand told him that Takeyo had gone for the big sleep.'

'And what did the hard nut say then?'

'Daniel Amolo claims that Stuart Takeyo rang his doorbell at two o'clock on Monday morning, so about two hours after Kristine had been killed. Takeyo had been terror-stricken and begged to borrow his passport because he didn't dare go home and get his own. Of course, Daniel Amolo hadn't wanted to give it to him, so he asked him why and did some digging as to why it was so bloody important for Takeyo to do a disappearing trick with another man's passport. But Takeyo had refused to say what had spooked him — he had been at his wits' end — but he promised to return the passport in a couple of weeks.'

'No wonder Takeyo was frightened if his family was in mortal danger and Kristine Ramm had been murdered, on top of everything else.' *What was it that just struck me?* Frølich had the scent of a stray thought; something he had just said had triggered an association, but he couldn't pin it down. *Being frightened.*

'Eventually Amolo gave in and lent him his passport. Then Takeyo ran down the staircase and raced off to the airport either that same night or early the following morning. Stuart Takeyo, alias Daniel Amolo, bought tickets, first to Amsterdam and then to Nairobi.'

'Did he pay cash?'

'Not with a credit card anyway.'

'Where did he get the money from?'

'That same question crossed my mind too,' Gunnarstranda smiled. 'How pleasing.'

'What's pleasing?'

'The way your mind works. Never mind that though. The point is that Takeyo didn't get any money from Amolo — that's what he claims anyway.'

What's this burning sensation in my guts?

'And we know,' Frølich reasoned, somewhat panic-stricken. 'We know that Takeyo couldn't have got hold of this money himself. His bank card was in his flat, and he hadn't touched his account for several days, and when he did, he only took out money for food. Only one single item has been registered, at the till of the local REMA 1000 supermarket.'

'Well, according to Pedersen, Takeyo had been dressed in Rasta gear when he came to the pub for a job. Something's amiss here. How would Pedersen get the idea of hiring Takeyo to play an AIDS worker when he's togged up as a Rastafarian? Natty dread, mon. And so on.'

'I went to see Evelyn Sømme — you didn't go, so I

did. And she said Takeyo asked her for advice,' Frol-ich said.

'And I'm saying, we're getting warmer. I was sitting at home scratching my head,' Gunnarstranda went on, ignoring Frølich's little snipe, 'and I was thinking: if Pedersen was murdered, it was because someone had something to gain. Well, the swindle took place long before Takeyo was murdered. However, there must be one person, or maybe more, benefiting from the elimination of these three — Kristine Ramm, Stu-art Takeyo and finally Freddy Pedersen. But Africa? I thought. Where does Africa come into the picture? Well, the simplest thing is to ignore the murder in Africa. What is relevant for our work is the crimes committed against Kristine Ramm and Freddy Ped-ersen. And then I realised I didn't know anywhere near enough about Pedersen. So, I rang Sørli, who knows a lot more, and he sent me various files, and do you know what I found out?'

Why am I beginning to feel sick? Frølich wiped the sweat from his brow. His hand was trembling. 'No idea,' he whispered. *What is this? Is it a fever? Malaria?*

Gunnarstranda grabbed his briefcase, placed it on his lap and opened it. From it he took out an old num-ber of *Kapital* magazine, which had holes punched in it to slot it into a ring file. 'Here,' he said, pointing to a photograph.

The picture was black and white and showed four men in suits and ties in a small conference room, each with a laptop in front of them on the round table. 'I've never met Pedersen,' Frølich said, wiping sweat away again. 'I've no idea what he looks like.'

'This is a photo from a press conference announc-ing the founding of an IT company in the spring of

298

1996. Here are the four owners. Pedersen's sitting on the right. But what made me go to the vinmonopol to buy some champagne is the man sitting on the left, the second along.'

'Who is it?'

'Jan Groven,' Gunnarstranda grinned. 'I looked at this photo,' he continued with some satisfaction. 'And it all came together. Until I saw this, I thought Pedersen had killed Kristine. Bloody inconvenient that Pedersen's died, isn't it. But then this photo turns up and it all makes sense. Groven was an engineer and had a job in the peace corps until he stopped sometime in the eighties. He stopped, but stayed on in Africa. What do you think he was doing there?'

'Working?'

Gunnarstranda shook his head.

'He wasn't working?'

'He was creating work places. Jan Groven's a bloody entrepreneur. It says that here. In 1996 he is introduced as someone who is well-known for his dynamism and energy, and creating employment in poor countries.'

Again, Frølich felt unwell. Gunnarstranda's voice came from far away:

'What it doesn't say here is that a few weeks ago he was in negotiations regarding his personal debts and was on the brink of going bankrupt.'

'Bankrupt?'

'Yes. There are companies that can find that kind of information. Did you know? Well, Groven's ridden out that storm — thanks to help from Stuart Takeyo. Look at the photo and think: Takeyo had to do someone a favour because some black-magic types were threatening his family. Think: Takeyo took Kristine to

299

a meeting with Groven in a car park. Groven asks to speak to Kristine alone. Don't forget Groven is the African man's father figure. Takeyo trusts Groven one hundred per cent. So Takeyo leaves them alone for a few minutes. When he returns, Kristine Ramm dies in front of his very eyes — killed by the man who gave Takeyo the opportunity of a lifetime. Imagine what goes on in his head when he sees Kristine die and Groven tells him to go home and take care of those who mean the most to him. He jumps on a plane and flies to Kenya to protect his family. He thinks he is safe. But he isn't, not when you two arrive, you and the journalist. You faxed us a report saying that you were being spied on, didn't you? By this prostitute who was told you were a Norwegian policeman, together with a Norwegian journalist?'

'She isn't a prostitute,' Frølich said. 'She lives in a big house owned by Kisumu Grand Fisheries.'

'KGF.' Gunnarstranda stared through the windscreen. 'KGF is the same as Inborn Fisheries, which is the same as Jan Groven. The woman is Groven's eyes and ears down there. When she found out who you were, Takeyo became a real danger for Groven. Takeyo knew something Groven didn't want revealed at any price. Until you and the journalist showed up in Kenya, Jan Groven had parked Takeyo miles away from Norway, hoping he could be spared. But that was a misjudgement too. Takeyo chose to play the good boy, travel home on someone else's passport to protect his family against Groven's allies. In this way Groven was rid of a witness. But Takeyo must've suffered torment at the loss of his girlfriend. What was more, he realised that the only defence he had against Groven was the fact that he'd been allowed to live and could tell the truth. So, he made an alliance with the journalist Lise Fagernes. The good boy was beginning to become disobedient and would have to be eliminated. It was the woman by the swimming pool who ordered Takeyo's death, on behalf of Jan Groven.'

I feel sick, Frølich thought.

Why?

Because the same people have threatened . . .

'When I took the statement of his partner, Liv Inger Sømme, she told me she and this man had been out in an open boat on the infamous Saturday when Takeyo had to play a role on the *Loveliss*. It was pouring down that day, Frølich. The only day for weeks there had been a deluge of rain. Why would they be out in an open boat in the pouring rain? Of course, Groven wanted to see with his own eyes that Takeyo was doing what he had been told: to pay off his debts. He had to act the scientist, the expert on AIDS and HIV, so that Groven earned money on the Pharmanor company instead of losing it. Groven knew about the arrangements for picking up Kristine and Takeyo in a boat on the Saturday. Groven made sure he was close by — on board his skerry jeep. Liv Inger Sømme recognised Takeyo in the dinghy. But unfortunately for Groven she was alone when I visited her at home. She told me about the boat trip — and the snowball began to roll.' Gunnarstranda stopped talking and stared at Frølich in astonishment. 'What's the matter, Frølich? Are you ill?'

Frølich was clinging to the steering wheel with both hands. *Her source. Jan Groven is her source. Lise must've spoken to Jan Groven. He must've known she was in contact with Takeyo. He is the only person who could organise a hit on Stuart Takeyo, the only person who could elim-*

301

inate Ibrahim Suleiman, because he had someone who could tip off the police about where he was hiding.

'I'm not ill,' Frølich groaned. 'I'm just bloody stupid. She's the next victim on the list.'

'Who is?'

'Lise must've been in contact with Jan Groven.'

'Of course. Otherwise Groven wouldn't have known that Takeyo was being disobedient.'

Frølich made a grab for his phone, dropped it, caught it again and passed it to Gunnarstranda. 'Call her. Lise Fagernes.' He started the car.

Gunnarstranda grinned. 'Isn't it much better if we go to his place and simply arrest him to stop him doing any more damage?'

★ ★ ★

That evening Lise Fagernes sat staring into space. It took time to absorb the shock. She was forced to view her actions in a new light. She was angry, furious at herself for not having seen the link before, furious because she had allowed herself to be used.

The only thing her brain was capable of handling was that she had to turn this situation around. She had to make use of what she had found out. But how? And how to get her revenge?

She had to confront him. She might be wrong about what she had deduced — but was it really possible for her to have made a mistake?

For probably the twenty-fifth time she went through the case in her head, everything she had done, everything they had talked about, the words they had used.

On her stereo Marianne Faithfull was singing 'The

Ballad of Lucy Jordan'. Lise got up and turned down the volume. What should she do? Get drunk? No. She had to think clearly. The only way to rid herself of tensions was a decent run. And she needed one. She hadn't run as much as a hundred metres while she was away. She glanced at her watch. It was past midnight. Was it too late? No. She was as tense as before an exam, and outside it was still light. It was warm, a so-called tropical Norwegian night of twenty-plus degrees and probably the same temperature in the water.

★ ★ ★

'It's late,' Gunnarstranda said when the car stopped.

Frølich checked his watch. 'It's early,' he said, switching off the engine.

They sat staring ahead. Then Gunnarstranda's phone rang. 'Please keep it brief,' he said.

Frølich faced him, resigned.

'Excellent,' Gunnarstranda smiled. 'Sleep well. You've earned it.'

'Since when have you started being nice on the phone?'

'That was Lena Stigersand. She's run a match on the Kimberley case. And bingo. It transpires that one of the witnesses in June last year mentioned a particular name in the interview. Guess which one.'

Frølich opened the car door. It felt like night in the lower part of Holmenkollen. No cars on the road, hardly any lights in windows, just muted light and two car doors slamming as they got out. A dog started barking in a garden nearby.

'We're waking people up,' Frølich said.

'It's not my dog,' Gunnarstranda said drily. 'And you haven't guessed yet.'

Slowly they walked down the path leading to the part of the complex where Groven had his house.

'The answer's Groven. What does the jury say?'

'The jury says your answer's right.'

'Are the people who live here rich?' Frølich wondered aloud. He studied the cars as they passed.

'Richer than us.'

At that moment they heard wheels screech in an underground garage. A broad garage door hummed open. A car engine whined. The two policemen exchanged glances. A dark-blue BMW shot out and up the ramp. As it passed, the light outside the door shone on the driver's face for a brief instant.

'That's him.' Frølich immediately set off running. He sprinted back to the car. But Groven's BMW was already a long way down Olaf Bulls vei. The red brake lights lit up just before the bend, fifty metres down the hill. And Frølich's car was facing the wrong direction. He threw himself inside and slammed the gear into reverse. The wheels spat sand. He almost collided with a No Entrance sign. The engine screamed as he slammed the car into gear. Groven's red lights were nowhere to be seen. Frølich glanced in the rear-view mirror. He could see Gunnarstranda standing with his hands in his pockets, staring after him with a blank expression. A second later Frølich accelerated away.

* * *

Frølich was way behind but was in no doubt that the red lights ahead of him belonged to a dark-blue BMW. He crossed the Smestad intersection on

304

amber and was two hundred metres behind Groven, who stayed in the left lane as he raced down Sørkedalsveien. Groven wrenched the car left on amber at the Majorstu intersection. This man knew he was being followed. Frølich braked to avoid two young ladies in short skirts staggering across the road. Then he turned left on red. By then Groven was already a good way up Kirkeveien. The man bore right down Suhms gate. Frølich stamped his foot down hard; his tyres squealed in front of the traffic crossing. He saw the rear lights of Groven's BMW disappear over the brow of Norabakken hill. Then it was past Bislett Stadium and on to St. Hanshaugen.

The car was gone. Frølich braked at the Ullevålsveien crossing and looked left and right, unsure which way to go. There was no traffic in any direction. He took a risk and continued along Waldemar Thranes gate. He drove slowly. On both sides of the road there were parked cars. On the left a BMW was parked behind a red Golf. Could it be Groven's car? No one was inside. Frølich drove on, still at a snail's pace. What should he do? He had to try Ullevålsveien or maybe Geitmyrsveien. Frølich turned right into Bjerregaards gate. *Idiot! You should've checked the BMW's bonnet to see if it was warm.* He accelerated as he rang Gunnarstranda's phone, continued up Akersgata and back, into Waldemar Thranes gate. The phone rang in his ear. He stopped by the BMW and got out. The bonnet was warm. This was Groven's car. But where was he? There was no one around. Then he saw. There was a gap in the line of cars. The car in front of Groven's had gone.

★ ★ ★

Lise Fagernes had to search for a while before she found any clothes to run in. She took her bikini and a dry towel, then dashed down the stairs and out to her trusty Corolla. She unlocked the door, threw the rolled-up towel and bikini onto the back seat and got in. After starting the car, she switched on the radio. It was night, it was summer. Hip-shaking Elvis needed some music. It was time for 'Propaganda' by Norwegian pop group Briskeby.

Whenever Lise felt like running through forest and field, her immediate response was to run in the area she knew when she was a child. Heading toward Røa, she crossed the lights on amber, continued down Griniveien and looked up as she passed her childhood home in Røatoppen. The house was in darkness; her parents were probably asleep. She should go and see them; she hadn't seen them for a good four or five weeks. But not tonight. She drove on, across the Lysaker river and up to Fossum. She drove up to the barrier and parked. There were lots of other cars around. Lots of other people thinking like her, that the summer's night could be spent doing something other than sleeping, because when she bent down to tie the laces on her trainers, another car drove in and parked further down. She straightened up and began to run, up the gentle slopes to Lake Østernvann, trying to concentrate on other matters, everyday things such as visiting her mother and father next Sunday or ringing pregnant girlfriends, everyday things like men . . .

★ ★ ★

Lake Østernvann lay black and still and expectant on the edge of the forest. As she began to get her breath

306

back, she could hear some youths partying across the water. She continued at a walking pace to find somewhere to swim.

There are two peculiarities about a summer's night, she thought. One is the light: a kind of mist that slowly settles to form dew the following day. The green is darker than during the day, the tree trunks turn black instead of brown, and the air is no longer invisible, it quivers like a strangely accumulated transparency. And then there is the sound of silence: the absence of birdsong, the absence of car noises and the distant rumble of trains or planes; all that is heard is night-wanderers' lonesome words lost in the rush of air filling the space between the branches on the trees — and your own footsteps pushing the grass aside while fern leaves and obdurate brambles cling to your body.

It was while she was standing like this on the path and trying to express to herself what made this feeling special that the spell was broken: it was a kind of imbalance, a sudden draught in an empty room, she thought — something inaudible, like a tiny crack in white porcelain. Perhaps it was a sound, perhaps it was a movement, she couldn't put her finger on what it was — she just sensed something, something that shouldn't be there.

With her eyes wide open, she slowly swivelled round. The trunks of the birch trees resembled human figures frozen in mid-flight. But there was nothing out of the ordinary among them. She turned a little more and stared ahead. Then she waited a couple of seconds before quickly glancing back over her shoulder. At that moment she recognised the third peculiarity about summer nights: the light is less transparent than during the day. The spaces between the nearest trees are impenetrable.

And pretty menacing.

It had become difficult to move, walking any further seemed dangerous, foolhardy. As she considered this thought, she saw the grimness of it. Was it dangerous? No. It was all a question of not revealing your presence.

Revealing your presence to whom? Not the kids partying across the lake. Someone here? There wasn't anyone. And, anyway, nothing could happen, with the people across the lake. Armed with these thoughts, she forced herself to carry on walking along the path. But now the atmosphere wasn't good. The attention she had given to the aesthetics of the countryside was now concentrated on an unpleasant prickling sensation in her back — a feeling that she was being observed. *If perhaps I turn right round, I can establish beyond doubt if someone is there.*

She stopped and turned.

Nothing. The birch trunks were as stiff as before, possible hiding places. And the prickling sensation in her back was still there when she turned and again stared ahead of her. The sensation just grew and grew. And once again, when she was about to continue, she realised that the menace could equally well be lurking in front of her as behind. Still, she forced herself to carry on. She had a metallic taste in her mouth and her chest hurt. She was moving now like a completely different person, a woman almost in a headlong rush, sending panic-stricken glances over her shoulder, looking furtively left and right and behind her. She was bathed in cold sweat, sobbing, walking with quick, rigid steps, feet that wouldn't find the way. Her trainers had become slippery. She missed her footing, a leg slid sideways. And her ears were no longer able to pick up anything but her own sob-filled panting and the dreadful pounding of her heart. There were no other sounds until a bird screeched.

Then she came to a halt. Trying to hold her breath so that she could listen. But she heard nothing. She saw nothing. For a fraction of a second all she smelt was the nauseous odour of ether.

A Swim

'Did you see a red Golf?' Gunnarstranda asked.

'I think so,' Frølich said, pacing back and forth with his phone to his ear. 'There was a gap in the line of parked cars. I think a red Golf had been there. But I'm not sure. What are you driving at?'

'I'm with his partner right now,' Gunnarstranda explained. 'She says her red Golf is parked in Waldemar Thranes gate because she has a flat there.'

'Imagine that shit being able to find a free parking spot right outside.'

'Yeah, yeah,' Gunnarstranda yawned.

'Get the reg number and I'll organise a search.'

'Relax. I've already done it.'

'What shall I do?'

'If we look at the pattern, all the murders seem very well planned. But now he can feel we're hot on his trail and he's losing the plot. So, anything can happen. I think you'd better check that all's well with the journalist. She lives in Bjølsen, not so far from me.'

★ ★ ★

When she felt his fingers around her neck, she was still moving forward. The vile stench was everywhere.

'No!' she screamed and heard only his wheezing in her ears.

But when she fell, his grip loosened a little. At that moment she bit with all her strength.

'Owwww!'

The finger digging into her throat was gone.

She was free, she ran, down the path. The taste of blood in her mouth came back when she heard footsteps behind her. No other sounds. Only her panting and his steps coming nearer and nearer. She stumbled, but staggered on, onto the gravel track. Right? Left? That was as much time as she had to think before the air was knocked out of her lungs and she hit the track, shoulder first, down into the ditch. Her body rolled down. She hit her left hip on a rock. Her running top was pulled up her back, which scraped against twigs and sharp stones. She screamed in pain. Rolled down further. Received a blow to the mouth. Up she got. On she went. Suddenly she was kneeling in water. Supporting herself on her hands. Mud. Like digging in cold, lumpy porridge. A second later she could smell it and felt his hands around her neck. *The poison*, she thought, *Ether*. Her nose, mouth and throat were full of the same repugnant stench.

She threw herself forward. The hand with the poison lost its grip.

She heard him splashing as he waded after her. She tried to draw her legs up underneath her and stand. But was unable to. With an iron grip he forced her head and back down under the water. *He wants to drown me. I need air. Air! I need air.* She groped with her hands through the revolting sludge and found something hard. Her lungs were constricted. Her body ordered her to give them air. They were hurting. And then she could do no more. She let go; her muscles relaxed. *Air*, she thought. The pressure on her temples told her she was beginning to lose consciousness. That was when the pressure on her neck and head was released. The fingers of her right hand held the rock as he lifted her up. She drank in air and held the rock with both hands behind her head. She let her arms follow the movement of her upper body. Up. Higher up. Back. And hard down as her legs took off. The rock swung in an arc toward the sky. And smacked down like a club onto hard wood.

It slipped from her fingers as she swung round and fell into the water. Panic-stricken and squirming, she struggled to her feet. Her vision was clouded by the water and her wet hair. He was also getting to his feet. And he was bleeding from the forehead; the blood was dispersing in the water and covered the whole of his face. It ran in streams down both cheeks, collected under his chin and dripped continuously down his sweater and into the lake. She fought for breath and backed away. Lost her balance. Fell backward again and groped with her hands. This time they didn't find a rock, only a fat, blunt piece of wood. She stood up. Continuing to back away, feeling her clothes restricting her movement and her hair sticking to her face. He waded after her. Slowly. Blood was still running from the wound on his forehead. He lowered his head, cupped a hand for water and rinsed the blood from his eyes.

Soon she was up to her waist in the lake. The piece of wood she was holding behind her back was pathetic. She kept backing away and was finding it harder to touch the bottom with her feet.

'Shall we have a swim?' he whispered. Blood ran into his snarling mouth and reddened the recesses between his teeth. Blood ran from the corners of his mouth. He coughed up red saliva and washed his face with another handful of water. She stepped back two paces. Now she couldn't stand on the bottom.

'I'll hit you again,' she whispered. The tips of her trainers barely touched the muddy bottom. She pushed off and floated a couple more metres back.

'Come on then,' he whispered. 'Come and hit me.'

'Stand still,' she said, treading water backward. Her foot and leg met a hindrance. A huge rock in the water, she thought, gliding backward with her knees bent. She found solid footholds. Crouched down on the firm base while holding her head and upper body at the same height.

'Come on . . . Come on.'

'Stop!' she screamed, thinking: *It might tip backward, I might slip off, but if I can straighten my knees . . .*

'Coooome on then, come on . . .'

'Don't come any closer,' she panted, gripping the stick harder.

He was taller than her. He wasn't floating. He was wading, and the water reached up to his waist at first, then to his chest.

He let out a sick chortle. The drops of blood from his chin were mixing with the muddy water the way sour milk makes black coffee go turbid.

His eyes didn't veer a millimetre; his mouth was distorted into a grimace. And he spoke as if to a child: 'Is the man going to get you? Hm? Is the man coming for you? Hm?'

'Stay where you are,' she whispered.

'Eh? Aren't we going to have a swim?'

'Stay where you are!'

He fell silent.

She could see he was bracing himself.

'Don't you touch me,' she whispered.

The movement started in his eyes. His pupils widened a tenth of a second before he launched himself at her. She straightened up from her crouch and was taller than him. She swung her right arm with all her strength. Her hand arched out from her body and to the left. The end of the flimsy wooden club was like the point of a spear. Hard wood, heavy wood, which had been lying in the water for decades. And she brought it down with fury. She struck him on the temple. His roar was truncated as he sank into the lake. But a second later it returned as an echo, somewhere behind her. Then she heard nothing. Only a rushing sound in her ears.

His upper body floated face down, lifeless. A back and a head bobbing up and down on the surface. *He's dying*, she thought, panting for breath. *He's dying. He's drowning*, she thought again. I have to get away. Then she raised her head and saw two totally naked men standing on the bank.

Hermit Crab

He stood staring at the door. There was not a sound to be heard inside. But something was happening. The peephole in the door had at first shone yellow, now it was dark. Someone inside was giving him a thorough vetting. In the end, he had to cough and change position. Then the door opened a few centimetres.

'Hi,' she said wearily through the crack.

As though I were a door-to-door salesman, he thought, and said: 'Hi. I've brought you some flowers.'

She opened the door wider and took the box. Her face was creased, as though she had just woken up. She was wearing jogging pants and a big, woollen jumper. She just peered at him through the crack.

'I bet you'd never have believed,' he said with a wry grin, 'that a cop would ring your doorbell and bring you flowers.'

'Actually, I've stopped believing anything.'

'Well, I only wanted to find out how you were.'

'I can't ask you in.'

'Of course. Put the flowers in a vase and we can talk on the phone when you've recovered.'

'This is my shell,' she said.

'Mhm.'

'It's the only one I have. This flat. I'm the kind of crab that parks its rump in a shell and thinks it controls the world. I know I'm kidding myself, it's an illusion, but I can't help it, not after what happened. I can't let anyone in.'

'OK.'

'You think I'm crazy,' she said.

He shook his head vigorously. 'Me? No . . .'

'I can go out with you. We can go for a walk. Wait a minute . . .'

He stood staring at the closed door again. His phone rang. He looked at the display. It was Gunnarstranda. He switched it off. Then she was there. The same jogging pants and jumper. And trainers. 'Your phone was ringing,' she said.

'I switched it off.' He watched as she locked the door with first a Yale key, then the security lock and finally pushed the door to check it didn't budge. She faced him again with her Michelle Pfeiffer eyes. 'Shall we go?'

When they were outside, the heat hit them. The sun was shining from a cloudless sky. It was afternoon and the town was quiet. For a while they stood on the pavement, lost for words. She was chewing gum.

'We can go for a walk along the river,' she said and led the way, first down Bentsebrugata and then down the path between the green lawns. They found a bench with a view of the river Akerselva. She sat gazing at her shoes. He had no idea what to say.

'Gunnarstranda doesn't live so far away from here,' he said at length, 'closer to Bjølsen Park.'

'Will he live?'

'Who?'

'Groven.'

'Of course.'

'Will I be charged?'

He smiled. 'If anything can be called self-defence, then —'

'Don't laugh at me,' she interrupted.

'I'm not laughing.'

'I saw you. You were laughing.'

'I mean it. I'm not laughing. The point is no one will even think of taking out a charge against you. Jan Groven will be charged with murder and fraud and embezzlement, and also for the assault on you — I assume.'

'Not me. I want nothing more to do with this case.'

She had gripped his arm. He looked down at her hand, the short nails, now without a trace of varnish. 'I'll ask the public prosecutor to contact you,' he mumbled.

'Fristad?' she said, letting go of him. 'He's told me to find a solicitor.' She gazed at the river. 'He doesn't understand that all I want is peace and quiet. I don't want anything to do with the case.'

Neither of them spoke for a while. There was something she hadn't said, but it was in the air. He, Frank Frølich, was a part of the case. But she didn't say that. He sat still too, contemplating the water between the branches, glad that she hadn't said it. Two ducks were waddling around down by the bank. In the grey water there was a bike.

'It's hit me now,' she said. 'A kind of reaction. After all, I was alone with him several times. This feeling that I didn't understand anything and just allowed myself to be led. But I'm also struggling with the thought that he was serious. He had actually intended to . . .'

She sat on the bench as though frightened she would fall off. Her back was hunched; her gaze inward, reflective. Frølich raised a hand and stroked her cheek without thinking about what he was doing. He quickly withdrew his hand. But she didn't seem to have felt his touch.

'I blame myself for not having understood earlier,'

she said, 'and I'm trying to tell myself I had no idea he and Pedersen had plans to defraud and swindle others. To me, he seemed like an alright kind of guy, very alright.'

'It probably started as idealism,' Frølich said when she stopped. 'This company he built up and the medicines. I'm sure he set out to contribute something to the third world. The problems arose because of a lack of money and the realisation that they'd been tricked. The realisation that the medicine they'd risked everything for was useless and had no value. It had been an utter swindle, dog eat dog. And so he contacted Kimberley, and when he didn't get what he wanted, there was a chance with Stu —'

'Don't say his name,' she interrupted, upset.

Frølich said nothing.

She looked down for a long time, before wiping her eyes. 'The doctor calls it angst.'

He nodded.

'You said something about piecing together a surreal picture,' she said, 'that night.'

He nodded again.

'I think a lot about it. About it being something that will pass.' She breathed in and stared up at the sky, then slowly breathed out. 'The angst.'

'Time's a good medicine,' he said.

'It could've been me,' she said. 'Kristine, dead inside the car. It could've been me. That's how I think. And I struggle to accept that I could be so stupid and frightened. Actually, I didn't show much grit. I ran away from her. And while I was running I remember that I thought she . . .'

'She what?'

'That she seemed so lonely. It's so damned hard to

318

accept that I ran off.'

'Her death,' Frølich pronounced in a grave tone, 'is his responsibility.'

'I know that, of course. But it's so hard to come to terms with such things. Just the fact that, after having been so brutal, he has such luck,' she said finally. 'That the two men managed to drag him ashore before he drowned.'

'I lost him,' Frølich said. 'That's my nightmare. I managed to lose him. I followed him, you know, that night. But he spotted me. The world's cheapest trick. I sat looking at his bloody car for half an hour. But he'd hopped it. He had another car and drove up to yours.'

'They'd stripped off so as not to get their clothes wet,' she said. 'But I freaked out when I saw them wading toward me. I thought they were after me too.'

He nodded.

'The other two didn't enjoy such luck — Kristine and Stuart.'

They sat in silence, watching the river flow past. An elderly woman taking a fat, old golden retriever for a walk strolled toward them. The dog stopped and sniffed Frølich's trouser leg. It gazed at them for a few seconds before sniffing and moving on.

'And I'm ill,' she said, after the woman with the dog had gone. 'I take pills and feel like such a hermit crab.'

'Do you feel more relaxed now?' he asked.

She turned to him.

'Here, with me. Are you feeling more relaxed?'

She nodded. And they went back to watching the river.

'I've remembered a film I like,' he said out of the blue.

She looked up.

'It's about two pianists who for some reason can't make it. But then they find a singer ... Michelle Pfeiffer.'

She smiled wanly. 'We'll have to talk about that later,' she said.

'When?'

'When I've sloughed off my shell.'

We do hope that you have enjoyed reading this large print book.

Did you know that all of our titles are available for purchase?

We publish a wide range of high quality large print books including:
Romances, Mysteries, Classics
General Fiction
Non Fiction and Westerns

Special interest titles available in large print are:
The Little Oxford Dictionary
Music Book, Song Book
Hymn Book, Service Book

Also available from us courtesy of Oxford University Press:
Young Readers' Dictionary
(large print edition)
Young Readers' Thesaurus
(large print edition)

For further information or a free brochure, please contact us at:
Ulverscroft Large Print Books Ltd.,
The Green, Bradgate Road, Anstey,
Leicester, LE7 7FU, England.
Tel: (00 44) 0116 236 4325
Fax: (00 44) 0116 234 0205

THE ASSISTANT

Kjell Ola Dahl

Oslo, 1938. War is in the air and Europe is in turmoil. Hitler's Germany has occupied Austria and is threatening Czechoslovakia; there's a civil war in Spain and Mussolini reigns in Italy. When a woman turns up at the office of police-turned-private investigator Ludvig Paaske, he and his assistant — his one-time nemesis and former drug-smuggler Jack Rivers — begin a seemingly straightforward investigation into marital infidelity. But all is not what it seems, and when Jack is accused of murder, the trail leads back to the 1920s, to prohibition-era Norway, to the smugglers, sex workers and hoodlums of his criminal past, and an extraordinary secret.

THE HEMLOCK CURE

Joanne Burn

It is 1665 and the women of Eyam keep many secrets.

Isabel Frith, the village midwife, walks a dangerous line with her herbs and remedies. There are men in the village who speak of witchcraft, and Isabel has a past to hide. So she tells nobody her fears about Wulfric, the pious, reclusive apothecary.

Mae, Wulfric's youngest daughter, dreads her father's rage if he discovers what she keeps from him. Like her feelings for Rafe, Isabel's ward, or the fact that she studies from Wulfric's books at night.

But others have secrets too . . .

When Mae makes a horrifying discovery, Isabel is the only person she can turn to. But helping Mae will place them both in unimaginable peril.

And meanwhile another danger is on its way from London. One that threatens to engulf them all . . .

LEONARD AND HUNGRY PAUL

Rónán Hession

Leonard and Hungry Paul are two quiet friends who see the world differently. Content with their circumstances, they use humour, board games, and silence to steer their way through the maelstrom that is the twenty-first century. But things are beginning to change. There's a death in the family. Leonard is interested in a woman at work. And Hungry Paul has entered a competition with a sizeable financial prize. Should the pair choose to stick with lives of comforting predictability — or forge new paths for themselves?